D1527936

Once Upon A Rhyme

Book Two

Little Bo Sneak

Abigail Manning

Once Upon A Rhyme: Little Bo Sneak
© 2023 Abigail Manning

ISBN:9798398082654

Cover design by Karri Klawitter

Edited by Silvia Curry

"Little Bo Peep has lost her sheep,
and doesn't know where to find them.
Leave them alone, and they'll come home,
wagging their tails behind them."

prologue

"Come along, Evie. We wouldn't want to miss your appointment," Mother said in a sing-song voice that was somewhere between proper and frustrated.

Despite my greatest efforts to delay going to the dress shop, we were still nearly there on time. I tried spilling tea on my dress, hiding Mother's gloves, and even tangling a comb in my hair, but Mother simply threw a bonnet over my head and dragged me out the door. I hated bonnets, perhaps even more than I hated dress shopping for my tenth birthday celebration after I made myself perfectly clear that I wanted to go horseback riding. Mother said ten-year-old-ladies didn't ride horses; they rode in carriages.

I told her ladies were boring, but that only earned me another lesson in etiquette.

"Ah, look! The shop is just ahead. And look at that adorable display in the window!" Mother pointed at the shiny glass storefront, filled with neat rows of mannequins and fabric displays.

I followed the direction of her finger and

nearly stumbled as my jaw dropped at the horrific display she was gawking at. A bright yellow dress, just about my size, stood far too proudly in the center of the window. It had a frilly high neck, hideous rosettes down the sleeves, more ruffles than an angry duck, and worst of all... a matching bonnet.

"How adorable!" Mother awed as she dragged me toward the lacy shop of torture. "We should definitely have you try on that one."

I stared up at the sky, begging the world for a magic stone to fall from the heavens and grant me the strength to run back home until I was safely hidden in my secret blanket fort. It didn't even have to be a magic stone; even a minor distraction would do the trick since we were already almost late. I glanced around for any cracks in the ground I could trip on, or perhaps a conveniently lost child. My gaze darted wildly around the crowded street, searching as intently as I could for anything to save me from my doomed fate.

"Thief!" A shrill scream split through the air, shooting the biggest smile up my face. "Someone help! That man stole my pocketbook!"

My body buzzed with excitement as I locked on to the pocketbook thief, a dark-haired man with scary green eyes and a strange hunch in his posture.

"Oh, how terrible." Mother pressed a hand to her cheek, only pausing briefly until she noticed a few members of the royal guard spring into action. "I hope the guard can catch that man... Now, we better hurry along."

What? That's it!?

While I was grateful for the distraction, it was far too brief, but I didn't plan to keep it that way.

"Don't worry, Mother!" I yanked my hand from her grip, barely managing to pry my fingers free. "I'll go make sure the guard catches the bad man!"

I spun around, and barely felt Mother's hand graze the back of my lacy bonnet before I escaped into the crowd.

"What!? Evie, wait!" Mother reached out for me again, but I wasn't about to give up my chance at escape now. I sped up, ducking under the arms of an elderly couple as I followed the direction of the thief. "Evie, get back here!"

Mother's voice died off behind me as victory blossomed in my chest. I knew running off would earn me plenty of scoldings—and likely even another round of etiquette lessons—but if it kept me from wearing the heinous yellow cupcake, it was well worth it.

I'd only loosely been paying attention to where the thief actually went, but it was the busiest time of day in this district, which meant he'd probably try to disappear into the crowds in the marketplace. I turned the corner and found the pair of guards who'd been in hot pursuit already combing through the sea of people. They stopped a few shoppers to ask questions, and tried to funnel everyone else past them, but it seemed inefficient since the marketplace had two back alleys where a crook could hide.

Both alleys led to dead ends, and Mother always told me not to go back there because that's where the urchins live. But that never made sense to me, because my tutor always said urchins lived in the ocean. I paused in front of one of the alleys and glanced into the shadows. There definitely didn't appear to be any ocean back there, but it did smell kind of fishy, so maybe Mother was right after all.

A few people dressed in ragged clothes lined the alleyway, camped out in empty supply crates and covered in news pamphlets. I considered asking them if they'd seen any urchins, or if they would be willing to show me how they made their cool crate forts, but before I could introduce myself, a strange woman walked out from around the alley's corner.

She was blonde, wearing an oversized dress covered in patches and a bonnet, just like me. As she passed me, she gave me a brief smile, and her eyes gleamed in a wicked shade of green.

My breath caught as I recognized the color, then again when I recognized the obscure way the woman carried herself. Her posture was leaned too far forward, her hair looked too clean for someone in a dress that old, and her bag was the perfect size to carry someone else's pocketbook.

The thief is pretending to be a lady!?

I crept through the crowd and watched closely as the thief-turned-lady approached the guards. The guards glanced at her—or him, but never truly looked, and a second later, he was let past them. My jaw dropped as I followed behind the thief as close as I dared, watching them confidently stride toward the end of the market.

"Hey you," the guard called down to me, jerking me from my thoughts. "Where are your parents? Are you lost?"

I looked at the thief, and a fresh fire stirred in my heart as I decided today was the day that I, Genevieve Rayelle Palleep, would save the world.

"Yes, I'm lost!" I smiled up at the guard. "Hurry and catch me!"

I darted between the guard's legs and sprinted back into the crowd.

"Hey! Wait—" the guard called after me, but my disappearing act was far too advanced for his meager skills.

I squeezed past crowds and pushed through

clusters of shoppers until the masqueraded thief was right in front of me. I glanced back and confirmed that both guards were hot on my tail, then dashed forward and clamped my entire body around the thief's legs.

"What in the!?" the thief shouted, exposing his obviously masculine voice as he clawed at my arms. "Listen here, you little brat—"

The guards jerked to a stop in front of us, their eyes wide as the thief went silent.

"I-I mean, uh…" the thief cleared his voice, and in a mock-feminine tone, said, "what a cute little lady…"

One guard was already deadlocked on the thief's fake hair and even faker smile. "*Madame*, may we please see your bag?" the taller guard asked in a cold tone.

"Well, I…" The thief darted his eyes around the market, then in the blink of an eye, kicked me to the ground and made a run for it.

I fell back onto the cobblestone with a squeak, but my fluffy pink skirt padded me against any bruises. The thief only made it a few feet before the tall guard caught him, and the shorter guard bent down to help me.

"Are you alright?" he asked gently, but his eyes seemed more serious, like they were studying me somehow.

"Yes, I'm fine!" I said brightly, feeling beyond

proud that I had successfully escaped the dress shop appointment *and* saved the world, all in the same day. "Did you find the nice lady's pocketbook?"

The guard glanced back at his partner, who was currently pulling out the patterned pocketbook from the thief's bag. "We did, but it looks like you found it first."

My grin broadened. "I just noticed the lady had the same funny walk as the thief. Oh, and that his hair looked too clean to live with the sea urchins, and also that his eyes were scary."

The guard blinked at me and furrowed his brow—the same way I often saw Mother do whenever I tried to convince her I was allergic to lace.

"I see..." he said in a contemplative tone. "What's your name, dear?"

"Genevieve Palleep," I answered with a proud nod.

"You have a keen eye, Genevieve." The guard smiled, and something inside me knew it wasn't a normal smile. It was the kind of smile you saw before you received the type of news that made you even more excited than riding a horse for your birthday. "Let's get you back to your mother, but first, I want you to meet someone."

chapter one

Anyone who ever said that women talk too much has never been left alone in a room with a rich man.

I sipped my tea, hiding my eyes behind the porcelain just enough where I could safely roll them out of Lord Percy's view. He was attractive, I suppose, though it was obvious he knew it. His silk suit was freshly starched, and his blonde hair was slicked back with an expensive cream I recognized from the town's cosmetic stand. The nauseating, piney scent of the hair cream was unmistakable, and it almost hid the sweet floral scent of a woman's perfume lingering on his collar...

"Would you consider yourself capable of running a household, Lady Genevieve?" Percy asked with a pinched smile that made me wonder if it was powdered with cosmetics, too.

I fluttered my lashes and set my teacup down soft enough that it didn't clatter.

"I'm capable of running just about anything, my lord," I replied sweetly.

Lord Percy settled back into his armchair with a satisfied lift of his brow. "Is that so? What domestic skills do you possess?"

My eye twitched. I knew Mother had invited Lord Percy over in hopes of establishing a courtship between us, though I hadn't realized he'd been planning an interrogation as well. I shouldn't be surprised, though; Mother always tended to pick the men she believed would do their best to *tame* me.

I proudly folded my hands into my lap. "I'm afraid I'm not much of a domestic type."

"No domestic skills?" Percy looked as if I'd told him I enjoyed eating live snakes smothered in jam. "Then what use would you be as a wife?"

My smile stiffened and my eyes went to work, narrowing in on the white hairs stuck to his cuff from what appeared to be a Persian cat, the tiny dot of red wine on his jacket, and the brand of shoes he'd chosen to wear. He was almost too easy to read, but noblemen always were. They were all determined to be better than the rest, which really meant they were all the same.

"What use would you be to me as a husband?" I challenged.

"Clearly more than you'd appreciate," he huffed. "My family's mining business possesses more investors than a farmer does cattle. I'm obviously well-established, so I would be a more than an adequate provider, and my company is far more pleasurable than most."

"Is that what the women at the gentlemen's club, The Velvet Whiskey, told you?" I asked with an innocent smile.

Lord Percy's eyes went wider than the silver buttons on his coat. "I beg your pardon?"

"The Velvet Whiskey. You must have been there earlier today." I watched with sadistic glee as the proper lord squirmed in his seat. "I suppose it's easy to assume your company is enjoyable when you tip the barmaids to flatter you."

His neck turned red, and a delicious anger pulsed into his eyes.

"I don't know what you're insinuating, Lady Genevieve, but I am an honorable man," Percy said with a deep growl laced into his tone. "The Velvet Whiskey club is nothing more than a hotspot for gamblers and drunkards. I have never—"

"Do you own any pets, my lord?" I asked sweetly.

"W-what? No, of course not." He scowled.

"How curious..." I reached forward and grabbed his wrist, ignoring his mindless arguing as I flipped over his wrist for us both to see his cuff. "Because these white hairs here appear to be from a white Persian cat... a rather rare breed in

Reclusia. The only person I've ever heard of who is fortunate enough to own one is Sir Samson Velveten, the owner of the Velvet Whiskey."

He yanked his hand back, straightening his jacket with a clenched jaw.

Noblemen are so pathetic when they're backed into a corner.

"That's preposterous, this is only—"

"Oh, and there appears to be a small wine stain on your jacket." I pointed toward the pea-sized drop. "It's quite an interesting color, looks like a deep ruby-red shade, much like the house-made wine Sir Velveten makes."

Lord Percy's mouth split open like a gaping fish, his eyes darting between me and the tiny stain.

"Oh, pardon me, I've taken us off topic." I giggled with a toss of my blonde curls and a wicked smile tugging at my lips. "We were talking about what an impeccable husband you would make! I'm sure your gambling will serve as an excellent example for your future children."

He pushed up from his seat with his fists clenched at his sides in a manner that he probably intended to look intimidating but he came off more like a toddler mid-tantrum.

"I believe it's time for me to leave, Lady Genevieve," he seethed through his teeth.

"Oh? So soon?" I fluttered my lashes. "What a shame. I was just starting to enjoy myself."

He turned for the door with heavy-footed steps that didn't help him look any less like a fitful toddler. "What you *enjoy* is picking apart details that mean absolutely nothing," Lord Percy said with a tight growl.

I narrowed my eyes, my smile fading as I rose from my seat. "Every detail means something, my lord. Accepting that fact might help you win your next game of liar's dice."

His face went ashen, and his pupils shot to the size of an ink droplet before he spun around to face the door. I hadn't been entirely certain he was a liar's dice man as opposed to blackjack, but considering how naturally fibbing came to him, it seemed to be the most logical choice.

"Good day, Lady Genevieve." Lord Percy cleared his throat, then dashed out the door with an impressive speed.

I glanced over at the wall clock and calculated how long it had been since he'd arrived. Twenty minutes? Fifteen, if I didn't include how long it took for Dedra to get him settled in the parlor.

That might be a new record. Mother will likely—

"Evie!"

Oh, right on cue.

I settled back into the quilted sofa, neatly tucking my hands into my lap as I patiently awaited my darling family's wrath. "Yes, Mother?"

I smoothed a wrinkle in my satin yellow skirts as Mother stormed into the parlor as aggressively as an honorable lady of the house dared, quickly tailed by the housekeeper, Dedra, and a sour-faced Father. The trio lined up behind the tea table, each glaring with their own distinct look of disappointment. Mother was always the most intense, and therefore, the most entertaining to look at. Dedra was a close second, mostly because she always seemed to be the most baffled by my increasing record of how quickly I could make a suitor flee the manor. Father was only here because Mother always dragged him along. He would scowl, but ever since I cleverly avoided participating in the prince's bride competition a few months ago, he had long since given up trying to marry me off.

"Genevieve Rayelle Palleep, what in Reclusia did you say to Lord Percy to make him run out like that?" Mother was a master at yelling at people without ever truly raising her voice. It was a skill I admired, feared, and desperately wanted to learn. It was a good thing I received so many demonstrations from her to study.

I smiled sweetly. "We were only discussing our hobbies, Mother."

"Hobbies? What did you tell him!? That you enjoy tormenting young men?" Dedra huffed as she stacked the teacups.

"Only the tormentable ones." I shrugged as I bit back a giggle.

"Genevieve..." Father warned in his *'one more remark, and you'll be getting another week of etiquette lessons'* voice.

"Of course, I didn't say that," I relented as I huffed a loose curl from my eyes. "I merely asked him how he entertained himself, and he let it slip that he frequents the Velvet Whiskey club. When I continued to question him about it, the young lord became defensive and decided it was time to leave."

Dedra's jaw dropped open perfectly in time with Mother smacking a palm to her forehead.

"Evie..." Mother let out a tight breath as her palm slid down the front of her face. "You know better than to pry into a man's personal life."

"I also know better than to get involved with a gambler," I said tartly.

"Gambling is just a phase for many noblemen," Mother replied with a stern glare.

"Of course, it is." I rose to match her eyes. "Because those who don't stop don't remain noble. They squander away their wealth until they are no longer seen or heard from. So tell me, Mother, how am I meant to know the difference between a man who is noble and a man who is foolish when they both engage in the same reckless pastime?"

"It's not about the differences, it's about the similarities." Mother's voice raised with that practiced restrained yell. "They are still *men*. Men who are looking for a wife and whose families are affluent enough to take care of you, even if foolishness came for a season."

"You would have me marry a fool?" I asked with a twinge in my neck.

"I would have rather you married a prince." Mother's voice turned icy as she twisted back to the one point she knew I couldn't argue. "But you already did an excellent job of burning that bridge, didn't you, dear?"

I didn't answer. My blood burned beneath my skin, and my tongue itched to thrash behind my teeth, but I knew I needed to keep quiet. It was my job, after all. When questions remained unanswered, it was better to avoid them when brought back up.

"Why don't we all take a few minutes to collect ourselves." Father sighed as he rubbed his temple. "Evie, I expect you to write an apology letter to Lord Percy for your behavior today."

My legs stiffened. "Father, you can't be—"

"You heard your Father, miss." Dedra scolded as she tucked the tea tray under her arm. Ever since I weaseled my way out of the prince's bride competition, she'd taken to enforcing my discipline—something Mother and Father seemed to have no issue with. "I'll bring you up some stationery once I've put away the dishes."

The hot surge flowing through my veins was all too familiar. Wanting to argue, but knowing you had no ground to stand on, was one of the most dissatisfying feelings I'd come to know. Especially when, in truth, I had a perfectly solid argument that I simply wasn't permitted to share.

I didn't avoid the prince's competition solely to avoid marriage, though that was part of it...

"I'll be in my room," I clipped, whirling around on my house slippers as I moved away from the looming shadows of my family's ever-growing shame in me.

The Palleep estate usually felt too big, but after altercations with suitors, I always appreciated the long walk back to my suite. I forced a smile as I passed a few servants, trying to shove back the anger that was brewing behind my pearly teeth. Once I was safely shut inside my room, I pressed my back against the door and knocked my head against the sturdy wood.

How much longer must I wait? Surely, I didn't cause that much drama during the prince's competition?

I wandered into the room, finding myself stopping in front of the window as I met my stubborn blue stare. It had been months since I'd last heard from my handler, and I was far beyond antsy. I knew switching places with my handmaiden, Lacey, would cause at least a small stir, but I hadn't expected things to transpire as far as they did. Don't get me wrong, I was happy with how everything turned out for both my friend and Reclusia, but I also feared my meddling might be part of the reason why everything was so quiet.

A soft knock sounded just before Dedra pressed the door open. I didn't bother turning around to face her; I could already see plenty of her disapproving stare from the window's reflection.

"Here's your stationery, my lady," Dedra said as she placed the basket of supplies on my desk, "along with today's letters. If you wish to get back into your parents' good graces, I'd suggest looking through them. A few appear to be from potential suitors. Oh, and there's a stock update from your favorite dress shop as well."

The dress shop!?

My eyes widened in the glass as my heart leapt, and I fought the urge not to make a mad dash for the basket. I locked eyes with the neat stack of letters, instantly recognizing the shop's signature stationery.

"Thank you, Dedra. That will be all," I said plainly as I eagerly chewed my lip with each slow step she made toward the door.

Come on, Dedra, move it!

With the urgency of a snail swimming through molasses in the winter, she casually strolled out of the room and shut the door behind her. I counted to ten to ensure she'd had a moment to walk away, then broke away from the window to race for the letter. I snatched up the ivory paper, absorbing the moment as best as I could as I took in the crisp scent of ink and the parchment's smooth texture.

Finally.

I ran my fingers over the button-shaped seal before breaking it open, readying myself for the thrill of what was inside. The shop's name was neatly printed at the top, stirring my senses to life as I read the name of the crown agency that had employed me since I was a child.

Little Bows Shop and Dress Emporium.

I hadn't avoided marrying the prince because I didn't want to be his queen; I avoided it because it was my job to protect him and his future queen. It was already hard enough to hide my assignments from my family, but hiding it from a hovering husband would be nearly impossible. So, I couldn't marry, not yet at least. There was still work for me to do, and I was itching to get to it.

To our loyal customer,

We apologize for the delay in this season's restock. Unfortunately, a few of our cloaks have gone missing in transit. We are still hoping to have our collection ready as soon as possible, so to expedite the process, we'll be commissioning an extra supplier for our next restock.

You can expect an update on the collection as early as this week, so be on the lookout for our next shipment! As always, thank you for your loyalty to our brand.

Sincerely,

Little Bows

I read the letter twice to ensure I had picked up on everything wedged between the lines. It was another fetch request, like my usual assignments.

Ever since I was recruited as a child, my handler had recognized I possessed a skill for tracking down just about anything: people, magic stones, money, or anything else that could be lost or stolen. Because of this, my letters were often coded based on what object or person I was meant to be tracking down. Hats were code for runaway convicts, dresses were for black market goods, gloves were for horses, but cloaks were new...

Is it a play on someone's name? I don't recognize the name cloak from anywhere...

I read through the letter once again, recognizing that *shipment* implied I would need to travel for this job, and the mentioned update was likely going to be another letter with further details. The only other part that left me puzzled was the mention of the extra supplier... Usually, suppliers were code for other agents, who were used to convey information they had learned and thought might be of use to the next agent on the job. So why did the letter say they were commissioning another?

My fingers tightened on the parchment, crinkling the paper as the pieces crashed together in my head like a drunken joust. It had been months since I'd taken on a job, and years since I'd done more than track down a criminal's hideout from my maps at home.

'To expedite the process, we'll be commissioning an extra supplier...'

I held the letter up to the flame in my oil lamp, watching the fire dance across the ink as it enveloped the message one fleck of ash at a time. My blood simmered as I watched the word *supplier* be swallowed by the flames, wishing I could make the reality of the word burn with it.

They're sending me on a job, but they're sending me with a babysitter...

chapter two

I always hated how slowly time passed when the one thing you were waiting for didn't have a designated delivery date. I was meant to receive an update within the week, but I felt like no one truly understood how long a week could actually be until you were stuck wasting it away with stuck-up suitors and frustrated parents.

Fresh air blew in through the open library window, mixing the scent of grass and flowers with the library's dust. A few curls fluttered out from my hairpins, blurring my vision from the map collection I was studying.

I'm still not certain what a 'cloak' means, but I can at least study up on the topography around Reclusia before my chaperone shows up.

I thumbed through the pages, memorizing every curve of the Widowrush River, and every hill in the Weberell forest. We had just left the rainy season, so the rivers would be full and difficult to cross, and the forests would be thick with growth, making them an ideal escape route for anyone on the run.

Elaine strode into the library with a feather duster in hand, passing me a brisk smile before she set to work, pulling books to dust off their covers. I returned the smile, then adjusted my book to ensure the novel on dragon adventures was still placed overtop the atlas. It would have looked better if I'd selected a book on etiquette or even a romance novel to cover my true read, but that wouldn't fool anyone. Everyone in this manor knew I wasn't interested in jumping into domestic life, so pretending that I was would only draw their eyes.

Crown spies don't need eyes on them, but it's hard to hide in the shadows when your family keeps dragging you into the spotlight.

I scowled at the pages as I recalled the so-called *supplier* I was meant to be expecting. Admittedly, the events at the prince's bride competition were a bit flashy, but my name was hardly dragged into the affair... Alright, so maybe it was in a *few* kingdom news pamphlets, but for goodness' sake, it was months ago! Did they really find it necessary to keep me off duty for so long?

In the eight years I'd been working as an agent, I'd never once had a partner. Occasionally, I would receive intel from other agents to assist with my jobs, but I'd never actually met them beyond an encrypted letter. What will this incoming agent be like?

A sigh overtook me as I imagined a crabby old agent with a scraggly beard and a nasty scar running down his right eye from an altercation where he saved Reclusia from an imploding magic stone the size of a meteor. He'll probably have a limp from being stabbed in the leg by a Sarnoldian spy and an accent that is impossible to place after years of perfecting his false origins. Or maybe it will be a woman who's been mastering the art of disguise since she could see her own eye color, and be perfected in the art of etiquette, espionage, and maintaining perfect curls.

Basically, I can guarantee it will be someone who will look down on me.

I turned the books face-down on my lap, leaning back into the armchair as I let the soft bristle of Elaine's duster serenade me. I was fortunate to have been recruited at only ten years old, but that was just the thing… I was recruited, not bred for this line of work like many others. At only eighteen, I was still inexperienced, and it didn't help that my life as the young Lady Palleep made it difficult for me to perform tasks from beyond my bedroom walls.

It made sense why they would send me an agent with more experience, but at the same time, I wasn't ready to share the job. I may not have been the most seasoned, but my skills were nothing to scoff at, either.

I sat a little straighter as my internal pep talk drowned out Elaine's dusting.

That's right, Evie! You're no newbie. You single-handedly brought down two minor crime branches in the magic stone black market! And by sending your beloved handmaiden into the prince's competition, you uncovered another black market dealer whose daughter had been sent in to compete!

I smiled proudly, only vaguely noticing the puzzled expression on Elaine's face as she skirted around my chair to get to the farther shelves.

You don't need anyone's help, especially not from some grouchy, old—

"Evie, dear. Come down to the parlor. You have another suitor here for a visit!" Mother's voice echoed through the house, growing closer until she poked into the library to find me. "Ah, there you are, and thank goodness you look presentable. You best come downstairs. This gentleman appears to be the busy type."

The pride I'd placed in myself shriveled like a dying flame as I recalled that even if Evie was strong and resourceful, Genevieve still had to fall second-class to men with deep pockets.

"Were we expecting this gentleman?" I asked stiffly as I discreetly tucked the atlas and dragon novel onto a low shelf.

"Surprisingly, no." Mother giggled. "Though it's possible you may have met him before. He claims he spotted you in the capital during your time at the... *ahem* competition. Apparently, he was quite taken with you and has been looking for an excuse to travel to this part of the kingdom ever since."

Goosebumps dotted my skin as I imagined some slimy old nobleman ogling me while I traversed the castle. Any man who was willing to ride four hours in a carriage to meet a girl he'd never spoken to was either desperate or felt entitled to what he liked.

"Sorry, Mother," I said as I rose from my seat with a gentle smooth of my skirts. "But I'm afraid I'll have to decline his visit. Since I wasn't forewarned about his arrival, I shouldn't be expected to entertain him while I have other plans."

"What *other* plans?" Mother asked crossly.

"Shopping, of course." I smiled brightly. "I'm afraid I already have a dress fitting, oh... right about now."

I started for the door, perfectly content with wandering around the market for an hour while pretending I was out being pricked with pins. Unfortunately, Mother had no issue blocking my only exit.

She smiled with the sickly sweetness of a rotten peach. "Then I suppose you'll have to reschedule."

I mirrored her grin. "Now, would that be ladylike of me? To neglect an appointment for someone I had no prior engagement with?"

"Perfectly." Mother said with a thrash of her tongue. "Especially considering there's no need to go to the dress shop when this fine gentleman has already come prepared with a gift from your favorite boutique."

My breath caught in the back of my throat, and it took all my efforts to keep my smile from twitching.

No…

"A gift?" I swallowed dryly. "Which shop did it come from, specifically?"

Mother lifted her chin with a victorious glint in her sapphire eyes. "That little shop in the capital you're always so interested in. The Little Bows Shop."

For the love of…

"Very well," I clipped as I averted Mother's triumphant smile. "I suppose I could take a moment to at least meet him."

My legs moved mechanically as I made my way to the parlor, biting back a dozen curse words on my tongue. There were a hundred different ways the agent could have come into contact with me—acting as a servant, catching me in the market, pretending to be a long-lost cousin… Any of them would have been better than pretending to be a suitor.

Is this their way of punishing me for making a mess of the prince's competition?

When I made it to the parlor, I paused before stepping inside. I always felt prepared to deal with a suitor, but in this case, I was completely lost on what to expect or how to react. This wasn't a man I needed to pick apart and send home running in order to protect my hidden life. This was someone who was just like me, who was already expecting me to be a burden on their mission.

Perhaps I should pick him apart after all. He needs to know I'm not as dainty as my ribbons imply.

"He's right inside, my lady." Dedra motioned for the door, as if I didn't know how doors worked. "Why don't you introduce yourself, and I'll prepare some tea."

She slid past me toward the kitchen, and I waited until she was fully out of sight before I turned back to the door. My hands shook slightly, though I wasn't nervous. I clicked the door open and stepped inside the parlor, finding my gaze settling on the back of a dark head of hair.

The sound of the door alerted him to stand, and I quickly realized he was a good head taller than me, which wasn't surprising for a veteran agent. His hat was tucked under his arm, and his coat was nice, but not expensive enough that one would expect him to be associated with a mentionable family. He turned around to face my eyes, and suddenly, my assessment of him came to a screeching halt.

His eyes were a rich hazel shade, like a candied maple bar that was still glistening with the sticky glaze. I hated how intelligent they looked, as if they were loaded with mystery and knowledge that was kept behind a locked door and a charming smile. His skin was tanned, but not enough that one would assume he worked in the sun, and his build was sculpted better than most of the artwork I'd seen in the palace. He had broad shoulders and a thinned jaw that complimented his prominent features. He looked strong, agile, younger than I'd anticipated, and most surprisingly... handsome.

"Afternoon, you must be Lady Genevieve." The agent stepped out from around the chair to bow, and I caught the slightest rasp of an Ebonair accent in his tone, but only enough to assume he visited their kingdom for business. "My name is Shepherd Stocklan. It's a pleasure to finally meet you."

I watched his movements with the eyes of a hungry hawk, picking up on the slight dart of his eyes and the small bulge along his waist that likely held a weapon. On closer inspection, I could see the ends of his sleeves were slightly frayed, and his dark hair was combed, but not greased like Lord Percy's had been. He was portraying a lower-class nobleman that, while respectable, was also of little note to anyone within local gossip chains. His features kind of reminded me of my favorite agent growing up, Ryder Wolfe, with the same mysterious flawlessness that may or may not end in betrayal. He was definitely the agent I was waiting for, and he was good.

"Lovely to meet you." I motioned for him to sit, and he did so gratefully as I took the sofa across from him. "My mother tells me you brought a gift. Is this true?"

Shepherd's expression remained even, but I could see the twinkle pass through his eyes as he reached beside his seat for a satin hat box decorated with a vibrant pink bow.

"It is. I've heard you're quite fond of this shop, and when I stopped by, they said they knew exactly what you'd be looking for." He offered me the box with a smile that conveyed more than his voice.

I took the box with a grateful nod, as my eyes instantly landed on the familiar branding written across the top of the box.

"How very kind of you to bring it all this way," I said sweetly as I untied the bow and set the lid on the cushion beside me.

My blood pulsed as I spotted the note sitting atop the folded fabric. I picked up the card, and tried to remain composed as I scanned the lettering as fast as I could.

From us to you. We hope you enjoy our new supplier!

I frowned as I turned the card over in search of any further information, only to come up empty. The message was clear; my partner already knew the details of our mission, which meant I had to ask him.

I bit back a growl as I set the note aside to inspect the fabric folded underneath. At first touch, I could tell it was made of wool, which was strangely unseasonal considering we were just now exiting spring. I explored the fabric and found a hood and deep pockets sewn into it.

A cloak.

"It's lovely," I said as I folded the cloak and placed it back into the box. "Care to explain the significance of it to me?"

Shepherd's eyes tightened, but his polite smile remained as perfectly in place as a steel corset.

"Is now the best time to explain such things?" he asked with a drop in his voice that I found more attractive than I'd like to admit. "I believe your housekeeper was preparing tea for us. Perhaps we should save such detailed conversations for after she's served us?"

Ah, and so it begins. The first instance of this man believing his ideas are superior to mine.

I leaned back into my chair with an unladylike slouch, folding my arms and tilting my chin up as I glared at the man who dared doubt me on my own home turf.

"Dedra takes approximately ten minutes and forty-seven seconds to brew a cup of tea for a visitor and me; occasionally, it will take her eleven and a half minutes when she can't find her matchsticks—which I promptly hid this morning in anticipation of your potential visit. We've been speaking for three minutes, which leaves at least seven remaining before she returns with the tea, and leaves only six until she presses her ear against the door to gather as many bits of my conversation as possible to scold me about later." I picked up the Little Bow's shop card and twirled it between my fingers as I watched the *superior* agent's eyes widen with the most satisfying look of shock.

I flicked the card into the air, catching it just in front of my eyes as I turned the print to him that read, *I hope you enjoy our new supplier.*

"Now, what's the purpose of the cloak, and what are we meant to be finding?"

chapter three

"Very well, then. Right to business, I suppose." Shepherd's lips twitched into a brief smile that was gone before I could fully commit it to memory, but I was still certain I'd seen it to feel a flicker of pride within me.

If I have to work with this man, then I'm not going to let him run the show from the start.

Shepherd's eyes darted smoothly around the room, flaunting their warm hazel color as he slid a small scrap of parchment out from his interior pocket. He flipped it over for me to get a glance, revealing a pencil drawing of what appeared to be an everyday cloak with ornate buttons fastened around the neck tie.

"What is this?" I asked in a hushed voice as he carefully tucked the image back into his pocket. "I already told you we can speak freely for now. You don't need to keep speaking in shop codes."

"It's not a code." Shepherd's voice dropped, and my blood warmed at the deep tone.

Gosh darn it, he had a good secretive voice—

the kind that could be heard over any chaos but still only reach the ears it's meant to. I needed to work on my vocal skills...

"This is what we're looking for," Shepherd continued, drawing me out of my mental assessment of his voice. "A few weeks ago, eight wool cloaks were retrieved from the black market but were quickly stolen by a group of organized bandits. Our job is to retrieve them before whatever buyer requested them gets ahold of the product."

I furrowed my brows as I recreated the image of the cloak in my mind, trying to piece together why anyone would desire something made of wool when we were approaching the heat of summer.

"What's so special about these cloaks?" I asked, attempting my own secretive voice, that unfortunately, came out way too deep. I cleared my throat. "I mean, the black market usually only distributes magic stones, does it not?"

"Correct, which is why these cloaks raised quite the buzz around the market." Shepherd tapped the edge of his sleeve, running his finger along the fibers of the fabric. "According to our sources, the wool is infused with powdered, unrefined magic stones, making these cloaks some sort of magic-wielding material."

Oh, my stars... That is so cool.

"Magic stone-infused clothing?" I blinked curiously, trying to hide the excitement bubbling behind the surface. "What would something like that even do?"

My mind buzzed with ideas, thinking through all the different stones and how their uses could be incorporated into clothing. A strength stone might make someone's movement more powerful, or perhaps even act as armor? Would a fire stone make someone burn everything they touched? Or make their clothes immune to heat? Oh, there were so many inventive applications! It was no wonder someone wanted to buy it!

"We're not sure," Shepherd said in a heavy tone. "We don't know what type of stones they're infused with; all we know for sure is that they're unrefined, which means—"

"They're unstable," I finished for him. "I understand now. These cloaks could be intended to be anything from armor to weapons, but knowing how temperamental unrefined magic is, they're likely extremely dangerous."

"That's right." Shepherd leaned back in his seat with another cautious glance around the room.

His posture stiffened, and the intelligent look in his eyes seemed to increase tenfold when he went into agent mode. He looked entirely different from the polite gentleman who had greeted me when I entered the room. *Gosh, he really was good.*

"I've heard you're well-suited for tracking down lost items like this?" Shepherd inquired, breaking through my distracted thoughts once again.

"Well, I don't mean to brag, but I've never once lost a single stocking at the launderers that I haven't later tracked down." I straightened with a proud smile.

Shepherd looked at me kind of like a puppy whom he had commanded to sit, but instead rolled over, still slightly impressed, but also not sure if it should be praised.

"And... what about missing cloaks?" he asked.

My smile broadened as I leaned back in my chair with a mischievous glint in my eyes. "What do you know about their destination, the buyer, and the thieves themselves?"

Shepherd eyed me curiously, then shrugged as he counted off my questions on his fingers.

"Nothing, nothing, and it was at least five men, all dressed in dark gray from head to toe," he said with a challenging tilt of his head.

Oh, just you wait, pretty boy...

"They're from Sarnold, and are likely heading back that way, too," I said simply.

"What makes you think that?" he asked with a deliciously suspicious lilt in his voice.

"Simple. The majority of black-market deals occur within Ebonair, which I'm assuming is where the cloaks originated from, correct?"

Shepherd nodded. "Yes, the cloaks were first seized while they were passing the border into Reclusia."

Just as I thought.

"If they were going to Bellatring, they wouldn't have needed to pass through Reclusia, which means the buyer is either in Reclusia or Sarnold," I continued. "Reclusia is rich in walnut and alder trees, which produce our main source of black dye, while Sarnold's geography has a sparser collection of tannin-rich roots and bark, making pure black clothing more expensive to come by. This leads me to believe that our dark-gray clad bandits originate from Sarnold, and are likely returning in that direction to a buyer who sent them out to fetch it."

I desperately wanted to soak in the fascinated look on my new partner's face, but I didn't have time to enjoy the moment since I knew Dedra would be back soon.

"There's also still a chance the buyer is within Reclusia, but their escape route should be the same either way." I drew a mental image of Reclusia's map in my mind, recalling the hidden trails that would be accessible after the rivers flooded from the rainy season. "They'll be heading east, likely along the Amberlace road, either because it's a more discreet route to Sarnold or because it feeds back into the main roadways of Reclusia."

I completed the mapping in my mind, feeling satisfied with my reply as I finally took the moment to enjoy his reaction. When I settled on his gaze, I felt my pride shatter like a fallen teacup, scattering beneath the sting of his bored expression.

"Sounds like a good start," he said simply, as if my expertly detailed analysis of the thieves' whereabouts was as commonly discussed as the time of day. "We'll need to move quickly in order to make it to the Amberlace road before they go much farther. Will you be ready to leave two days from now?"

Two days?

I shifted in my seat as an awkward aura of sorts swept over me. I'd nearly forgotten that this mission required travel. How was I meant to disappear for weeks on end without raising suspicions with my family?

"I could be ready, but I'm afraid I haven't had the opportunity to develop a cover story for my departure." I glanced toward the doorway, signaling to Shepherd that I could hear Dedra's tea tray clatter at the end of the hall.

Shepherd nodded, then readjusted to his more poised posture. "No worries. Our handler anticipated it would be difficult for you to step away from your noble life, so she devised a perfect cover for us both."

I could hear Dedra speak with mother outside the door, likely only one quick chat away from stepping inside.

"And what cover would that be?" I asked hastily while smoothing over my skirts and straightening my posture.

Shepherd gave me a puzzled look that ruffled me a bit more than I'd like to admit. He seemed surprised that I couldn't already read his mind or magically know what our handler had planned, but it wasn't my fault I was barely given any information on this mission. I'd only had one conversation with the man, and it was already apparent that his expectations of me would be unattainable.

It's official. I don't like him.

"Isn't it obvious?" he asked in that annoyingly perfect, low voice. He quirked his brow, riling me up even further for making me look like a fool for not being able to deduce an answer with no given information. "We're meant to be courting."

The door swung open only a moment after

I nearly choked on my tongue. Shepherd had no trouble switching to a cheerful smile as Dedra swept in with a tray of tea, and Mother came in behind her. It took me an extra moment to scrape my jaw up off the floor and plaster on a smile, but I don't think it mattered because both Mother and Dedra were far more interested in the suitor who hadn't made a mad dash for the door yet.

"Pardon our intrusion." Mother smiled so sweetly, I half-wondered if she'd taken a shot of honey before stepping through the door. "I just wanted to welcome you to our humble home and let you know how honored our sweet Evie is to have caught your attention."

Shepherd rose from his seat to meet Mother's gaze, then gave a cordial bow before looking up with a smile so bright and charming that it could have easily blinded an unsuspecting victim.

"The honor is truly mine, Lady Palleep." Shepherd mirrored Mother's honeyed tone, once again pulling out a perfect voice for the occasion. "Your daughter is a wonder to behold, and I find myself fortunate just to be within her glowing presence."

Darn, he knows how to flirt, too. Is there anything he can't do!?

Shepherd turned his attention to me, and all thoughts fled as he smothered me with his adoring hazel eyes. There were very few times I was at a loss for words, but being gazed at by a man who barely even respected you as a spy, yet could somehow make you feel like you were the most stunning princess in all the lands, wasn't necessarily a moment I'd spent much time preparing for. A soft warmth flooded my cheeks, and I cursed my heart for its unprompted thud.

"Oh, look at you, Evie dear." Mother giggled with a proud clasp over her heart. "You're blushing! Is it possible this kind gentleman has actually captured your interest?"

Mother glanced between me and Shepherd while Dedra curiously looked up at us from where she was pouring our tea. My cheeks stayed hot, but it was more from frustration than the lingering effects of Shepherd's doughy-eyed stare.

Why... why of all the cover stories did the handler choose a courtship!? He couldn't have been a long-lost cousin? Or perhaps a new footman instructed to follow me around and do whatever I say?

I clenched my teeth while softening my lips into a girlish smile that I complimented with long, slow flutters of my dark lashes. I raised a nervous hand to the edge of my mouth and glanced up at Shepherd through my lashes, while simultaneously muttering every unladylike word I knew inside the back of my mind.

"Your company certainly has been pleasant, Sir Stocklan." I averted my gaze from his while twirling a loose curl, practically feeling Mother's excitement burn from across the room.

"Please, Lady Genevieve," Shepherd stepped in front of my seat and stretched his hand out to me, and I glanced up just in time to see his sickeningly amorous smile and rich gaze, "call me Shep. It's what those I'm closest to call me."

I took his hand, and he gently aided me to my feet as if I were as light as a feather. His hand lingered on mine, and the burning in my cheeks returned, but this time I didn't fight it since it made for a great show. Our touch lingered, and I gave my lashes a few extra flutters for good measure.

"Very well, Shep," I said with a soft gasp. "In that case, please call me Evie."

Every fiber of my body burned with pure humiliation as I locked eyes with my despised partner. He was good at flirting... too good, which meant I likely was one of many girls he had fawned over. Nevertheless, his act was still flawless, because Mother and Dedra were practically puddles on the floor as they melted from our swoony scene.

"How darling." Mother sighed. "I think it's wonderful that you two have clicked so well. Perhaps you'd like to spend a little more time together this week?"

That sounds horrible.

"What a wonderful idea, Mother," I said in a bright tone. "Would you care to join me on a stroll tomorrow, Shep? Then we can chat more about your dear family you were just telling me about and your upcoming plans to visit with them."

Shep's eyes gleamed, reflecting the man I knew was hiding behind the polished smile.

"I would be delighted." He raised my hand to his lips and placed a tender kiss on top.

I hated that he was perfect at that, too. Most men either lingered too long on a hand kiss, kissed too sloppily, or acted entirely awkward. Shep's kiss was flawless—gentle, sweet, and just long enough to display affection, while not long enough to overstay his welcome.

Curse you and your perfect kisses...

My jaw ached from the amount of clenching I'd been doing, but I managed to ignore the discomfort as I flashed a longing gaze when Shep dropped my hand from his.

"I look forward to learning more about you, Shep."

chapter four

The soft patter of rain echoed off Shep's umbrella as I cozied next to him to keep dry. It was just my luck that our stroll would land on a rainy day, but there was no time to put it off when we needed to convince my family as quickly as possible that we were infatuated with each other enough to validate me traveling to meet his family.

Dedra lingered about twenty paces behind us, sheltered under her own umbrella as she acted as a chaperone. Between the generous distance she gave us, and the ambiance of the rain, it was easy to chat without any of our conversation being overheard. I just had to be certain to throw in a good giggle every now and again to ensure I looked like I was enjoying myself.

"Not bad. That last laugh almost sounded real." Shep nudged me playfully, though I was fairly certain the jab was real.

"If it was real, then it wouldn't be true flirting, now would it?" I gave him a teasing smack on the arm with another fake giggle. I may have hit him a little harder than I should have, but to his credit, he took it like a champ. "Ladies don't *actually* believe men are funny; they only laugh to stroke their egos."

"Ah yes, because no man could ever possibly make a woman laugh," Shep said as he gently pulled me closer to keep the rain off my shoulder.

"I think it's more important for a man to make a woman smile than to make her laugh," I said as I darted my gaze toward the puddle-glossed ground, ignoring the fluttering in my chest as I pressed up against him. He may have been used to courting women, but I was far less desensitized to being pressed against an admittedly muscular man. "It's easy to make someone laugh—there are plenty of ridiculous things in this world that spark humor. But making someone genuinely smile is far more difficult and also near-impossible to fake. A man who can make a woman smile knows not only how to brighten her day, but how to make her day entirely."

I could feel Shep's eyes on me, but I kept my gaze trained on the puddles, pretending I didn't want to step in them, even though my boots could handle the rain.

"In that case, shouldn't you be smiling at me instead of laughing?" he asked matter-of-factly. "We're meant to convince your family that we're smitten with each other, are we not?"

Don't men know there is a difference between smitten and in love?

"Giggling is plenty," I said tartly through another flirtatious smile. "It takes far too long for a man to learn what makes a girl smile, so we'll have to settle for laughter. I'm hopeful we'll have my family convinced by the end of the day so we can hurry over to Everlow."

"Everlow?" Shep raised a brow. "I thought you said we would be taking the Amberlace road."

If Dedra wasn't watching us like a spectator at a horse race, I certainly would have rolled my eyes.

"Amberlace passes through Everlow," I explained. "With more rain, the roads will be flooded and difficult to travel by cart or wagon, so they'll likely need to pick up more horses or travel by foot. Everlow is full of farm fields and pastures, so they could easily acquire a horse, or find a barn to hide out in until the rain passes if they're traveling by wagon or on foot. Either way, I know a shortcut there."

The rain filled the silence as Shep took a moment to process my reasoning. It was so annoying the way he picked apart my responses, like he was looking for a flaw buried within them.

And even more annoying that I had to pretend to like him during it...

"Very well, then," Shep said decisively in the low tone that always seemed to accompany his deeper thoughts. "In that case, we definitely need to leave before the rain lets up. The farther we let those cloaks get away from us, the more difficult it will be to catch up to them."

Well yeah, but thanks for your approval.

"What else do you know about these cloaks?" I asked. "I know you said we don't have much intel on them, but do you really believe they're dangerous?"

Shep stiffened, and an uneasy shiver rolled down the back of my neck.

"Anything from the black market is dangerous," he said coldly. "There's a reason magic stones aren't permitted to be used unless they've gone through the refining process. The effects of an unrefined stone are far more potent, and if used the wrong way, they can leave a permanent curse."

"I'm well aware," I said softly, thinking back to my friend Lacey, who had endured such a curse for nearly all her life. She'd been my best friend for years, but she had gotten so good at hiding the effects of her curse that I never once noticed it until it was too late, and I'd accidentally placed her in severe danger.

It was fortunate I had the resources I did. Without revealing my true life to her, I managed to gather false documents and travel papers to help her escape the prison I'd trapped her in, but in the end, she didn't need them. She may have been cursed, but she still managed to carve her own path out of her circumstances.

And it made me want to do the same.

"Wrap your arm around me," I said as I looked up at him with a sweet smile.

Shep blinked at me, but didn't flinch at my command. "Pardon?"

"You heard me. If we're going to get those cloaks, we need to leave, so stop being a gentleman for two minutes and act like you love me." I latched onto his arm, risking a quick glance backward to ensure Dedra was watching.

Shep gave me a sultry smile, one that would have looked fit for a romance novel from afar, but up close, was clearly laced with mischief. He leaned close to my ear, lowering the umbrella just a touch to blind our faces from Dedra's view.

"That's a big ask. Do you really think you can handle it? Are you ready for me to treat you like a lover?" His warm breath tickled my cold ear, sending a ripple down my spine.

Wait, is he still fake flirting? If so, why is he hiding our faces from Dedra?

I met his eyes with an unshakable glare,

staring straight through his sweet mask and into the slick agent who knew exactly what I was asking for.

"Treat me like the partner you want to complete your mission with," I said sharply, cutting out all the nonsense as I shifted closer to him until our faces were only inches apart. "Whatever that looks like, get on with it. I'm not going to keep giggling aimlessly while there's a dangerous stack of wools waiting to curse innocents. Convince my family that I need to meet yours."

Shep's smile twitched, and for a brief moment my fearlessness wavered as my heart hammered like there was some sort of approaching danger.

"As you wish, my lady," he said in one of those perfectly low tones as he slid his arm around my waist.

I didn't fight the action, but my entire body turned hot as I pressed against the agent I had only met yesterday. I placed my hands atop his chest and allowed him to place a gentle hand under my chin as he tilted my face upward.

Wait a moment, is he about to...

My eyes widened and my heart went wild as he lifted the umbrella just enough to give Dedra a perfect view of his incoming kiss. My skin grew clammy and my eyes squeezed shut as I fought the urge to tremble. I know I had told him to do what it takes, but even my iron will was too fragile to stand up against a fake first kiss.

He inched closer to my face, and my fingers tightened against his chest, noticing a brief jolt of his heart as I clenched the fabric on his coat.

It's just a kiss, Evie. It doesn't mean anything... It's only for the mission.

I held my breath, awaiting the feeling of his lips against mine, but at the last moment, he lowered my chin.

My heart stopped beating entirely as he lowered my head and pressed a tender kiss on the center of my forehead.

My eyes shot open, and my body cooled as the gentle touch seeped through me. He may not have kissed me on the lips, but somehow, this felt far more intimate. Instead of proving he was attracted to me, he proved he cared. He was making me smile instead of making me laugh...

Curse you and your perfect kisses, Shep.

chapter five

"You want to visit Shepherd's family in Bellatrix?" Mother braced herself on the nearest piece of furniture. I wasn't sure if her shock stemmed more from our fast-tracked infatuation or the disbelief that her daughter was actually showing interest in a serious relationship. "I-I suppose it's not completely out of the question, but isn't this all a bit sudden?"

I tightened my grip on Shep's arm, ignoring the uneasy feeling in my chest as I forced another lovey smile on my face.

"Shep has to leave tomorrow morning," I said with a pitiful sigh. "His family will only be in Bellatrix for another few weeks before they have to travel overseas for business. This is my only opportunity to meet them properly before they leave for what could easily be months."

Not the worst story we could have come up with, but there's definitely still a few cracks Mother could tear into.

"Why don't you simply meet them when they return?" Mother asked.

Yep, there's the crack.

"A few months may seem long, but it will allow you both more time to court and truly get to know each other before meeting Shep's family." Mother looked back at Father for support, but he seemed more puzzled as to why Mother was thwarting an opportunity to get me out of the house.

She may have wanted me to wed, but she was still my mother and wanted what was best for me.

Of course, she had to pick now to be cautious...

Shep placed his hand atop where I clutched his arm, sending sparks through my skin with his tender, yet firm, touch. He was far too talented at expressing appropriate amounts of affection. The touch may have been minimal, but his fingertips knew just how to expertly brush against my arm, and he had well-mastered gazing at me with a look that held desire, but not demand.

If I wasn't doomed to find a husband before, I was definitely doomed now. Shep was giving me far too unrealistic expectations for what to expect in the future.

"Lord and Lady Palleep, if I may..." Shep stepped forward, gliding me up alongside him as if we were already attached at the hip. "I understand that our courtship has been brief, and visiting my family is a big step, but I beg to remind you that I have not merely fallen for your daughter on a whim."

His grip on me softened so he could look down into my eyes with his hazel stare that I was trying to pretend looked more like dirt clumps than sparkling amber, but for goodness' sake, why did they have to sparkle so much!? He reached out to brush a curl from my eyes, letting his touch linger on my cheek just long enough to cause my skin to burn.

I held my breath, trying to keep my throbbing heart in check as it fought between the urge to tell him to back off or completely swoon.

"I first saw Evie months ago," he whispered, smoother than silk. "She was disguised as a handmaiden at the time, yet she still infected my mind like an ailment with no cure. When I discovered she was actually a noblewoman, I only found myself more fascinated by her and her selfless heart. Most women would do anything for a chance to marry a prince, but Evie... She gave up her spot for a girl who would have never had the chance otherwise."

He lowered his hand from my cheek, and I realized I hadn't been breathing the entire time.

Had he actually been at the palace while I was disguised as a servant? Or was he truly that good of a liar?

His spell had completely enchanted my parents and Dedra. They were as much at a loss for words as I was, and Mother's hand was pressed overtop her heart as if she feared it would burst free. Shep smiled at them, sliding his arm free from me so he could take my hand instead.

"I have already waited months to be with your daughter," he said as he respectfully bowed his head to my parents. "If I must wait months more, I will, but I humbly request to be spared the agony and granted the chance to welcome her into my home as you so generously welcomed me into yours."

Agony? Just how many romance novels did this man read on his way over?

"You know, my lady," Dedra leaned over to whisper less than discreetly in Mother's ear, "I truly do believe his affections are sincere. They were quite sweet on each other during their stroll..."

Father's brows shot up, and my face burned as I felt a phantom of the kiss Shep had left on my forehead.

"Tell me, boy," Father said in a grisly voice as he approached Shep with a towering glare. "What exactly are your intentions with my daughter during your visit?"

Oh boy... Perhaps his kiss wasn't as perfect as I

thought.

"To be entirely honest, Lord Palleep..." Shep glanced between Father and me with an impressive lack of fear in his eyes. "I wish to introduce her to my family and gain their approval of our relationship so, if your daughter is gracious enough to accept my hand, we might wed as soon as they return."

Did he just say that with a straight face!?

My ears burned hotter than a peppered stew as I battled against every fiber in my body not to shrink back in pure humiliation. A few days ago, I was the mighty Genevieve Palleep who struck fear into the hearts of suitors, and now, here I was, begging my family to let me visit another man's family.

Oh, how the mighty have fallen...

"Oh, please let me go." I swallowed back the urge to vomit as I managed my most heartfelt plea. "If I don't go now, there's no telling how long our courtship will be drawn out. I suppose I could always go unmarried for another few months, or perhaps years..."

"W-well, I suppose if you both truly desire this." Mother cleared her throat, and Father, after giving him one final look of warning, backed off. "We can allow you to go with Shepherd, with a chaperone, of course."

Mother nodded toward Dedra, but before she

could say anything to secure her spot on the trip, I clasped my hands together with an excited squeal.

"Might I bring along Elaine? Oh, she'd make such a wonderful companion on the journey, alongside Shep, of course." I smiled at my fake love, and he returned it with a perplexed, *what are you up to* narrow in his eyes.

"Elaine?" Dedra asked with an arch of her thin brow.

"Yes, of course!" I said proudly. "Don't you remember? Elaine was meant to escort me to the bride competition as my handmaiden before she grew ill, and Lacey had to fill in. As much as I adored having Lacey, I was so disappointed for poor Elaine. But now she has a new opportunity to join me on an adventure. Shall I let her know to start packing, or would you prefer to share the news with her yourself?"

I blinked curiously at Dedra, who only stared blankly at me, then turned to Mother, who only offered her a shrug.

"I suppose I can inform her," Dedra relented, and I gave an excited giggle.

Perfect. I can get away from Elaine, but Dedra…

"Wonderful! I'll start packing right away." I started to pull away from Shep, but a slight tug on my wrist pulled me back.

I spun around to see what he needed and felt

my heart stiffen behind my ribs as I found myself cornered under another one of his endearing gazes. He held me there for a minute, just long enough to let my cheeks grow red as he gently raised the back of my hand to his lips before pausing only a breath away.

"I'll see you first thing in the morning, my dear Evie," he said in a voice so obnoxiously perfect, I'm fairly certain even the wilting flowers on the tea table perked up.

He pressed the kiss to my hand and my skin pulsed under the soft brush of his lips. I know I told him to do whatever it took... but perhaps that was ambitious of me. Didn't he know that women, even spies, had disobedient blood pumping organs!?

"Until tomorrow," I said with a smitten smile as I slowly pulled away, being certain to look back over my shoulder a few times to really sell the longing.

Once I had disappeared from the parlor, I found my feet flying toward my room. My heart was out of control, racing with pent up tension, embarrassment, and obnoxious flutters that needed to be dealt with immediately. I slammed myself into my suite, not bothering to catch my breath as I whipped out my suitcases and began stuffing them full of an even mixture of practical dresses and frilly gowns I'd be expected to wear when meeting other nobles. My heart rate refused to simmer, still blazing after all the sweet touches, whispers, and gooey-eyed looks Shep had seared into my brain.

How am I supposed to focus on the mission when my partner is so distracting?

I slammed the suitcase shut, then rushed over to grab my secret stash of maps from underneath my closet floorboards. The maps were covered in notes and scribbles from years of marking criminal hideouts, safe-houses, and natural landmarks. I shut myself inside the closet and sprawled the maps across the floor to try to refocus my mind on the hunt instead of the hunter I was paired with.

The cloaks were heading for Sarnold... but who in Sarnold would want weaponized clothing? Sarnold already had the strongest military force out of all the surrounding kingdoms, so unless the king was simply collecting power, it wouldn't make much sense for him to hire measly crooks to oversee a black-market deal. The deepest veins of the black market ran through Ebonair, though no one has been able to track the true hub of the market. It's possible that any sales required someone on the inside with intel to the market, which meant a knowledgeable crook could be just as useful as a trained operative.

Is Sarnold looking to get stronger? Or is someone within Sarnold looking to overpower their own kingdom?

I folded up the maps and tucked the Ebonair and Bellatrix one away, while keeping out the detailed Reclusia and Sarnold maps to bring along. Theorizing about the use of the cloaks was a good distraction to my current partner problem, but it wasn't the job I was assigned. The wool cloaks were my objective. This was my opportunity to prove that even if Shep was talented at playing the role of lover, my talents lay in tracking what no one else could find.

I'll find the lost wools, then we'll see who's the most useful.

chapter six

"Are you sure you have everything?" Mother flitted around the carriage, inspecting it for the fourth time to ensure I hadn't forgotten a single hatbox, trunk, or cloak.

"Yes, Mother, I'm certain." I gave her a reassuring smile as I ran through my mental checklist to make sure I hadn't forgotten any maps or tools. "We'll only be gone for a few weeks at most. It'll be shorter than my visit to the capital."

Mother bit the edge of her lip, smearing the lipstick onto her tooth.

"I know, it's just that..." She glanced over at Shep, looking him up and down as if searching for a flaw she had yet to discover.

Shep stepped forward with a hand placed across his apparently flawless heart. "I can assure you, Lady Palleep, I will treat your daughter with the utmost care and respect, as will my family."

Mother's teeth released her lip, and the last bit of reluctance faded from her eyes as she let out a long sigh.

"You know I truly am happy for you, Evie. It's just that..." Mother was interrupted as Father placed a tender hand on her shoulder, pulling her close.

"This is a bit sudden for all of us," Father continued for her. "But what your mother is trying to say, is that even though we always want to be around for your happiness, we won't stand in the way of it."

Mother nodded, her eyes glossing with tears as she looked at me with a tender pride that I felt terribly guilty receiving.

I hope she doesn't take the news too hard when we dramatically break off our courtship after the mission.

"Thank you, Mother, Father." I pulled them both into an embrace, squeezing them a little extra hard like I always did whenever I was sneaking off for a mission.

My jobs were never particularly dangerous, but I've had to pull a knife on more than one occasion. Hunting down convicts and stolen goods wasn't a task that often put me in the line of fire, but that didn't mean I wasn't going to give my parents an extra squeeze in case I didn't come home.

"Be sure to write us every day," Mother sniffled, dabbing her eyes with a handkerchief before any tears could escape her lashes.

"Of course," I said, stepping toward the carriage where Shep was already holding the door open for Elaine and me. "I'll see you both soon."

I gave them one final wave goodbye, then stepped into the carriage behind Elaine. Shep remained outside for a moment, likely to show one final impressive display of chivalry before whisking me off into the countryside. It struck me as humorous how the last time my family had sent me off in a carriage, I was secretly planning to swap places with my handmaiden, while this time, the entire trip was secret and I had a handmaiden to deal with...

I smiled over at Elaine, who was already settled onto the padded bench seat and cozied up in her knit shawl. She hadn't been exactly enthusiastic to join us as our chaperone, but like my previous handmaiden, Lacey, had discovered, it was difficult to refuse a request from Dedra.

Shep joined us in the cabin and signaled to the driver to head off. The snap of the reins rang through the air as the whole carriage jerked to begin our journey.

"Are you excited, my dear?" Shep asked, his curious eyes gently drifting toward Elaine.

He's wondering what I'm planning to do about her.

"More than I can say," I gushed with an overdramatic sigh. "I have so many plans I want to do with your family, but perhaps I'll indulge you in my ideas once the journey has begun to grow dull."

Shep gave me a discreet nod, responding with a clean smile. "As you wish, Evie."

At least he knows how to listen.

Time passed painfully slow as we journeyed through the town and moved from the cobblestone roads to the pebbly dirt ones. I watched out the window as the homes outside grew smaller and less ornate with every passing street. The first day in the carriage passed about as peacefully as one could expect, and we ended up resting at a reputable inn not far from the city. Elaine and I shared a room, but once she was asleep, I lit a candle to take another look at my maps.

Just a little farther, then we'll need to split off.

We started the next day with an early breakfast, where Shep told stories about his family's pet horse that felt so real, I had to wonder if any of the story was actually fake.

We hopped back on the road, and I counted the trees as we made it just far enough away from home that I finally felt ready to enact the first stage of our mission.

It's time to dismiss Elaine.

I glanced over at Elaine, who was staring blankly out the window, looking out at the passing trees and letting her eyes droop as they blurred together.

"Now, should be far enough." I broke the silence, causing Shep to jerk up from the book in his lap and Elaine to tear her attention from the window.

"Far enough for what, my dear?" Shep inquired as he tucked the book aside.

I turned to Elaine, my doughy-eyed facade vanishing as I caught the older woman's startled gaze.

"Did you need something, my lady?" she asked.

"Elaine, do you remember that time when I was fifteen, and you caught me sneaking out of the manor through the kitchen window past dark?" I asked bluntly, causing both Shep and Elaine to stiffen, as if I'd just confessed to murder.

"M-my lady..." Elaine darted her eyes to Shep. "I do believe you requested I never speak of—"

"One month's salary was enough to buy your silence then, and you've proven able to keep the incident between us," I continued, digging into my boot, where I found the hefty bag of gold coins I'd stashed earlier. "Today I am prepared to offer you two months' salary for your silence once more."

Elaine's jaw dropped, and Shep nearly choked as he sucked in half the air within the cabin. I knew this wasn't the most *discreet* way to go about accomplishing our mission, but it was either this or faking my own abduction, which would only draw *more* attention to the wild Lady Genevieve.

Shep cleared his throat. "Evie, are you—"

"Hush, dear." I flicked him an overly-sweet smile. "The ladies are doing business."

Shep's jaw snapped shut, and Elaine narrowed her eyes at the two of us before settling her gaze on the bursting bag of gold coins. I could practically feel the rage steaming off Shep behind me, but I would have to deal with dousing him later.

"My lady, what exactly are you planning on doing?" Elaine bit her lip, still ogling the coins as she squeezed her hands in her lap.

"Nothing dishonorable, if that's what you're fearing," I said with a calming lilt in my voice. "In exchange for the gold, we'll drop you off at an inn where you'll remain until we return. Each day you'll send out a letter to my parents, addressed from me."

I reached into the interior pocket of my cloak, pulling out a stack of sealed and addressed letters that were tied together with a pink ribbon.

"M-my lady, I couldn't—"

"You can." I pressed the letters and the pouch of gold into her lap, causing the woman to stiffen. "Upon my return, I intend to gift you with three of my finest necklaces back at the manor. That should be more than enough to pay off the bank loans you accumulated for your daughter's medications."

Elaine's gaze shot to me, her pupils wider than a black pearl that was slowly being submerged behind her glossy tears. I could hear Shep shift behind me, though I was too fixated on Elaine to pay him any mind.

"Y-you... you know about my daughter?" Elaine asked, her voice choked from her welling tears.

"I had a strong assumption," I said kindly, recalling the extra hours I'd seen her work, the books on medicinal herbs she'd borrowed from the library to read on her breaks, and when I'd overheard her asking the parlor maid, Sarah, if she could cover her shift to take her daughter to an appointment. "I noticed one of the bank loans sticking out of your pocket the other day. Has her health improved since the treatment?"

"It has. She's made a miraculous recovery, but the cost was..." Elaine's face flushed, and she averted her gaze to the items in her lap. "My lady, are you certain this is a good idea?"

She looked back at Shep, who quietly watched our exchange with crossed arms and a look that was a mix between puzzled and pleased.

"If you can promise me your silence once more, I couldn't think of a better idea to help us both." I took Elaine's hands and curled them around the letters and gold sitting in her lap. "Will you allow me an adventure, Elaine?"

I held my breath, watching every twitch, blink, and glance from Elaine as her hands finally relaxed overtop the gold.

"Very well, Miss Evie." She sighed as she rubbed her damp eyes. "I will do as you wish, but only if you can promise me you'll return unharmed."

"That's not a promise I can easily make, Elaine," I answered honestly as I recalled the brief moments I'd had to go on the defense. "But I can promise I will take on this adventure with caution. But just to protect you..."

I reached over to the bundle of letters and pointed out one on the bottom with a soft pink envelope.

"If for some unforeseen reason I don't return, use this letter to protect yourself. It claims that I ran away from you to elope with Shep, outside of your knowledge."

Elaine bit her lip as she brushed her thumb against the letter I hoped no one would ever have to read. "What about him?" She tilted her head toward Shep. "Should I be concerned about letting you run off with a suspiciously perfect gentleman?"

Shep caught my eye, robbing me of my breath for a moment as the loving mask of a suitor fell and revealed the intensity of the spy beneath.

"From what I've seen, the only suspiciously perfect one here is Miss Evie," he said, keeping his eyes locked on me.

What is that supposed to mean?

I averted my gaze, turning my attention to the window as I cracked the carriage door open to shout up to the driver. "Please take us to the nearest inn."

"Yes, my lady," the driver called back as the carriage adjusted to a new track.

"Are you absolutely certain you want me to stay behind?" Elaine asked over the clatter of the carriage wheels.

"Positive." I beamed. "Besides, I'm sure you're long overdue for a vacation."

. . . .

Once we arrived at the next inn, we dropped Elaine off and informed the driver we would be upgrading to a more comfortable carriage in the morning, then sent him home with a hefty tip. I left nearly all my luggage with Elaine in her spacious room, only bringing along a single shoulder bag with some spare coins, my maps, and a few other essentials.

I changed out of my frilly yellow day dress, and put on a more simplistic light blue dress with a corseted top and a dark gray cloak to blend in as we approached Sarnold. My hair still held the curls from the updo Elaine had spent nearly an hour on this morning, so I did my best to tame it back into a more simplistic braid before bidding Elaine farewell and meeting Shep outside by the front of the inn.

He was waiting right where he said he would, with his pressed silk tunic replaced with a more rugged cotton shirt and his starched slacks swapped out for a more modest pair of trousers. Without his waistcoat, his sculpted form was far more visible through the thin cotton shirt, surging a strange heat in my chest.

"You certainly clean up well, my lady." Shep smirked as he gestured to the dark brown horse he had acquired in my absence. "Your carriage awaits, my dear."

Oh great, I got a partner with a knack for showmanship.

I pushed past him, tightening my bag over my shoulder as I made my way to the horse.

"You can cut the theatrics. We made it out of my family's line of sight, so you should be safe to treat me like a partner instead of the main character in your upcoming romance novel." I fluttered my lashes at him with a sarcastic smile.

"Are you certain?" Shep folded his arms with a devilish laugh. "You seemed rather comfortable taking on the role of my beloved. I'd hate to break the immersion for you when you played it so convincingly."

"What?" I spun around, heat flaring in my cheeks as I met his ridiculous grin. "I was only mirroring *your* affection. You're the one who kissed me in the rain!" I stomped my foot, kicking up a cloud of dirt and scuffing my boots.

Shep's smile didn't fade, but his eyes gleamed with that same annoying look he had when he thought he knew more than me. He took a slow step forward, kicking back some of the dirt as he leaned down to my ear.

"And you're the one who begged me to do it," he whispered, singeing my nerves with a single breath.

"I *asked* you to up your game because I actually knew what I was doing," I hissed as I pulled back a step. "My family wasn't going to let me leave simply because of a fleeting crush."

"And you did a great job of handling things on your own turf, my lady." Shep thanked me in a tone that was just a note closer to mocking than it was genuine gratitude. "I must say, your plan with the servant had me put off, but I'm impressed how it came together."

"Thank you," I clipped with a tilt of my nose. "Navigating my environment just happens to be what I do best, as I *displayed* when acting as your lover."

Shep smiled, his hazel eyes crinkling with the most infuriating gaze that was just a little too tall and a little too pleased. Oh, how I wanted to smack some respect into his pretty face, but this was my partner—a partner who had unfortunately kissed me.

"Very well then, navigator." He took another step closer, closing the distance between us as if challenging me to bend to his smile the same way my infatuated act did. "Where should we start looking first?"

I didn't budge, keeping my gaze locked on him even as I had to crane my neck to match his towering height.

Just you wait, Shep...

"The local watering hole," I said coolly. "All livestock has to drink at some point. We'll find information about our missing wools there."

chapter seven

Did he really have to get only one horse?

I locked my jaw as we bounced along the trail with Shep's arms wrapped around me to reach the reins. Despite assuring him I was fully capable of sitting behind him and remaining stable, he insisted that placing me in front would be more comfortable for the horse.

Unfortunately, I don't know much about horses, so I couldn't prove he was lying.

Curse you, Mother, for never letting me attend horseback riding lessons as a child...

We had spent another two days riding since dropping off Elaine at the inn, only stopping to swap out horses and rest at a questionable inn with only one room available. Shep offered to sleep in the stable, which I was more than happy to comply with since I wasn't necessarily feeling open to sharing a room with my obnoxiously attractive partner.

Shep clearly had been well-trained in handling a mount, which only aggravated me more. After successfully carving the path of our mission's success for the last few days, I was finally placed in a position where I truly needed Shep's help. I knew it would come up eventually —that's what partners were for, after all—but I had hoped to establish at least a little more dominance over him before the situation arose...

The horse made a small jump, forcing me to lean back into Shep, and his arms tightened around me and the reins. For a moment, he was completely embracing me, slamming my heart into overdrive as I hastily shifted forward and out of his touch.

How am I supposed to prove my worth to this guy when, at every turn of our mission, I am forced to fall into his arms!?

The least our handler could have done was send me an ugly partner...

"You said the tavern should be at the end of this road, right?" Shep leaned close to my ear to ensure I heard him over the clatter of hooves.

My ear tickled from his warm breath, sending me back to the moment when we were huddled under our umbrella in the rain, and surging up the desire to elbow him back a few inches. The air was just as warm as it had been then, but instead of the crisp scent of rain surrounding us, the earthy fragrance of the forest flooded my senses, reminding me this was no place for snuggling.

"Yes, it's the only tavern in this area that isn't highlighted on public maps," I said as I shimmied forward on the horse, only managing to chafe my thighs in the process. "Should be a local hot spot for the more *private* folk around these parts, and a great place to pick up intel."

"I see." Shep slowed the horse's steps to a walk as the first dim glow of the tavern came into view beneath the fading sun. "Shouldn't be too difficult to squeeze some information out of some rowdy drunks. I'll swing inside for a bit and see what I can learn."

I whipped my head around, nearly clocking him in the jaw as I turned to glare at him.

"*You'll* go inside?" I scowled. "What am I meant to do? Sit and keep the horse warm?"

Shep chuckled as he pulled the horse up to the edge of the path. "You said so yourself, it's not exactly a *proper* establishment."

"Yes, and?" I prodded.

"And..." Shep eyed me as he dismounted with a bemused smile. "You're a very intelligent woman, Evie, but you're still a lady."

"A lady who can handle herself just fine, thank you." I slipped off the horse, landing a little more awkwardly than I had intended, but with a smooth recovery.

I'm not about to let Shep steal my thunder after it was my idea to visit the tavern. No, sir. If the agency wanted to send me a babysitter, then I was going to send him back with too much time on his hands.

"Evie, I can handle this. I just need to buy a few drinks and get some information," Shep reasoned, his gaze tightening on me with what almost felt like real concern.

"Ah, you see, that's the difference between you and me." I dropped my hood and tugged the leather strap off the end of my braid to fluff out my golden curls. "You have to buy drinks to get men to talk, but if I step inside, I'll be the one they ask you to buy drinks for."

I winked, and Shep shook his head with what appeared to be a bitten smile.

"You're impossible, you know?" He stepped forward and reached his hand around my waist. I froze for a moment, wondering if he was going in for some sort of embrace, but relaxed when I realized he was only reaching for the reins to tie off our horse.

He kept eye contact as he wrapped the reins around the branch just above my head, standing so close I could smell the lingering scent of the cologne he'd worn as a fake noble.

"I'm a spy," I said softly. "Aren't we meant to be unwavering?"

"Yes, but I'm your partner," he huffed as he tugged the knot above me, letting his arms fall, but not making any move to step away from me. "We're meant to look out for each other."

"What makes you think I need looking after?" I asked with a prim lift of my brow. "Just because I'm a small, dainty lady doesn't mean I don't know what I'm doing."

"Alright, my lady. Then prove it." He gave me a sideways smile, the type that should have made me annoyed if I wasn't already so flustered by his close proximity. "We'll both go inside, and whoever gets intel on the missing wools first gets to call the shots for the rest of the mission."

A thrilling spark shot down my spine as a smile curled my lips. This was exactly what I had been hoping for—a chance to prove my undeniable usefulness and run this mission like it was mine all along. This pretty boy wasn't going to know what hit him.

"You're on." I brushed past him, giving my curls one final flick as I headed toward the tavern. "Just don't pout when I ask you to keep the horse warm later."

I waved over my shoulder, then adjusted the laces on my dress to emphasize my curves. Genevieve Palleep may not have gotten out much, but Evie spent a fair portion of her training observing how people walked, talked, dressed, and behaved—and the best place for observing people in their truest form had always been at a tavern.

There were many ways to get information out of a person, but the best way to do it was in a manner where they didn't even know you were asking. No one liked to be interrogated, but every man loved to be fawned over. Fortunately for me, I was born perfectly adorable. But adorable didn't cut it in a place like this; I needed to be desirable.

Well, at least a little bit. I want them to talk to me, not drool over me.

I stepped through the doors and was instantly slammed in the face with the sour smell of ale. Oak floors, littered with sticky puddles and the remnants of shattered bottles, sprawled underneath me, with the occasional missing floorboard to really complete the look. A long bar stretched across the far wall, covered in even more suspicious sticky substances than the floor, and tables full of patrons were scattered across the rest of the room.

The back corner was packed with half-drunk lumbermen, who were still covered in wood shavings and sawdust. They were chatting at full volume, clinking their drinks and gulping down bowls of questionable stew. The men at the bar seemed even louder, mainly because they had to shout down to the ends of the bar to get anyone to hear them. It was noisier than I remembered, but the chaotic, yet relaxed, atmosphere was all the same.

It's good to be back to work.

"Hey there, little miss." A tall, burly man with a squared jaw and a fierce scar trailing from his neck to his collarbone met me by the door. He had dark gray eyes and was far more attractive than most tavern dwellers I'd come across, with a tall pint of ale in his hands. A few of the other men he was seated with peered from their seats at the bar, each eyeing me like a rabbit who had stumbled into a fox den. "If you're looking for a spot of tea, you've come to the wrong place."

The men behind him laughed, and I lifted my chin as I approached my greeter with an unyielding glare.

"The only thing I'm looking for is a hard drink and a soft chair." I wrapped my fingers around the man's pint, pulling it slowly to my lips without breaking eye contact.

I barely let the drink brush my lips, but that was all it took to catch everyone's attention. It admittedly smelled better than the flowery wines served at estate parties, but it was still bitter, so I only faked a swallow. I released the pint back to its burley owner, who was now looking at me as if he'd just watched the rabbit devour a lion.

"Thanks for the drink." I wiped the edge of

my lip with a devilish smile. "Now, how about that chair I was asking about?"

Just then, I heard the door creak open behind me, but I didn't have to turn to know it was Shep. After spending so much time right up against him, I was no stranger to his presence. The burly man glanced over me to narrow his eyes at Shep, and for a moment, I wondered if he was going to question his sudden entrance as well.

"I suppose *your* seat is open," I said with a coy smile as I brushed past the man to move toward the bar. "Thanks for the warm welcome."

The men clustered around the bar laughed and called to their companion as I slid onto his abandoned stool. The man whipped around, forgetting all about Shep as he followed behind me with a grisly laugh.

"What's your name, little lady?" he asked as he yanked a stool out from the scrawny blonde man sitting next to me, causing him to crash to the floor. He sank down onto his newly acquired stool, setting the pint down on the counter with another splash of sticky liquid.

"Call me Lyla," I said as I hooked my finger around the rim of his drink and slid it closer. "Now should I just call you barmaid, or do you actually have a name?"

He laughed, pulling his drink out of my reach as he snapped his fingers and spurred one of the men on the edge of the bar to rush back behind it.

"The name's Lex, and as a matter of fact, I am the barmaid." He nodded toward the man who was scurrying behind the bar, and a second later, a pint of my own was sloshed in front of me. "This is my tavern."

"Well, Mister Lex," I leaned forward, catching his eyes as I looked up at him through my lashes, "what's a fine businessman like yourself doing out here in the middle of nowhere? Can't get any regulars off the main road?"

A burst of laughter echoed behind me, and I snuck a glance back, only to find Shep at the head of the commotion. He looked like a completely different man from the one I'd seen in the woods a second ago. His shirt was halfway unbuttoned, his hair tussled, and a drink was held high in his hand as he proposed a toast to the table of men he already had eating out of his palm. My cheeks burned as my eyes drifted toward his half-buttoned shirt, revealing a sneak peek at a set of sculpted abs that would make even a nun blush.

He glanced up from his toast, catching my eye as I turned back in my seat to face Lex, who was also perplexed by Shep's growing popularity.

Drat... he's good at this, too. I need to focus.

"I'm not really fond of the clientele in that area," Lex said in a low voice as his focus slowly shifted back to me. "I prefer the patrons who have more interesting stories to tell."

He rested his hand on the sticky bar top, grabbing another swig of his drink with his free hand. He glanced at my untouched drink, but I pretended to be too interested in him to notice. Faking a sip of the owner's drink was one thing, but drinking from a cup specifically made for me was a risk I wasn't planning on taking.

Even though he was entertaining his own party, I could still feel Shep's eyes burrowing into the back of my head. I didn't have to look to know he was watching me, waiting for me to slip up or reach for the drink just so he could swoop in and save me.

Keep dreaming.

"Interesting stories, hmm?" I traced my fingers along Lex's arm, earning an impressed whistle from one of the men around us. "Which ones are your favorites? I heard a rumor about some black-market goodies coming through town and have been really sucked into the gossip train lately."

Lex let out a low chuckle, setting his drink aside as he leaned in closer to meet me with his dark stare. "Black market? Haven't seen any of those shipments pass by in a while, but I have a great story about a soldier who thought he could best me with two of his lackeys."

I narrowed my gaze on the bead of sweat that

crossed his forehead, the slight inflection in his voice, and the goosebumps that prickled the arm I was tracing.

He's lying...

I continued to smile and nod at his story as I started taking a closer look at the men around the tavern. Only three were wearing cloaks, but none of them were made out of anything heavier than cotton. The cloaks weren't in plain sight, but there had definitely been some contraband passed through here. I just needed to confirm it was the cloaks.

"Oh, good grief," I interrupted Lex's story as I wobbled in my stool, catching the edge of my gray cloak underneath the leg. "My cloak is snagged. Don't you just hate it when your cloaks don't do as you wish?"

I laughed, watching Lex intently as he forced a smile across his face.

"They can certainly be a hassle." Lex cleared his throat, sharing a brief glance with the other men around the bar before diving back into his story.

Got you.

"Excuse me, miss."

I fought the urge to grimace when I recognized the familiar voice.

Not now... I'm finally getting to the good stuff.

"Can I help you?" I turned to face Shep, doing my best to give him a *'don't you dare sabotage me'* look.

"Sorry to bother you, but you came in before me, right? I think I saw your horse pull loose from its post." Shep's voice was calm, but for some reason, he was glaring at Lex like he had some sort of murderous intent. "I can show you if you'd like."

Guess he wants to talk.

I started to move from my seat, but was halted when Lex placed an arm in front of me. "The lady hasn't even been able to enjoy her drink yet. Why don't you be a gentleman and take care of the horse for her while she keeps us company."

The friendly smile on Shep's face melted, as an icy glare passed through his eyes like a frozen blade. I'd seen many of Shep's faces at this point, but none were quite as intense as this one. I sat fixated in place, unable to move as Shep's shadowy presence infected the room like a surging storm.

"I don't believe I was asking *you*," Shep said sharply, his hand twitching near his belt where I suspected he kept a blade.

Oh boy...

Lex rose from his seat, still standing in front of me as he sized up to Shep with a flock of men rising behind him.

"Under my roof, everything is my business." Lex cracked his knuckles, and a few of the men started chanting behind him in hopes of edging a fight.

I bit back a groan. *You really can't take men anywhere, can you?*

I pushed to my feet, shoving Lex aside. "Will you boys stop fussing before my blasted horse runs away!?" I grabbed Shep by the arm, flashing him a dirty glare before dragging him behind me toward the door. "We'll be back as soon as this pest shows me what he's talking about."

Shep narrowed his eyes at the charming nickname I'd given him, but I hardly felt bad when he was the one who nearly started a barroom brawl when I was only moments away from learning what direction our cloaks were heading.

I pulled him outside, and my lungs celebrated the clean air that was free from the reek of booze. We didn't stop until we were tucked safely out of sight behind the trees, and my adrenaline began to stir as I realized I had already won our challenge by walking away with information. It may not have been a direct answer to where the cloaks were heading, but I had confirmation that we were on the right track.

The sun had already dipped behind the trees, and the first chirps of crickets were starting to serenade the evening as I whirled around to face my beaten opponent with a smile.

I opened my mouth to solidify my victory, but at the exact same moment, he opened his as we spoke in perfect unison.

"The cloaks were here."

chapter eight

"What? How would you know that?" I asked.

Had he been listening in on my conversation? That cheater!

"The men I sat with said a group of men in fine cloaks passed by last night." Shep narrowed his eyes on me with a suspicious twitch in his brow. "How did *you* learn that information? Were you spying on my conversation?"

What!?

"As if I'd need to," I huffed. "Lex, the tavern owner, seems to have a lot of run-ins with black-market goods. He gave me a reaction when I brought up the cloaks, so he definitely knows they're not ordinary fashion statements."

"You got a *reaction*?" Shep smirked. "So, what you're saying is that you don't have intel, just a hunch."

Why you little...

"It's not just a hunch. He knows something about the thieves, and I would have found out more if you hadn't so rudely interrupted." I clenched my fists, practically vibrating with the urge to thump him on the forehead.

"You should be thanking me for stepping in when I did," Shep said. "Did you see how those men were looking at you?" His voice tensed, and he looked on the verge of swearing.

"I saw how *you* were looking at me," I countered as I jabbed his shoulder. "Is it so difficult for you to trust your partner to do their job without hovering?"

"I don't know, is it?" Shep folded his arms. "You certainly didn't seem keen on letting me do my job earlier, remember?"

"Because it's my job, too." I bit the inside of my cheek, fighting the urge to shout and draw any attention from inside. "I'm not going to be pushed to the side just because you think I can't handle myself. Lex knows something about the cloaks that we haven't learned yet, and we're not going to find out just standing out here in the dark."

Shep rubbed his temples with a long breath, pacing across the grass as he sputtered out a few of the swear words he'd tucked away earlier.

"Fine, *we* will talk to Lex," Shep said.

"*We?*" I frowned. "Sorry to disappoint you, but I don't think you necessarily made as good of an impression on him as you did your drinking buddies. He won't talk to you, but he might talk to me."

"I don't need to be his friend to make him talk," Shep said starkly. "Besides, we tied in our little bet, so we both have to lead the mission."

Ugh, why didn't I say my information quicker!

"Although..." Shep crept forward, making his way back to the tavern, but stopping beside me to meet my ear. "If your hunch about the owner is wrong, then it would appear that only one of us actually walked out with intel."

I turned to look at him, getting a full view of his side profile, which was almost more attractive than his full face. "Don't get cocky," I said as I turned to follow him back to the tavern. "I'm rarely ever wrong about people."

"Oh, yeah?" Shep side-eyed me. "What about that handmaiden of yours? The one whose lies you famously fell for?"

"I said *rarely*," I grumbled. "It's hard to read people who are always lying, because you can't find enough glimpses of the truth."

"What about me?" Shep asked as we approached the door. "I lie a lot. Is that why you don't particularly like me?"

No, I don't like you because your sole purpose in being here is to undermine me.

"You're still easy to read," I said. "You're someone who always thinks they're the best in the room. You're confident, considered trustworthy, and have a little bit of a dark side you keep under wraps."

We stepped through the doors, and Shep brushed past me to head toward the bar, whispering in my ear as he went, "You're right about one of those things."

The hairs on my neck stood as he moved past me, and I swallowed dryly to keep my face from reacting to his never-ending lack of suaveness. After I collected myself, I turned my attention back to the bar, where Shep was already chatting up some patrons. I scanned the room in search of Lex, but he wasn't where I'd left him. In fact, he wasn't there at all.

"Where's Lex?" I asked the scrawny man pouring drinks. "I didn't scare him off already, did I?"

The man slid a pint of ale across the table to Shep, who caught it without even turning his head. "As I told yer friend, he'll be back in a moment. He told me to make sure you had a fresh drink while he was gone. Looked like he was just taking out the trash."

The trash?

I flicked Shep a glance, and to my relief, he was already looking at me with the same tension I felt. The bartender went to fill another pint from the barrel, and I wasted no time grabbing

Shep by the wrist and pulling him away from the bar.

Shep followed me as smoothly as a serpent, racing alongside me as I pushed back out of the tavern doors.

"He's making a run for it," I said under my breath as Shep and I ran around the back of the building.

"That, or he's trying to hide something from us." Shep sprinted alongside me. "You were right, Evie."

Something inside me glowed from his acknowledgment. Slowly but surely, he was having to accept that I wasn't some frilly lady in search of an adrenaline rush. This wasn't a pastime for me; this was my job.

Something moved in the forest, just beyond the light of the tavern's windows. Shep and I turned to follow the noise, and a second later, the slight sound turned into the noise of running feet. He was trying to escape.

"Stop!" Shep called after the culprit, skillfully ducking under branches and vaulting over fallen logs like he'd been doing it since birth.

I fell behind, unable to navigate the forest's terrain quite as efficiently in my dress and cloak. I tried to keep him within my sight, but the woods were clear enough that they could run at full force, leaving my shorter legs in the dust.

Usually, my small size made it easy to escape through forests, but chasing someone else was a completely different story. Shep disappeared, and the sound of close combat rang through the air.

"Shep!"

My heart stiffened in my chest, and my lungs pulsed like the air was too thin as I raced through the never-ending woods. They were too fast, and I couldn't even see them anymore, but the sound of fighting was growing louder. I'd done so well staying ahead of Shep. I thought I had finally proven I was capable of taking the lead, but when things got serious, I was still doomed to fall behind.

My dress snagged on a bush, and I turned to tug it loose. The sound of combat grew quiet, and my tugging ceased as the terrifying silence permeated the forest. The absence of sound clawed at me, leaving me stiff as all the worst-case scenarios filtered through my mind. The soft hoo of an owl caused my head to jerk, and the squeak of a squirrel nearly sent me sprinting. There were still sounds, but they were the wrong ones. What had happened to the men?

Is Shep okay? Did something happen?

My hands quivered as I reached for the dagger in my boot. I took a cautious step forward, my heart slamming into my ribs as fear for Shep's safety gnawed at me from the inside.

What was I supposed to do if he got hurt? I could defend myself, but I couldn't fight off someone as strong as Lex. I bit my lip as I moved deeper into the woods, my heart sinking as the crashing realization of Shep's words hit me square in the chest.

If Shep is hurt, it's because of me.

I had insisted on taking over a job he knew he could handle. If I hadn't been so stubborn...

I heard a shout come from somewhere in the woods, but I couldn't tell if it was Lex or Shep. My heart went into overdrive as I spun blindly around the woods. I never got lost—that wasn't even a word in my vocabulary—so why couldn't I find them now? My head spun, too dizzied by the thought of Shep being pummeled into dust by Lex. I had to find him; he needed help, and I had to—

"Lyla! Are you there?"

Shep!

I jolted at the name, nearly forgetting it was the alias I had given Lex earlier. Despite the wrong name, there was no denying Shep's voice —his perfect voice that always knew how to convey exactly what he wanted the other person to hear.

He needed help.

"I'm coming!" I followed the sound and discovered I had actually passed them when Shep tackled Lex behind a tree. Shep was on top of Lex, pressing the side of his face into the dirt with a dagger pointed between his shoulder blades.

Relief poured through me the second I saw that Shep was unharmed, and I found myself grateful that it was too dark for him to see how truly worried I must have looked.

"Get off me, you maniac!" Lex sputtered into the dirt, his face red with rage as he squirmed. "I'm just taking a blasted walk!"

"Is that so?" Shep used his foot to kick at a discarded bag that had fallen to the ground, nudging it in my direction.

I tucked my dagger back into my boot and reached for the bag. It only took one look inside for my breath to catch and my fingers to brush against the familiar texture of the heavy winter material.

Shep grabbed Lex's hair to lift his head, so he could see the bag's contents. "Then why aren't you wearing your cloak?"

chapter nine

Found one.

I unfurled the cloak and shook out the wrinkles to get a better look at it. The wool had been dyed black, and the ornate button at the top was engraved with some sort of seal that looked like a twinkling star. The fabric itself didn't look unusual, but upon closer inspection, I could see a soft golden shimmer within the wool. It was fairly subtle under the moonlight, but I could only imagine how it would glitter under the sun.

Magic stones...

There was no denying the glitter of magic, but I had never seen it woven into another material like this before. It looked as if someone had powdered the unrefined stones and somehow infused the wool before crafting the cloak. It was incredible, and likely more powerful than I could ever imagine.

But what does it do?

"Never took you for the glitzy type, Lex." I held out the cloak to him, allowing the fabric to sparkle in front of him. "I sure hope you have some bejeweled boots to match."

Lex squirmed beneath Shep's grip, but the cool touch of a dagger behind his neck was all Shep needed to stiffen him up.

"If you want the blasted wool, then take it! Just get off me," Lex growled. "I don't want anything to do with it or the freaks who wear them."

Now we're getting somewhere.

"What *freaks*?" Shep asked. "Where did you get the cloak?"

I watched with fixed attention as Shep calmly pressed the blade into Lex's tanned neck. Shep was so collected, and his movements with the blade were incredibly precise. He knew exactly how much pressure to apply to intimidate his prey without actually breaking the skin, and not to mention his voice... At the bar, he had spoken in a higher pitch, with a slight Reclusian accent that made him seem approachable to the locals, but now his pitch had dropped to a low and practiced growl—the type that rings in your ears even hours after you've left the conversation. I had thought I was fairly decent at interrogations, but Shep... He was downright scary.

"Hey! Watch the knife, buddy!" Lex's voice wavered, his eyes darting to me as if expecting a little sympathy from the dainty little lady. "It wasn't just me, alright! There was a whole group of us. The leader is the one to blame."

The leader?

"What's his name?" Shep asked as he smoothly moved the blade to a different spot on his neck to increase the illusion of pressure, yet still not drawing a single drop of blood.

"Heck, if I know!" Sweat beaded across Lex's face, his tone frantic. "He barely even let us see his face, let alone know his name. All I know is that he offered each of the men a hefty sum of coins in exchange for swiping some cloaks from a royal military shipment."

Shep's eyes narrowed like a preying viper, and a cold chill rushed through my blood. "I'm bored with asking all the questions. Start telling me everything you know, or I'll entertain myself by carving doodles into your back." He traced the blade down Lex's spine, keeping a firm hold on the back of his neck. "What do you say, Lyla? Would you like me to draw you a rose? Or perhaps a butterfly?"

He met my eyes, and I froze. He looked so serious... I'd always known he was good at playing different roles, but this role I hadn't yet read the script for.

"I..."

"I'll talk, I'll talk!" Lex cracked before I had

to think up a reply, his entire body shuddering under the brush of the blade.

Shep lifted the blade back toward his neck, still keeping it just a touch above his skin in case he decided to twitch. "Go on."

"It was all just a side job. The leader came through the bar and asked if I knew any men strapped for cash," Lex explained. "I told him I was never a man to say no to some extra coin, and he had me join his little gang. There were eight of us in total, counting the boss. He told us that all we had to do was swipe some fancy cloaks and help him get them to Sarnold. After that, he'd pay us. But I didn't follow through with the rest of the job..."

A cold breeze swept through the forest, but the shiver in Lex's voice felt too intense for just a chill. I looked down at the sparkling cloak in my hands, and the same dark chill seeped into my fingertips.

"What happened?" I asked.

"I escaped," Lex said with a sharp breath. "I'm not sure what happened exactly, but after we acquired the cloaks, the other men started acting... off."

"Off, how?" Shep pressured.

"I don't know! Just bizarre!" Lex said hastily. "They stopped speaking to each other unless spoken to, their emotions seemed to vanish entirely, and one by one, they started acting like they'd abandoned their humanity all together, and it all started when they put on those blasted cloaks."

He nodded toward the cloak in my hands, scuffing dirt on his chin as he did so. The wool suddenly felt a lot heavier, and the uneasy feeling I'd noticed had increased like a slow boil.

"He told us wearing the cloaks would make us stronger, but the second I felt something funny messing with my head, I took the rags off and made a run for it," Lex continued. "I figured I would resell it back on the market when I had a chance, but I hadn't expected anyone to come sniffing around for it."

He shot me a dirty glare, and I returned it with the same sweet smile that had won him over in the tavern. He rolled his eyes.

"Where did the rest of the men go?" Shep asked.

"I already told you, they're going to Sarnold." Lex scoffed. "I think they're crossing the border at the river with the ferry boats."

The Willen port?

"Lyla? Do you know where that is?" Shep looked up at me.

"Oh please, don't insult me," I said as I folded the cloak back up into the bag. "I bet it's about a two days' ride from here. Tell me, Lexy, dear.

Were your friends walking or riding horseback?" I knelt at the level of his dirt-smeared scowl.

Lex didn't look very pleased with his new nickname, but another press of Shep's blade stopped him from arguing. "They were walking. There were too many of us not to stand out on horseback, so we stayed a bit off the path."

"Perfect, thank you, darling." I patted his cheek, then rose from the ground to catch Shep's eye. "We need to get going. If my hunch is correct, which it often is…" I glanced down at Lex with a proud smile. "Then the group we're looking for is taking shelter in a sheep pasture for the night."

Shep lifted a brow. "A sheep pasture?"

"That's right." I popped my hands on my hips. "Believe it or not, most large groups of bandits hide amongst animals. Open pastures allow good visibility for keeping a lookout, and animal sounds help mask their presence. There's a large sheep farm only a few hours from here that would have been far too tempting for them to pass up if they were traveling all the way to Willen's port."

Shep blinked at me, and opened his mouth as if to ask another question, but in the end, he decided to keep his mouth shut. It would seem he finally discovered just how futile it was to strike up an argument with any of my plans.

"What should we do with him?" Shep finally crawled off his back, grabbed Lex by the scruff of his neck, and jerked him up into a sitting position.

"He's not part of our mission." I gestured to my freshly acquired bag. "All we were instructed to do was retrieve the cloaks. We can alert the guard of his involvement when we return, but for now, we can't waste time dragging him along with us."

Shep studied me for a moment, his intelligent eyes entangled with mine as if I had spoken in some sort of riddle. "What's this? You're not insisting I drag him back to the capital while you carry on by yourself?"

My hand tightened around the bag's strap as I recalled the fearful moments I'd spent in the woods alone, and the terrifyingly skillful way Shep had intimidated Lex.

"Why would I insist on something like that?" I asked innocently.

"I thought you'd jump at the opportunity to lead the mission on your own." Shep gave me a knowing look, and a devious smile cracked the edges of his lips. "Have you finally accepted that you need my help?"

What!? I don't need his help! I just need his agility skills, and perhaps his interrogating skills, and I still need to learn how he manipulates his voice in the same way a master musician tunes their instrument...

"I've accepted that you have uses, but then again, so does my toothbrush." I turned my back to him, already starting toward the horse, all while secretly hiding the humiliation seeping into my cheeks.

Why is it so frustrating to admit I need help? Is it because I don't want to be seen as weak, or is it because I don't want to be seen as weak by Shep.

"You're not too bad yourself, Lyla," Shep said behind me as I heard him release Lex from his blade. "You're lucky the lady doesn't want me to bring you in. Just remember, that you have until we get back to the capital to clean up your act when the soldiers come to put this place on the map." Shep's warning earned a grisly huff from Lex.

"Just get out of my sight before I decide to stop being so friendly," Lex growled, though the threat felt pretty empty after seeing him get tackled by a man half his size. "Just do me a favor and burn those cloaks when you find them. I'm not sure what magic they're using, but it's not something anyone should ever play with."

Lex's voice faded behind me as I moved deeper into the woods, and Shep fell into step behind me. Despite not looking back, I could still feel the intensity of Lex's gaze burn into the back of my head. The tavern owner was no daffodil, but something about the cloaks had him shaken. I looked down into the bag, watching the innocent sparkle of the wool.

What dangers do you contain?

"I'm sorry for earlier." Shep startled my gaze up from the bag, shocking me with how much sincerity was in the same voice that left me petrified earlier. "I shouldn't have doubted your instincts. You were right about Lex, and I should have taken you more seriously."

A soft throb echoed in my chest, reminding me of the moments Shep had spurred the same reaction during our fake courtship. For someone so good at acting, I hadn't expected the true side of his sweetness to feel so different from his act.

"I'm sorry, too," I said shyly as I tucked a stray curl behind my ear. "I shouldn't have been so stubborn about going into the bar. I'm sure you could have handled it on your own."

Curse you Shep, for making me admit my own stubbornness. Your perfectness is a mighty foe, indeed.

"Maybe..." Shep cast me a side-smile, his eyes twinkling in the starlight like an amber-toned magic stone. "But I think we handled it best when we were working together. Maybe this whole partner thing will work after all."

"Oh, won't my parents be thrilled." I laughed.

"They'll be so happy to hear that I'm capable of playing well with others."

"I think you do more than just play," Shep said in a low tone that sent a warm ripple through my blood. He gestured to the bag on my shoulder, catching my eyes with one of the glances that could only be described as offensively attractive. "You make the rules. Now, let's see if the game master can track down the rest of the players."

My cheeks burned as the lights of the tavern came back into view.

If I truly made the rules, then I wouldn't be so affected by my teammate.

chapter ten

Once again, I'm left wondering why we couldn't have picked up a second horse.

Our trusty steed carried on through the moonlit path, easily guided by Shep, whose arms were *once again* wrapped around me. The soft bounce of the horse and the cool night air threatened to lure me to sleep, but I needed to stay awake in order to guide us to the pasture.

"Is this the turn?" Shep asked when we reached a fork in the path.

"Yes, take a left here, and then it should be straight for another hour or so. After that, the pasture will be a bit off the trail." A yawn breached my defenses, too strong and forceful to hold back.

"You should rest," Shep said in a light voice. "I can wake you up when we're closer to the next direction."

Before waiting for me to reply, he shifted his arms around me to move them from the sides of my arms to my waist. He moved closer, pressing his torso against my back so I could brace myself against him and sleep. My heart pattered as I felt his warmth envelop me, robbing me of my breath and any future yawns.

How can I possibly get any sleep while using his rock-hard chest as a pillow!?

"I should stay awake." I swallowed shyly. "The directions are just an estimate; I'll need to see the path to know for certain we're going the right way."

Shep didn't shift back, and I could practically feel the doubt radiate off him like a campfire's heat.

"Your directions haven't been wrong yet," he countered. "If you're tired, you should sleep. We can't have that clever little mind of yours getting too sleep-deprived, now can we?"

He thinks I'm clever?

I shrunk back a bit, allowing my back to press against Shep one inch at a time. Despite being as strong as he looked, he was strangely comfortable to lean up against. His arms fit snuggly against my sides and kept me from wavering, and his chin tucked perfectly on the top of my head. My heart fluttered violently, quickly proving that no amount of exhaustion would be enough to let me actually sleep cradled in my partner's arms.

"Good spies don't need sleep..." I yawned

again.

"You're right, but *smart* spies do." Shep pressed his arm against me as we hit a bump, steadying me before I even had a chance to slip. "And I already admitted that you're clever."

So, he did mean it...

"What about you?" I looked up at him through sleepy blinks, admiring how even from an upward angle, he still managed to make my heart stutter. "You're not sleeping. So what kind of spy does that make you?"

He remained quiet at first, his eyes fixated on the path ahead of us, his muscles tightening around me as if I'd somehow tugged on a nerve.

"A foolish one," he whispered. "But that's nothing new."

"What?" I sat up a touch, doing my best to turn and look at him, but struggling to move with his restrictive hold on my waist. "You're not foolish at all. Your quick thinking stopped Lex from getting away with one of the cloaks, and it even helped us learn where the others are hiding."

Shep smiled, but it wasn't his usual mischievous one, or even his perfected swoony one that had won over my family. This smile was raw, exposed, and far too broken to actually possess any joy.

"I may have done well today, but I'm still a

long way from proving myself," he said with a dejected laugh.

Proving himself?

"What do you mean?" I asked softly. "It's not like someone like you has anything left to prove."

A cool wind brushed through his hair, exposing his deadlocked eyes. "Actually, I have plenty..."

Is he joking?

"I don't understand." I let my thoughts slip out with a quiet breath. "You're practically perfect in everything you do. What else is left?"

"Trust," he whispered, sending a brisk pulse through my bones. "Or more specifically, convincing the crown that I'm still trustworthy."

My breath hooked. "*Still* trustworthy?" My memories flashed to the intense manner in which Shep had interrogated Lex and the terrifying way he had handled the blade. "Did you do something to break their trust before?"

Who exactly am I working with?

My entire body went rigid, but I was too stunned to move. While leaning up against Shep, I could feel his heart patter, growing with intensity before he finally let out a long breath.

"I didn't do anything, but my father did," he said coldly, his voice stripped of all kindness as he tightened his grip on the reins.

His father?

"Was your father some sort of criminal?" I'd heard of a few cases where spies with less than respectable family ties were recruited into crown agencies. Their ties to shady family businesses often made them more useful for uncovering dark trade secrets, but at the same time, they were kept on a tighter leash to ensure they weren't trying to explore both sides.

Is that why Shep was recruited?

"Actually, he was a spy," Shep explained, snuffing out my theory in an instant. "One of the best, as a matter of fact. When he was working, the black market was a mere spark of what it's fanned into now, mainly kept under control by his work alone. The Reclusian king personally trusted him and even permitted him to train up the youngest apprentice ever recruited."

I swallowed, "You?"

"That's right," he replied starkly. "I was four when he first started teaching me how to lie. He taught me everything he had ever learned, which is why the crown hardly trusts me now..."

He straightened behind me, like someone had prodded him with a hot coal. Shep's story remained incomplete, but I didn't need him to finish to put the pieces together with the history I already knew.

Three years ago, my handler went quiet for

nearly six months due to a high-clearance spy who had betrayed the crown.

"You're Ryder Wolfe's son?" I sucked in gasp the second I spoke the words, wishing I could pull them back into me. This wasn't a scab I should be picking at.

"Huh... Been a while since I heard his code name." Shep chuckled dryly. "His real name was Conall Ryde, but I just called him Father. If I'm being honest, I always knew he was up to something behind the curtain. His payments were always a bit too high, and his methods were always a little more intense than the situation usually required." He glanced down at the bag on my shoulder, staring at the acquired cloak. "Admittedly, it's a difficult habit not to pick up on when you know the tactics work."

My blood chilled as I suddenly became acutely aware of the blade tucked inside his belt as it grazed my lower back. Those interrogation methods he'd used... they'd come from the nastiest traitor in the kingdom.

"Once Father showed his true colors and escaped the kingdom with Reclusia's secrets, the entire security system had to be overhauled." Shep repeated the tale I knew all too well.

In the six months the agency was quiet, all our communication methods were recreated. Before the Little Bows shop, I had received letters from a local charity that had tragically gone bankrupt after Wolfe's betrayal. All the magic stone vaults had to be moved or rebuilt, and even the prisons had to change their routines. The entire foundation of Reclusia's silent security had been crumbled by a single man the king trusted far too much.

I'd always wondered how one man could convince so many people to trust him, but after meeting Shep... I'm starting to understand.

Now that I thought about it, it was terrifying how much of Shep's skills lined up with the traitorous agent. His ability to walk into a bar and befriend a half-dozen men was beyond impressive, and his ability to convince a family to let him run off with their daughter was nearly unheard of. He truly did possess every skill his father did, but the question was, would he use his talents differently?

"So you were put on probation?" I inquired. I knew I shouldn't be picking at old wounds, but this wasn't the type of conversation I could leave unfinished. Being nosey was always my specialty, but this was more than just digging for gossip. Shep was my partner, and working together meant trusting each other moving forward.

"Unfortunately, yes." Shep sighed. "For the first year, I was kept under house arrest. They wanted to see if my father still cared enough to come back for me or, at the very least, send a message. But he never did... After spending all that time raising me to be his perfect prodigy, he had no trouble leaving me in the dust."

Something inside me cracked, scattering shards throughout my heart as I listened to Shep's dipping voice. For the first time, his voice wasn't perfect... It still conveyed only what he wanted me to hear, but the strength he was lacing into his tone was too fake, too theatrical for what his pounding heart was telling me.

"How long did they keep you from working?" I bit my lip, recalling how awful it was to be left in the dark for only a few months after making a mess out of the bridal competition.

Working as a spy was what gave me purpose, what got me up every morning and gave me the energy to put on a frilly dress and bow. That life was a part of who I was, but unlike Shep, I still had another life to fall back on when my secret life went quiet. What would it be like if working as an agent was the only life you knew, and suddenly, it was gone?

"Three years," Shep said in a dark tone that was so quiet, I was certain I misheard him.

"Wait, did you say *three years*?" I did the math in my mind, scrunching my brows together as it added up. "But that's how long it's been since Wolfe... I mean your father's betrayal. So that would mean—"

"This is my first mission since." Shep filled in the blanks as the pieces came crashing together in my brain. "That's why I have to prove myself, Evie. This is the first chance I've had to show the crown that I'm not like my father."

Oh. My. Kingdoms...

"That's why we're partnered up...?" My jaw dropped indelicately, and I think I may have even swallowed a bug, but I was too shocked to even care. "All this time, I thought the handler was sending me with a babysitter because they didn't trust me to handle a mission on my own..."

"Is that what you thought?" Shep chuckled, the first warm sound I'd heard from him since this discussion began. "Sorry to break it to you, darling, but I'm not babysitting anyone. As a matter of fact, you're likely meant to be keeping an eye on *me*."

I nearly fell off the horse. My entire body jumped as I tried to whirl around, accidentally elbowing Shep in the ribs a couple of times and causing him to jerk the reins. "What!? You really weren't looking down on me the whole time!?"

The agency hadn't sent me a shepherd... they'd sent me a blooming sheep to watch!

"Well, I do look down on you, but that's more of a height issue than anything else..." He smiled wryly.

"Shepherd!"

"I'm only teasing." He laughed, filling the forest with the warm sound. "But no, I never once looked down on you. I'm not sure how I even could have when you were always so... perfect."

Me...? Perfect?

"But... But I... Oh kingdoms, I'm going to kill our handler after this is over." I pressed my palms to my eyes with a long groan. I would have happily stayed hidden behind my palms for the rest of the day, but apparently, Shep had other ideas, because he let one hand go from the reins to peel my hands from my face.

His touch was gentle, just like it had been when we were fake courting, and his warm hazel eyes reflected the sweet smile that felt far more real than it had before.

"Did you really think I thought myself better than you?" he asked with a sultry voice that outshone even the soft hoots of the owls.

"Well... yes," I admitted with a flush of my cheeks. "I thought you were sent to me because the handler didn't think I was good enough."

He lowered my hand back to my lap, letting it go with a soft brush against my palm as he reached for the reins. "You? Not good enough?" He tightened his arms around my waist, surrounding me in his warmth. "I suppose some spies are so good at lying that they deceive even themselves."

chapter eleven

After about an hour of riding, we stopped to let our horse drink and stretch our legs. While it was important for us to make good time, no spy could be fully functional if they dismounted with a nasty leg cramp.

I kneeled beside a stream's glassy water, admiring the moon's silver reflection as it illuminated my silhouette. The crisp water tasted as sweet as nectar on my parched tongue. It was the first drink I'd had since nearly sipping Lex's ale, and the bitter taste had still stuck to my tongue even though I never drank it.

Shep knelt beside me to grab his own drink. Even while we were both kneeling, he towered next to me. It was so strange how someone who had been tucked away for so long still felt so powerful. He was like a sword that had been stowed away in its sheath for years, never once having its blade dulled, but also not receiving any practice. Was he really ready to be back out in the field after all this time?

"The nights are getting warmer," Shep

commented, and he scooped some water into his palms to wet back his hair. I had to keep myself from staring as the sparkling water dripped off his face like crystal beads in the starlight.

Why does he always have to look good!?

I looked down at my reflection in the water, knowing for certain that if I tried to wet down my hair, it would only end up looking like a ragged mop.

"I bet it feels nice being out and about again," I said while standing to stretch out my legs.

"That it does," Shep said with a quiet smile. "It feels different than it did before, though. Perhaps it's because I have you with me this time."

I watched as he stretched out his legs and paced back and forth. He didn't act like he was out of practice, but now that I knew the truth behind his history, it was more obvious to see he had been left out of the field. He didn't look nervous, per se, but he was antsy. It was like he was itching to have a chance to run at full speed but was stuck at a walk in the meantime.

"Is this the first time you've ever worked with a partner?" I asked. "Other than your father, of course."

He stopped his stretches, and for a moment, I wondered if I had poked a nerve by bringing up his father. He folded his arms as he gave me a thoughtful look that appeared as if he was mentally recapping all his previous missions. The longer he thought, the more I wondered just *how* many missions he had been included in.

He has been working since he was a child... but still.

"I've worked with others in the past, but you're my first true *partner*," he finally replied with a teased smile.

"True partner?" I tilted my head. "What is that supposed to mean?"

"Well, I've had other partners before, but that's a generous term for them," Shep clarified as he eyed me down with a humorous light sparkling off his eyes. "They didn't necessarily carry their own weight like you do, nor did they go out of their way to try to prove they were better than me."

Oh... So he put that together, huh?

"Who said I was trying to prove I'm better? Did you ever consider that maybe I just *am* better?" I asked with a coy lift of my chin.

"Oh, like how you were so much better at catching Lex when he ran away?" Shep lifted a brow as he took a step closer, intentionally using his height against me to look superior... *Curse my dainty height...*

"You mean, when Lex had a chance to run away because *you* didn't believe he was involved with the robbery?" I straightened the best I could to measure up to him. He may have been tall, but my personality could stretch higher than most mountains when I instructed it to.

"Right, how could I forget?" Shep tapped his palm on his forehead. "That was right after *you* nearly got carried away in your act and accepted a drink from a strange barkeep that eyed you like you were his next mark." He shifted in front of me another step, our shoulders squared... well, as squared as they could be when his sat a good few inches higher than mine.

"Did you really think I was foolish enough to touch that drink?" I asked stiffly. "I may not have the same endless list of mission experience that you do, but I'm not daft. Those men could look at me however they pleased; they were never going to get anything out of me other than some eye flutters and a smile."

Shep's eyes met mine... Those frustrating eyes that, even now, still looked at me like they knew what was best. "They shouldn't look at a lady that way," he said in a deep, rich tone.

A soft wind rustled between us, fluttering the damp ends of Shep's hair over his stern gaze. Looking him dead in the eyes stirred up my heart as memories of our fake courtship reeled through my thoughts.

"But I'm not a lady out here," I said in a rooted

tone. "I'm a spy. And sometimes spies get looked at differently."

"Not while I'm watching." Shep's voice dipped so low, it was almost a growl, causing my heart to stutter in more shock than anything. "You see, that's how I know I truly see you as a partner. I can't walk away from you when I sense you're in danger. A partner is someone who is too valuable to the mission to lose."

My blood slowed, paralyzing me as I tried to piece together what Shep was saying. "You... you think I'm valuable?"

His lips quirked into a slight smile, and my chest did that annoying little flutter thing that always makes me wonder if I'd swallowed too much air.

"Why do you think I pulled you out of the bar when I did?" he asked. "I couldn't watch my partner flirt with such scummy company, especially not when I foolishly thought the job was already done."

My ears pricked up, and I bit back a grin. "So you admit you were foolish to pull me out when you did?"

"I was wrong to assume we had all the information we needed," he said as he stepped back from me, keeping our eyes locked as he moved closer to the horse. "But I don't regret getting you out from under their eyes."

What is that supposed to mean?

He turned his attention to the horse, and offered me a hand to help me mount, but I was still lost in the end of our conversation. I was feeling a little frustrated, a little confused, and admittedly, a little proud to have received the proper title of *partner* in Shep's eyes.

Though it's not like I really needed to prove myself to him. I already know I'm fabulous, and it would seem the agency thinks so too, especially since they partnered me with their problem child.

I accepted Shep's help up onto the horse and he followed after me, cozying back up behind me as we took our spots on the saddle. His arms braced around me like they had before, and something about his protective nature tickled the back of my mind. He didn't *have* to look out for me. He knew I was capable of handling myself, yet he still felt the need to watch my back. He didn't look out for me because he thought I needed it. He did it because he truly saw me as valuable.

I didn't need to prove my worth to anyone, but I was still glad Shep already saw it.

chapter twelve

We dismounted on the edge of the pasture, tying the horse off on a rickety fence post that loosely marked the edge of the property. I had stared at this location on my maps for years, but this was the first time I'd actually seen it.

The pasture itself was a lot bigger in person, but the stables and sheds looked just as suspicious as I'd always imagined. Their windows were framed but not glassed in, and their doors were locked with simple wooden latches—it was a fugitive's playground for the perfect game of hide and seek. And then there were the residents...

"Kingdoms, that's a lot of sheep..." Shep whispered in my ear as we both looked out into the fluffy hoard of woolly livestock. "Are they trying to amass an army?"

At least two hundred sheep dotted the pasture, most clustered into a massive herd of white at the far end of the field.

"What? You haven't heard about the ongoing great fluff war?" I tilted my head at him, and he humored me with an eye roll.

"Ah, how could I have forgotten? The Woolly War of the West, right?" He said it so seriously, I nearly choked on my own tongue.

"I'm pleased to know you're well-educated in such influential events within our kingdom," I said through a bitten smile. "Now, let's be careful not to stir the feud any further as we retrieve these cloaks. I don't want to hear a single lamb bleat about you offending them, got it?"

"Wouldn't dream of it, my lady." He pressed a hand over his heart, then gestured toward the pasture with a teasing glint in his eyes. "I'll follow your lead."

I pulled my cloak over my head and climbed over the lopsided fence. The grass was short from all the sheep's grazing, which left a clear view of the entire pasture from one end to the other. I crept out from the cover of the trees, trying to get a better view of where our thieves could possibly be hiding.

Let's see… There's a horse stable on the far end, which would provide good shelter, but it's cornered and would make escaping difficult. The hay bales on the other end aren't a bad option, but I'm not sure a group of seven men could all fit behind them. In the middle of the field, there's…

I sucked in a breath, blindly grabbing Shep by the arm and jerking him back until we were safely under the tree's shadow.

"What is it?" Shep ducked his head to sink deeper into the dark.

"Look, in the center of the sheep herd." I pointed toward the fluffy pile of snuggling livestock, and sitting just in front of them, was a man in a glistening black cloak. "I think I found the nightguard."

Shep followed the point of my finger, and his eyes narrowed on the shimmering cloak. The man wearing it was slouched against a tree stump, with his hand resting against a sword hilt, and his eyes drooping like he'd counted too many sheep for one day. I looked past the watchman and saw a few other men sleeping amongst the sheep not far behind him, each bundled up in a black cloak.

"Looks like we found our wools," Shep said in a low tone. "Nice work, Evie."

A gentle warmth spread through my core at his compliment, radiating a small smile on my lips. It was strange how his praise felt different than it did before I learned about his past. At first, I accepted his compliments as points awarded in my favor that helped me prove my worth as an agent, but now... now it was just kind words from my partner.

I wonder if he appreciates compliments, too?

"Let's move in from the side." Shep plotted

aloud. "The lookout doesn't appear to be paying great attention, so if we can surprise him, I think I can knock him out before he makes a peep."

The intensity in his voice sent a slight shiver through me. It was strange watching him work now that I knew who he'd been trained by, and how long it had been since he'd been in the field. I'd never thought about it until now, but he might be a bit out of practice...

"Are you sure?" I whispered. "That sounds like a pretty specific technique. Do you think you can pull it off?"

Shep snapped his head in my direction, piercing me with an offended look. "Are you doubting my *no peep* move?"

"No peep?" I scrunched my brow.

"Yes, that's what I lovingly nicknamed it after Father made me practice four times a day on passing guards for a whole year." He stepped around me, slinking through the shadows as he made his way to the guard's blind spot. "Just because I've been kept in the toolshed for a bit, doesn't mean I'm rusty."

He moved soundlessly through the grass, flaunting his perfect stealth skills like they were in bold print on his resume.

Is it wrong to be jealous of his traitorous father? Because, for kingdom's sake, he was an excellent teacher...

I followed behind him, tiptoeing over any sticks as I tried to study the light movement of his boots and his natural draw to the shadows. Watching him sneak through the dark probably gave me the same buzz that normal women received while watching men claim the dance floor in a ball. Shep's form and grace was just as skillful as any nobleman's waltz, but there was something more alluring about it... Maybe it was the silence, or the elegant way the shadows moved with him, but either way, I don't think I could ever be enraptured by a man in a formal setting again.

Once we arrived at the perfect angle, Shep stepped out of the shadows, sneaking up behind the quiet guard, and I followed two steps behind him. With each step he took, I placed my foot in the same spot, doing everything I could to remain as silent as possible.

We passed by more snoozing sheep, and a few awake ones who gave us curious looks between chewing mouthfuls of grass. A sheep behind me bleated, causing us both to stiffen as we waited to see if the sound would draw the lookout's attention. When he didn't bother to look back, we continued forward, one painfully quiet step at a time.

When we reached the main collection of sheep, I could finally see the entire group of men, all passed out in a snoring circle. Nearly all of them were using their cloaks as blankets, but one had his balled up underneath his head as a pillow. Removing them wouldn't be an easy task...

"Wait here," Shep mouthed to me as he crept up behind the lookout with even steps.

I bit my tongue as I tried to steady my heart to keep it from beating too loudly. Shep crept up behind the man, then hunched down to where his head rested a touch above the tree stump. He raised his elbow and, with one quick, silent hit to the side of his neck, the man was out cold.

My jaw dropped open with an audible *whoosh* as I watched Shep catch the man before he could thump against the ground. Shep steadied the man with one arm and unbuttoned the cloak with his other before gently lowering him to the grass. Once the man was down, he whirled around to face me with a grin prouder than a toddler showing off his latest mud-pie.

I scooped up my jaw and gave him a taut nod.

I admit it... that was cool.

Shep folded up the cloak in his arms, then pointed toward the other sleeping men. We exchanged a knowing look, and crept closer.

Two cloaks down, six to go.

Shep narrowed in on a man propped up against a shoulder bag, and I approached a man who was sprawled out in the grass between two well-fed sheep. The cloak was draped over top him like a bedsheet, and fortunately, he didn't appear to be pinning it in place anywhere with his limbs.

I can do this... Just use slow, gentle movements, just like an embroidery project!

Borrowing the dainty touch of Lady Genevieve, I peeled the cloak off my sleeping victim one inch at a time. I started at the base of his chin, slowly revealing his untrimmed beard and filthy cotton jacket with each lift of the cloak. Never in my life had I watched a man's breathing so closely, but by the time I slid the cloak off the bottom of his boots, he was completely undisturbed.

Phew, I might actually have to thank Mother for my embroidery lessons after this. Holding a needle steady is far more challenging than a wool cloak.

I slung the cloak over my shoulder and made my way toward the next bandit. Shep was still working on the same cloak he'd started with, encountering a few more difficulties with the snuggly thief.

Using the same slow tactic as before, I removed a second cloak, and just as I went for my third, Shep had collected a total of three, including the guard's. After I had managed to wiggle the shimmering cloak's hem out from under the man's boot, we had officially acquired all but one of the mysterious wools.

Shep crept up to me, placing the three cloaks he'd acquired into my arms with the three I had. "Take these back to the horse," he whispered softer than a cricket's hum. "I'll try to get the last cloak, but just in case he wakes up..."

He looked over toward the last bandit, whose head was pinning the cloak down as a pillow. He wore a thinner cotton cape as a blanket with the hood tucked so far down over his eyes, he probably wouldn't even see a fire if we lit it in front of his face. Swiping blankets off men was one thing, but stealing a pillow...

He might need to pull out another 'no peep' move for that.

"Right," I whispered with a soft nod. "Be careful."

I adjusted my grip on the stack of cloaks, slinging some onto my shoulders, and bundling the rest up in my arms as I carefully maneuvered out of the cluster of sleeping men and sheep. The wool was thick and heavy, and the exhaustion seeping into me made it feel like I was sinking deeper into the ground with each step.

You're almost done, Evie. Once Shep gets that last cloak, we'll both get to return home with undeniable proof of our abilities.

Shep would finally be able to work again, and perhaps this job will show the handler that I'm capable of doing more than just marking maps from behind closed doors. I'd forgotten how much I enjoyed splitting off from Lady Genevieve to fully immerse myself into the Evie I adored. I wouldn't even mind if they had to pair me with a partner again. I wonder if Shep and I would be able to work together again after this...? I suppose we could always keep up the ruse of our courtship to validate more travel together, but then again, that would mean he'd have to treat me like he loves me again...

My skin felt hot against the cool night air, and I scolded myself for letting my mind run wild on so little sleep. I'd nearly made it to the edge of the pasture when I decided to look back and see how Shep was faring with the last cloak.

My heart skipped a beat when I saw the concentration on his face. It was hard to see from where I was at, but it looked like he was trying to swap out the cloak for one of the men's bags.

That won't work. He needs something just as soft...

An idea clicked in my head, and I looked down at my cotton cloak.

He can use my cloak. But first, I need to stash these.

I wished I could shout for Shep to wait for me, but he was too focused on his task to even look my direction. I needed to hurry. If he even flinched in the wrong direction the man would spring awake, and we'd have seven angry thieves on our hands.

I found the horse, and slung the cloaks over his back, then spun back around. I ran as quietly as I could through the first half of the field, then slowed as I drew closer to the sleeping men.

I started untying the gray cloak from my neck, but only managed to tangle my fingers in the knot as I looked back at Shep. He was lifting the man's head now, just barely hovering it above the fabric as he attempted to reach for the folded-up cloak.

He's going to drop him!

Shep was doing an impressive job of keeping the sleeping man's head steady, but it was a peace that was only a fracture away from shattering. I snuck closer to him, hoping to help steady the man's head or slide the cloak out from under him, but I didn't even make it into the sleeping circle of men before the Great Woolly War of the West officially broke loose...

Baaa!

One foul-mouthed sheep bleated louder than any rooster had ever crowed, startling half the men to wake and causing Shep to jump back from the cloak and man entirely.

I smacked a hand over my mouth, biting back a gasp as the bleary-eyed men fastened their gazes on the bloodthirsty sheep, and then onto Shep.

No!

Shep remained crouched to the ground, his whole body tensed and ready to pounce as the man overtop the cloak slowly rose from his sleepy daze. I took a nervous step back, waiting for Shep to jump the man with his dagger and pull off another terrifying display of force. But he didn't move...

The man's hood slid to his shoulders, giving me a view of the back of his dark hair and squared shoulders. He didn't say anything, didn't even do more than sit up, but when Shep locked onto his face, all the color drained from his skin, and for the first time, I saw his perfection fully disappear.

"F-father?"

And then everything went white.

chapter thirteen

Father...?

The blast of white faded in a rich gold light before dimming entirely, and the men stirred from their sleepy stupors, now fully aware of both me and Shep. The light must have been from a magic stone, like some sort of signal to wake the others up in an instant. My lungs clamped shut as all breath fled my body with one pointed look from a tall, bearded man with what appeared to be a blinded eye.

Shep had staggered back a few feet, his eyes dazed and arms quivering as he stared at the man with the last remaining cloak; the man he'd called Father.

"Shep?" I called to him, taking a step back as I reached for the concealed blade in my boot. The men seemed to have noticed their distinct lack of cloaks, and the one with the blanched blind eye pointed a jagged finger straight at my heart.

"Thief," he growled, his voice coarser than a redwood's bark.

"Shep!" I called again, my legs twitching, unsure as to whether I should rush to his side or run back to guard the wools.

Shep broke free from his shock, his eyes blinking rapidly—likely stunned by the gold blast of magic. He scrambled to his feet; his face twisted in horror as the man who'd set off the flare jumped to his feet in front of him.

I still couldn't see the man's face, but his towering height, sculpted build, and tensed shoulders were all I needed to predict that this man was the infamous *boss*. His hair was shaggy and dark, with a hint of sideburns tracing his profile. He didn't bother to pick up the cloak as he stood or even put it on, but the way he casually stood beside it was almost more intimidating than if he had held it close to his chest.

"*You.*" Shep pulled a dagger from his belt. The silver moonlight shadowed most of him, but it was impossible to miss the fury eclipsing his flawless features. "Evie, get out of here!"

He didn't even bother to look at me, just waved his hand toward me to run as he squared up to the man I feared was the most dangerous spy to ever cross this kingdom.

I can't just leave him here.

"Shep, you can't—"

"Go!" He growled like a beast that had been set free from a lifelong prison, chilling my blood and forcing my legs into action.

The second I started running, I could hear the rest of the men follow after me, their boots scuffing through the grass like a pack of bulls. I risked a glance back to check on Shep and found that only the criminal's boss and the sleeping guard were left behind. The man Shep faced was calm and still, like he was a fellow traveler having a pleasant conversation. Shep, on the other hand, was crouched in a battle pose, not mistaking his opponent's leisure for weakness for even a second.

If that's really Shep's father...

"Catch the wench!" the burly man with the blind eye called behind me. "She's not going anywhere until she tells us where those wools went!"

I turned my attention back to where I was running, trying to push Shep out of my mind. He could take care of himself... I just needed to remind myself of that. Right now, I needed to not get caught and not lead them back toward the wools.

There's what...? Five men chasing me? Guess it's time to beat my record.

I snatched up the end of my skirt while running, tying it in a quick knot around my hips to let my legs move faster. The men were definitely stronger than me, but I doubted they were faster, which meant my best chance was to not get cornered. I may not have been able to catch Lex in the woods while chasing him and Shep, but running and dodging was a different story. My mother would agree that I was obnoxiously good at slipping away.

I darted straight into the trees, moving toward the thickest part with the lowest branches. The cool night air breezed through my hair, chilling my breath as I panted with each increase of speed.

"Cut her off! She's heading south!" One of the men's voices echoed through the trees. His command was loud; so loud that I was certain it was *intended* for me to hear it.

I continued south, not veering off even the slightest. I could hear the woods rustling around me, but they were too far to hear clearly. My heart pounded, racing with my ragged breaths as I slid behind an oak tree. It was foolish to stop running for even a minute, but I couldn't convince myself to flee too far from my partner.

Should I go back for Shep? If I can sneak back around the other men, then maybe I can—

A twig snapped a few feet behind me and out popped the half-blind man and another tall, tanned crook, both wielding short blades.

Oh, drat.

I jumped back to my feet, but only managed

to spin around before one of the men snatched me by my hair. I screamed, cursing myself for letting my feminine instincts react in a way that entertained my captors.

"Look here, we caught a little girl." The half-blind man laughed, jerking me around to meet his lopsided gaze. "Bet cha' thought you were clever sneaking off with our wools, but I'm afraid our boss isn't the type you can outsmart."

My skin went clammy as Shep's pale face flashed through my mind. "And who exactly *is* your boss?" I lifted my chin, ignoring the extra pain in my scalp as the movement yanked my hair. I tightened my grip on the dagger in my hand, trying to keep it tucked behind my back in case they hadn't noticed it yet.

"Hey, we got a feisty one!" The second man sneered, flashing his own blade in the moonlight as he pointed it an inch away from my chest. "If she's so interested in the boss, then perhaps we should let *him* question her about the wools."

"Are you daft?" The man squinted his good eye at his companion, tugging the ends of my hair with him. "The boss doesn't want to be handed *your* dirty work. Now are you going to get her to talk, or shall I?"

The second man rolled his eyes, raising the dagger to just under my chin as his buddy gave my hair an extra tug for good measure. There were many things I could handle in my line of work, but having someone abuse my hair... Oh, he was going to pay for what came next.

"Start talking, missy," the man with the blade hissed. "Where did you put the wools? And who sent you to find them?"

I glanced between the two men, slowly moving my dagger to my side as I calculated the best swing of the blade. The answer was clear, but I was still hoping to find a better option.

"Hold on." The other man yanked my hair again, and I cringed as I felt a few strands snap. "What's that in your hand?"

Forgive me, my beautiful tresses...

In a flash of metal, I swiped the dagger over my head and cut through the ends of my beautiful golden locks. The tension pulling against my scalp vanished, and I took advantage of the men's shock as I pushed straight past them back into the woods. Loose strands of hair fluttered around my face, and I bit my lip as I tried not to look at their uneven lengths.

They'll pay for this.

The men were still following me, but I wasn't about to sacrifice my golden locks in vain. I jumped over logs, climbed over branches, and slipped through the narrowest spots I could find. The men seemed to have learned from my last escape, because they were cutting more corners now, intentionally hunting down the more direct paths while I was looking for the difficult ones.

Not good.

I made a quick decision to climb, selecting the tallest tree I could find and scrambling up like a hunted squirrel. I only made it halfway before the tree started to shake, forcing me to latch my legs around the trunk so I wouldn't fall.

"Come on down, little lady!" one of the men called from below, but I was too focused trying not to slip to look. "Just tell us where the wools are, and we might even let you live."

I dug my nails into the bark, wishing I'd picked a thicker tree instead of a taller one that they could shake so easily. A harsh *crack* echoed below me, and I looked down to see that the men had successfully bent the trunk enough that it was starting to splinter.

They're going to knock the entire tree down.

Crack.

The tree moved more, its slender trunk wavering like it was caught in a wind tunnel.

"Last warning!" one of the men shouted, his voice laced with sick laughter.

My heart pounded as I shut my eyes, silently hoping that Shep had managed to escape and would be able to make it back to the cloaks on his own. I thought back to the man I had seen facing off against him, wondering if it truly was Wolfe.

Would Shep be able to handle him on his own? What if he had other magic stones on him? Or what if he used the cloak against Shep?

I felt sick, partially from the shaking of the tree and partially from the fear that chewed me up and spat me out. Just when I was starting to enjoy having a partner, I realized just how horrible having one could truly be, especially when you cared about their well-being.

Crack.

The tree shook as one of the men delivered a nasty kick to it's weakening trunk. I could feel the entire trunk bend, slowly tipping to one side as my entire world tilted. There was no choice; I needed to climb down.

Falling from this height could easily kill me, but at least if I climbed down, I'd have a chance at fighting my way past the thieves again. I tucked my dagger back into my boot, making sure the handle was poked out enough that I could easily retrieve it. I started crawling down the tree, moving as fast as I could as I felt the uneven weight shift further to one side.

"Hah! Now that's more like it, come on down so we can have a little cha—"

The voice cut off, silencing as quickly as it came, as if someone had choked his lungs dry. I looked down at the ground. I was only a mere ten feet above where the two men. But they were no longer threatening me mercilessly; they were staring blankly at the tree.

What?

I froze, pausing my descent as I watched the men step back from the tree. Their determined scowls vanished, leaving their expressions cold and dead with their eyes as glassy as a moonpool. They stared at the tree for a moment longer, and then, without a word, left me in peace and walked back into the woods like dogs to a whistle. I watched them from the treetops, waiting to see if they would snap back to their senses or at least say something as they silently moved back into the woods. When they left my view, I jumped back to the ground, staring off into the trees to see if there was something I had missed that had coaxed them into leaving.

"What in the...?"

"Evie!" Shep's voice flared my heart, and I spun around to see him running straight for me.

"Shep! Are you—" I gasped as my eyes landed on the fresh red cut across his cheek, and another slashed across his arm. "You're hurt!"

I untied the knot my skirt was bunched up in, not hesitating to tear off a strip of fabric into a makeshift bandage.

"It's nothing," Shep said, trying to wave it off.

"It's only a scratch. What about you? Are you alright?"

Ignoring his insisting, I grabbed his arm and wrapped the strip of fabric around the slash. "Just an awful haircut." I winced as I noticed his eyes drift to my choppy ends. "What happened just now? One moment those men were about to knock me out of a tree, and next..."

"They just stopped," Shep's voice was cold, and my fingers froze overtop his bicep mid-wrapping. "I'm not sure, but I'm glad you're alright."

Didn't Lex say something about this? About how the men were acting off when he left?

Shep placed a hand on mine, which was still over his temporary bandage I'd fastened. His cool touch was far too rigid, like he was trying to tell me something he wasn't actually ready to speak. I looked up at him and felt my heart still. His eyes looked different, like someone had stolen a piece of the Shep I knew and replaced him with a cold, dead version that was still shaking on the inside.

What had happened back there?

"Shep..." I breathed, keeping my hands pressed against his wound. "That man... you called him Father. Is he...?"

I couldn't finish, the broken look graying his vibrant eyes already answering any questions I had. He was barely injured, but it looked like he'd

143

been through war.

"Yes," he said sharply. "It would seem the leader of this group is none other than the spy who trained me."

My heart skipped a beat, unable to tear my gaze from his locked jaw and bleeding cheek. Ryder Wolfe... It was really him. What was he doing swiping black-market goods for Sarnold? A drop of blood dripped from Shep's cheek, and the sudden urge to punch his father square in the nose stirred beneath my skin.

What kind of father does this to his only son?

My fingertips stirred to life, tightening the bandage and tying it off into a knot. I pulled out a handkerchief from my bodice, raising it to Shep's face and wiping the stream of blood with gentle dabs.

The more I looked at Shep, the more I realized there was an absence in his stare, as if a chunk of him had been torn away and left back among the sheep. I let my hand rest on his cheek, wishing I could do something to make him whole again. There was only one way to get back what Wolfe had stolen... and that was to hunt him down and take it from his sleazy grasp.

"Well then." I gripped his eyes with the blazing fire fueling my newfound energy. "I think we've found our opportunity to prove your loyalty to the crown. Let's drag in the last cloak while it's still tied to his throat."

chapter fourteen

We made our way back through the trees to where we'd left our horse, stopping to check our surroundings every few feet to ensure we weren't being followed. When we finally made it back to the horse, I was relieved to find that all the collected cloaks were right where I'd left them.

Seven down, one to go.

I grabbed one of the cloaks off the horse's back, inspecting the stitching to find that it possessed the same gold glitter as the cloak we'd taken from Lex. It also had the same twinkling star seal on the button. I thumbed through the other cloaks, noticing all the same details. It was strange how warm they felt. Instead of trapping heat like a regular wool cloak, they seemed to almost radiate heat like a slow-burning candle. I'd come across a few unrefined stones in my life, but the magic in these cloaks felt stronger... more concentrated, like it was one disturbance away from bursting into flames.

"It's a good thing we grabbed as many as we

did," I said as I folded the cloaks back into a stack. "These are powerful. I can't imagine how much stronger those men would have been if we had to face them while they were cloaked in the magic."

I folded up the last cloak, and offered the stack to Shep to inspect, but he held his hand up to stop me.

"Maybe it's best if you hold onto them." He sighed, his entire demeanor had deflated ever since his encounter with the crime boss. "With my fath— Wolfe involved, I don't want to give the agency any reason to believe I had any hand in using the power within the cloaks."

He tucked his arms against his chest, like he was compressing a wound that was still bleeding out of him. The powerful, intimidating agent I had been desperate to out-perform was now afraid of being accused as a crook. It was so strange to see him like this, and for once, I hated being the strongest one between us.

"But Shep, you had nothing to do with the robbery. You were even under watch when they were stolen. They couldn't possibly accuse you of having any hand in your father's business." I tried to hold out the cloaks to him once more, but he took a step back, as if they were opposing magnets repelling each other.

"I know." He gave me a smile, but it was only a fragment of his usual charm. "But I've spent the last three years doing everything I can to disassociate myself from that man, and I'm not about to risk even bringing back a fleck of the mud from his boots. Besides..." he looked at the cloaks, his smile fading as guilt swallowed him whole, "I'm the one who failed to retrieve the last cloak, so you should be the one to keep the rest safe."

My arms tightened around the wool bundles, causing the warm buzz of their energy to seep into my skin.

Did he really think that?

"What are you talking about? You didn't fail at all." I stuffed the cloaks into the saddle bag, using a little extra force to shove the bulky fabric inside the leather pouch. "You're the one who knocked out the guard with that awesome *no peep* move. Which, by the way, I'm going to need you to teach that to me."

I folded my arms, and Shep let out a soft laugh that sent a warm ripple through my chest. It was good to see a real smile on his face again.

"Is that so?" He cocked his head, slowly turning back into the Shep I knew. "I suppose I could teach you a few pointers."

"Nuh-uh." I wagged my finger at him. "Not just pointers; I need a *full* lesson. If those bandits hadn't gone crawling back to their master when they did, I would have been smashed like a fallen bird egg! If I knew a move like that, I might have been able to prevent the tragedy that is my hair."

I ran my hands through the jagged ends of my locks, cringing as I noticed their uneven trim. Shep laughed again, closing the distance between us as he reached out to inspect my choppy haircut. He ran his fingers through my hair, sending a pleasant shiver down my spine. As he pet the scraggy ends, I realized that, despite the fact he was only inches from my face, I no longer felt uncomfortable in his presence. If anything, I was at ease having him close to me again, like nothing had changed and he was back to his usual self.

"I don't know, I kind of like the new trim," he said quietly, flicking my hair in front of my shoulder. "It suits your personality a lot better than the clean and proper cut."

I scrunched up my nose. "Are you calling me dirty and vulgar?"

"No." He chuckled. "I'm saying you're more untamed than one would presume, a bit of a wolf in sheep's clothing."

"Ah, is that an official diagnosis from a *shepherd*?" I lifted a brow.

"It's an observation from your partner," he countered, brushing past me as he started to untie the horse's reins. "I think we can both agree that you're a hunter, not a follower."

"I'd say I'm more of a tracker than a hunter," I said with a tilt of my nose. "Hunters go in for the kill, while I'm better suited for simply tracking down what's missing and leaving the dirty work for someone else. Though I suppose I'm not afraid to defend myself if needed... I guess I'm... well, I'm..."

"You're a herder," Shep said as he helped me back onto the horse.

I looked down at him with a furrowed brow. "A herder?"

"You're good at keeping track of what you're meant to, excellent at hunting down what's lost, and if someone tries to threaten your flock..." He made a slicing motion across his throat with his thumb and a devilish smile. "I certainly wouldn't want to cross blades with you. Any woman with the guts to cut her own hair in battle isn't one who should be underestimated."

I reached for my lopsided locks, feeling a strange sense of pride in the trim I had despised only moments ago. It was odd how Shep could make calling someone a *herder* feel like a compliment. Was it because of the title? Or because of how well he seemed to understand who I was beneath the life of Lady Genevieve?

"Come on." Shep braced himself to mount behind me. "Let's put those skills of yours to use. We still have one more sheep for you to herd."

He winked at me, and I rolled my eyes, though admittedly, I still smiled. He swung his leg over the horse's back, and I felt my heart flutter impermissibly as Shep braced me around the waist until we were both steady.

"At least now we know who we're up against," I said with a clear of my throat as I tried a little too hard to steady myself on my own so Shep wouldn't have to keep holding me.

His hands stiffened just before he pulled them from my waist. "That's true, though I must say, I already miss the bliss of ignorance."

He flicked the reins, and our mount started off toward the path. A dull pain settled in my heart, aching for the partner I was still learning how to support. I chewed the edge of my lip, letting the silence settle over us as we started along the path.

"I'm sorry about your father, Shep," I said softly. "And that you have to face him again now."

"The man we're facing now isn't my father," Shep said coldly, his chest stiffening behind me like a plank of wood. "He looked too different... too much like the criminal who had ruined my life for the last three years."

He took in a shallow breath, like speaking ill of his father somehow pained him like a prick in the ribs. I noticed he felt warmer now, much like the magical cloaks, and he was buzzing with an unkept energy that was ready to be let loose.

"I need you to find him, Evie," he whispered, his voice somewhat strained. "I need you to find him so we can stop him together."

The hairs on the back of my neck prickled, and my heart pounded with the severity of his tone. Shep was always intense, but this felt different... This wasn't just a job anymore; this was personal for him.

And for me, too. Shep is my partner, and he's hurting because of his numbskull father.

"They'll be heading for the Willen port," I said. "They're too far northeast to turn back now and take a different route to Sarnold, so they'll have to cross the river at the port."

Shep's knuckles tightened on the reins, turning them white as the first light of dawn kissed the top of his skin. "Which way?"

My stomach fluttered at the simple question. It wasn't complicated to find your way to the port along the trails since any eastern route would lead back to the river... Shep knew that, but he also knew I could get us there more efficiently than his generic guesses.

He trusts me... Was trust always this attractive of a quality? Or have I just been pressed against this guy's abs for too long?

I swallowed, wetting my dry mouth to try to

push away my intrusive thoughts while I studied the path ahead of us. We had a mission to complete. We may have tracked down seven of the wools, but one was still loose, and nothing got away on my watch.

"Forward."

chapter fifteen

The sun crested over the trees with an unforgiving amount of light. I squinted my eyes, biting back a yawn as the first sign of rooftops came into view. I'd pulled plenty of all-nighters in the past, but usually, I wasn't being rocked on the back of a horse and cradled in the arms of a man who would shame any teddy bear.

Shep was tired, too, though he did a far better job of hiding it. Aside from the slight shadow under his eyes and the occasional yawn he snuck under his breath, he seemed as sturdy as ever. We dismounted our trusty steed as the port town came into view, taking a moment for me to swing the stuffed saddle bag— where the cloaks were all hidden—over my shoulder.

"We need to find a better place to stash these," I said as I adjusted the bag strap. "We should leave the horse in a stable so he can rest. Also, I don't think my carrying this overstuffed bag is exactly *discreet*."

I tucked a loose corner of wool back into the bag's flap, feeling the warm aura of the fabric brush my fingers.

"Does this town have a bank?" Shep asked with a scratch of his chin, just above where the first signs of stubble were starting to shadow under his neck. My heart fluttered in my chest as I imagined what Shep's chiseled features would look like with a full beard.

Wait a minute, am I into beards? Or is this just another Shep thing...?

"Y-yes." I pretended to cough as I tried to distract him from my reddening cheeks. "Willen is actually fairly populated, so there's a bank, a couple of inns, and even a town hall."

"Perfect." Shep nodded, thankfully not noticing any of my strange infatuations with his stubble. "We can purchase a bank locker to store the cloaks for now. It won't be the most inventive hiding place, but not even Wolfe can organize a bank heist in the span of a day."

"I can't say it would surprise me if he could," I huffed. "But if you think it's a good plan, then I'm all for it. Let's drop off the horse first, and then we can visit the bank. I doubt our bandits have even made it half the distance we covered since they were traveling on foot. That should give us a few hours to scope out the area and plan."

I started heading toward the edge of town, but only made it one step on to the path before Shep snagged me by the arm.

"Hold up there for a second, Miss *Lyla*." Shep whirled me around, forcing me to face his roguish chin. "We need covers if we're going into a town. I think it's best if we state we're together."

My brows shot up. "You mean *together*, together?"

Oh no... not this again.

"Why not?" Shep grinned. "It wouldn't make sense for us to be traveling together in a courtship without a chaperone, so I think we're going to have to go all in and claim we're newlyweds on our honeymoon."

"N-newlyweds!?" I nearly choked.

"Well, we could always draw some wrinkles on you if you'd rather be an older couple?" He squinted, likely imagining me with gray hair and saggy skin. "You'd make a cute little old lady."

"You say one more word, and you won't live long enough to be a charming old man." I cracked my knuckles.

"Oh, you think I'd be charming?" Shep stroked his emerging whiskers. "I suppose I do look fairly dapper in a top hat."

"Shep!" I swung a fist at him, and he caught it with ease. I knew he would, and even if he let me hit him, it would be nothing more than a playful tap, but at least I finally had his attention. "Are you done playing around, or shall I go into town by myself as a young widow?"

I lifted a brow, earning a smug grin from him as he unfurled my fist with his fingers and gently gripped my hand. My skin tingled at the familiar sweetness of his softer touch, sending me back to the moments we first met. He raised the back of my hand to his lips, pressing a tender kiss on the top. I rolled my eyes to hide my blush, but the pounding in my heart was so strong, he could probably feel it in my fingers.

Darn you, Shep... I thought we were done with this!

"I wouldn't dream of letting my *darling wife* go into a new town alone." His tone dipped, low and sweet, like a thick, sugary syrup that coated you from head to toe. "Lead the way, my dear."

I pulled my hand from his, secretly missing his touch the moment my fingertips fled his. Part of me hated that this side of Shep was an act. Curse him, he really knew how to make my heart flutter...

"How about I lead the way, and you lead the horse." I gestured toward the reins with a sweet smile. "Let's save the hand holding for after, Mister..."

"Luther." Shep tipped his head. "Mister Luther Herder at your service, my dear Lyla."

"Herder, huh?" I folded my arms. "Bet you're patting yourself on the back for that one."

"I don't have to be the only one." Shep gave me a mischievous smile, pointing a thumb toward his back like he expected me to pet him like a Labrador.

"I'm your wife, not your mother," I scolded. "Plus, that's just plain weird."

"Newlyweds are always weird," Shep reasoned as he followed behind me with the horse in tow. "Not to mention, *affectionate*."

He brushed up alongside me, leaning down by my ear as I tried to focus on the ground. It was as if he was a daffodil and I was his sun, constantly reaching closer to me at every chance he got. My heart did a backflip as he reached back for my hand, singeing my skin around his hot touch.

It wouldn't be so bad if it wasn't fake...

"Fine," I clipped, accepting his hand in mine. "But we're only fooling the public this time, not my close family, so don't go overboard like last time."

"Overboard?" Shep laughed as we stepped out into the main road. "Lyla, my dear, I don't think you know what overboard really is."

His sultry voice speckled my arm with goosebumps, and I faked a shiver to pretend I was merely cold.

"You *kissed* me in the rain," I said through gritted teeth, forcing a smile up onto my face as we came into view of the locals.

Shep tightened his hand around mine, the movement both gentle and assertive as he pulled me a few inches closer to his side. "That wasn't a kiss," he whispered, sending another round of goosebumps across my neck. "A display of affection, sure, but a real kiss... I wasn't sure you could handle *that*."

I snapped my gaze to him, cheeks burning as I battled between feeling flustered and aggravated that he thought I was incapable of handling something. He met my gaze with his infamous smirk—the one that challenged me to test his assumption.

"I thought you were done underestimating me?" I murmured as we stepped onto the cobblestone streets. My ears burned as I screamed at myself for antagonizing him.

This isn't an arm-wrestling contest we're talking about, Evie! It's a kiss! You know, that one thing you've never really done before...

"There's a difference between underestimating you and respecting you," Shep said in a wistful tone. "And I respect you too much to fake something as real as a kiss."

I opened my mouth with a quick retort planned but ended up swallowing it whole as his soft gaze melted into me with the doughy look of fresh love. Kingdoms, it felt so real... Every fiber of my body filled with the warm flood of his attractive gaze like I had gulped down a pint of warm honeyed tea.

I should have said something, should have teased him or made a joke to imply that such things as *real kisses* were juvenile to a proper agent like me. But I couldn't make a joke, couldn't even meet his gaze without feeling like my heart was going to tear free from my chest. Shep was too good at playing this role, and apparently, I was too good at falling for it.

I should have suggested that we pretend to be cousins instead...

We stopped at the stable first and handed over our valiant mount for a much-needed rest before making our way toward the bank. The bank itself was a rather impressive building, with limestone walls, reinforced with steel vines and flowers that elegantly laced around the building. The streets were crowded, filled with travelers of all nationalities and the occasional sun-tanned local carting around their fresh catch of the day.

The air was thick and humid with the sweet smell of the river close by and the occasional pungent waft of fish. Shep kept hold of my hand as we crossed over to the bank, his grip on me actually proving to be rather helpful in the dense crowds. I kept the saddle bag close to my chest, never letting my eyes leave it as Shep guided me through the streets. We should have been a few hours ahead of the bandits, but that didn't mean someone else couldn't still be interested in stealing a petite girl's bag.

When we finally made it to the bank doors, we stepped inside, where the humid, fishy air vanished entirely. The bank was far quieter, almost as much as a library, with only the soft scribble of quills and the occasional flutter of paper echoing around the open space. The air was crisp and clean, with the fragrance of ink and lingering perfume brightening my senses.

"Good morning, sir." A stout banker with a starched silk vest and a crooked pair of glasses smiled at us. "Is there something I can assist you with?"

"Ah yes. You see, my wife and I have just eloped and planned to spend our honeymoon over at Sarnold's beaches." He flicked me a warm smile, and I mentally praised him for coming up with a smooth story. "The elopement wasn't exactly planned, so my wife grabbed a few too many belongings on her way out. We were hoping to purchase a locker to store them in until we make our return home."

The banker looked me up and down, keeping his smile plastered on his face as he inspected my scraggly haircut, torn skirt, and muddy boots. I certainly fit the description of a runaway debutant...

"I remember being young and in love once." The banker chuckled. "I would be happy to set you and your bride up with a locker, Mister..."

"Herder." Shep smiled a little too broadly at the pseudonym. "Luther Herder, and my new wife, Lyla."

I smiled sweetly, and the man tipped his head. "Mr. and Mrs. Herder, please follow me."

The banker led us behind the main desk, pausing to unlock the back door with a well-worn brass key, then directed us to a row of steel lockers, all mounted to the wall. I inspected the walls, doors, and even the ceiling, pleased to find that they were all reinforced with steel and stone, and the back door even had a heavy lock on it.

"This one should be empty." The banker swung open the thick metal door, about the size of an apple box. "Will it be big enough for your belongings, or would you like to purchase two?"

"This should be perfect," I said as I pulled the bag off of my shoulder.

"Yes, this is just what we were hoping for," Shep smiled as he pulled some coins from his pocket and placed them in the banker's palm. "We'll go ahead and rent it for the week, though I'm not certain we'll be gone that long."

"Not a problem," the banker said as he happily counted the coins. "I'll leave you two to set the code. Place your items inside and then twist the dial to any six-digit combination of your choosing. Just be certain to choose a number you won't forget. These vaults are near impossible to break back open otherwise."

His warning sent a wave of ease through me, calming my fear of something happening to the cloaks while we were away.

"We won't forget it, thank you," I said.

The banker stepped back out into the hall, giving us a moment alone as I stuffed the bag of cloaks to the very back of the locker. The locker was spacious, and just a bit dusty, but it seemed sturdy enough to hold up to a sledge hammer which was all I could really ask. I glanced inside the bag one final time, counting the cloaks to ensure all seven were inside. Once I felt assured we hadn't lost any in the market, I swung the door shut with a heavy *thud*, then began twisting the dial to a six-digit combination I was certain I would never forget.

"Are you sure that's a number you'll remember?" Shep asked as I put in the last number and latched it closed.

"I'm positive."

"Must be a pretty important date then," Shep mused, stuffing his hands into his pockets as he looked at me with his all-knowing eyes. I should have expected him to notice I inputted a date.

"What happened on the thirteenth of June when you were, what... ten years old?"

He did the quick math in his head, and I was impressed that he remembered my age correctly. I glanced around the room, ensuring the doors were sealed, and there was no chance anyone could be listening in.

"It was the day I became a spy," I whispered, causing Shep's eyes to flicker with light. "The day my life truly gained purpose, and the day I knew I had more to look forward to than just becoming a rich man's trophy wife."

I'll never forget that date... That was the date Evie first became her own person, and not the person others wanted her to be.

"An important date indeed," Shep said softly as he took my hand in his. "I suppose you can say that day ensured you and I would someday meet."

My breath hitched in the back of my throat, robbed by the fact that he was saying something like this outside of the view of prying eyes. *This wasn't part of his act.*

"W-what about you," I said dryly. "What was the date you first became a spy?"

I caught his eyes, my heart jumping around in my chest like it was punishing me for changing the subject. Shep may have been charming, handsome, talented, and the best spy

I'd ever met, but he was just that... a *spy*. I couldn't possibly let myself get attached to him any more than a partner should. Spies weren't designed to stick together.

"This past Sunday," Shep said assuredly, his eyes twinkling as his grip on my hand tightened.

I scrunched my brow. "Sunday? But that wasn't even a week ago, you've been a spy for—"

"Before Sunday, I was a spy of my father's creation," Shep explained. "Sunday was the day I met you, and the day I discovered *my* purpose. Father wanted me to be a spy who was strong and powerful, but working with you showed me that I wanted more... I want to be a spy who is quick-witted and clever, whose skills with combat and deceit can get them out of tough spots, but whose intelligence prevents them from being cornered in those spots from the start. Sunday was the day you introduced me to the man I never knew I wanted to become."

"You want to be like me?" I breathed, unsure how to process his answer. The son of the great Ryder Wolfe—and the man I desperately wanted to outshine only a few days ago—was inspired by how I lead my life and training.

"I want to try." He brushed his thumb against my palm, sending a shudder up my arm. "Though, I might need some lessons."

A smile brushed up my lips, filling me with

butterflies as I bit the edge of my lip to suppress it. "I'd be happy to teach you what I know, but..." I motioned toward the dagger concealed behind his belt. "In exchange, I want *you* to teach me how to handle myself better in combat. Starting with that *no peep* move, of course."

Shep laughed, turning toward the door with his hand safely tucked in mine. "You've got yourself a deal, Mrs. Herder."

chapter sixteen

When we stepped back out of the bank, the thick humid air plastered against my skin like a layer of cool sweat. The main street was even busier than before, now filled with shopkeepers setting out market stands to appeal to travelers. The sweet fragrance of ripe fruit and the savory smell of roasted chicken skewers melded together like a brilliant collage of flavors. My stomach growled, reminding me that I hadn't eaten since that whiff of ale I hadn't even swallowed at the tavern.

"Care to do a little shopping, my dear?" Shep asked, offering his arm out to me with a voice ten times sweeter than the sliced honeydew on the fruit carts.

I accepted his arm with a gentle flutter of my lashes, doing my best to look in love and not newly-infatuated as I had been in front of my parents.

"That sounds lovely, Luther." I giggled. "There are so many things I would like to try, and not to mention some interesting cosmetics I want to browse."

I pointed at a stall filled with face powders, hand creams, and hair dyes, earning another smile from my fake-husband.

"Of course, but why don't we start with some breakfast? You'll be able to think through your shopping better on a full stomach." He guided us toward the fruit cart, my mouth already salivating before we arrived.

The wares were much cheaper here than they were just outside the capital, so we both bought some slices of honeydew, pears, grapes, and a few apples for the road. I took an unashamedly large bite of honeydew, not even caring as the juices dribbled down my chin and onto my dress. The sugary fruit danced on my tongue, instantly refueling my energy, even without having had any sleep.

"Do you like it?" Shep offered me his handkerchief with a chuckle, but I was in too much bliss to consider how unsightly I looked.

"It's delicious," I mumbled through another bite as I accepted his handkerchief and dabbed my chin. My stomach growled for something savory, and the herby scent of the steaming skewers drew me in like a sailor to a golden siren. "But I think I want to try some of those chicken skewers next."

"What are we waiting for, then?" Shep guided

me to the chicken stall, and we picked out two juicy skewers that made the entire mission worth every moment.

The two of us ate until we were bursting at the seams, then we inspected the rest of the market stalls to pick up some fresh clothes that didn't make us look like we were chased by a bear on the way here. I stopped by the cosmetic stand and picked up a jar of inky black hair dye. It would be difficult to disguise Shep from his father, but I could at least mask my shiny blonde locks.

Before finding a place to change, we stopped by the ferry docks where three large wooden ships with wide balconies and tall smoke-stacks puffed out orange vapor, the color of refined fire stones. According to the dock men, the ships only carried passengers across the border every other day to prevent from overworking the stones, with tomorrow morning being the next departure.

Perfect, that means our thieves will be stuck in Willen until the next departure. Even with all these crowds, that's still plenty of time to find them.

"We should probably find an inn for the night, considering the next departure isn't until tomorrow," Shep suggested with a smile that was far too easy-going for what he was saying.

An inn? With Shep?

"Do you think there are any decent ones nearby?" I asked, my heart hammering as the situation I was in slowly began to crash upon me.

We were acting as a married couple... which meant we would have to share a room. Me. Share a room. With Shep.

"I saw one with some lovely windows that faced the main street." Shep pointed back toward a two-story inn across from the bank. "Should be a great place to rest up and observe the market."

Oh... He just wants to find a place to start a stakeout... I knew that.

"Right," I said a little more shakily than I intended. "What a great idea. Why don't we head there now, so we have some time to freshen up."

"Of course, my dear." Shep offered me his arm again, and I gripped it like it was an oiled fish, barely touching him and keeping a safe distance.

My heart strained from all the flipping, flopping, and somersaulting Shep's act had put me through. The worst part of it all was that part of me wanted to like it... a small part, of course. An itsy bitsy, minuscule, nearly undetectable part that kind of, sort of, liked having Shep look at me like I was his treasured love.

But kingdoms, that part of me was loud...

When we arrived at the inn, I'd managed to adjust my grip on Shep to actually look like I liked him and wasn't terrified of sticking too close to him like a hungry mosquito. The inn was quaint and polished with wood floors, fresh wallpaper, and a tidy desk at the far end of the room.

"Welcome to the Rosemary Inn," said a bright-eyed woman with a tightly wound braid slung over her shoulder. "Are you looking for a room today?"

I gulped at the singular use of the noun.

"Yes please. Is there any chance we could get one of the rooms overlooking the street? The view looks spectacular." Shep flashed his signature smile, and the woman gave me a look that said, *well, aren't you lucky.*

"Of course, sir." She dug through the desk drawer to produce a brass key with a room number engraved on the handle. Shep counted out a few coins on the desk, and the woman slid the key to him. "All rooms come with a complimentary meal at suppertime. I hope you enjoy your stay."

"Thank you, we will." Shep placed his arm around my waist, sending a soothing ripple up my spine that simultaneously dotted my neck in goosebumps. "Let's see our new room, my dear."

I nodded mutely, my tongue too dry to actually form anything that wouldn't have sounded like a tipsy sailor.

Warm sunshine filtered into the room from the expansive window, casting golden rays across the *singular* bed. I quickly reminded myself that it was unlikely we'd even be spending a full night at the inn, since the thieves we were hunting should be arriving in town within another hour or so. But even with that assurance, the bed was still there... Maybe if I threw all the pillows on the floor, it would look more like a dog bed and be less intimidating?

"There's a washroom in the back," Shep called, shocking me out of my strange plotting as he poked his head behind the wood-slatted door. "I'll go ahead and change. The window has a good view of the market and the street, so we shouldn't have any trouble spotting our thieves."

"Right. Got it." I cleared my throat, focusing my mind back on the mission as I pulled a wooden chair up to the window in perfect view of the street.

Why am I acting so weird around Shep? It's not the first time we've faked a relationship, although last time we had a chaperone...

When Shep emerged from the washroom, he looked just like the Sir Shepherd I had first met at my family's estate. His dirty shirt with the blood-stained sleeve was replaced with a clean black tunic, and his new tan trousers fit him exceptionally well. His hair was combed, and the stubbly beard he'd been growing was completely gone, showcasing his perfect jawline I had nearly forgotten to appreciate underneath his shadowy beard.

How dare I ever think he needs a beard…

"I can take over if you'd like to freshen up," Shep said as he set his soiled clothes on the bed, as if it were simply just a piece of furniture and not a massive reminder that we were very much an unmarried couple alone in a room.

Shep stepped up beside me at the window, and the fresh scent of rosemary-lemon soap brushed my senses. He made an attractive rogue, but seeing him cleaned up…? Oh, kingdoms.

"Thanks, I'll try to be quick with the hair dye." I stood from the chair to grab my spare clothes we'd found at the market, but only made it halfway to the washroom before Shep stopped me.

"Hold on a second, Evie." The sound of my real name sent a flutter through my chest. "Before you go, could you give me some quick pointers… On what I'm looking for, I mean."

I set the pile of clothes down, tilting my head as I turned back to Shep. "What do you mean? You're looking for the thieves we saw."

"Well, yes, I know that…" Shep ran a hand through his freshly combed locks, wafting the scent of rosemary and lemon through the air. "But you seem to be rather good at noticing the details I often miss. I know what the men look like, but that's only if they haven't changed their appearance since we last saw them. I guess what I'm asking is... how do you notice the unnoticeable?"

He looked shy, but only barely. There was just enough red in his cheeks and misdirection in his eyes that I couldn't help but smile at his request.

"If I teach you, you have to keep your promise to teach me your tricks as well," I reminded him as I popped my fists on my hips.

"I wouldn't dream of stiffing you." Shep laughed. "As soon as you teach me how to locate our crooks, I'll teach you a trick of my own."

"The *no peep* move?" I asked eagerly.

"Maybe..." Shep said, causing my shoulders to deflate. "There are a few basic moves you need to master before we can work up to that one, but I promise to teach you when you're ready."

"Fine..." I huffed, turning back to the window to inspect the crowd below. "What you're looking for are people who look like a stereotype but are missing a key element."

Shep furrowed his brow. "Alright... can I have an example?"

I studied the crowd for a moment longer, picking out a good traveler to prove my point.

"There, the pregnant woman with the tall-laced boots." I pointed. "What do you see that's off about her."

Shep studied her for a moment, following her steps with his eyes and narrowing in on her leather boots. "Her shoes look far more expensive than the rest of her attire. Perhaps she's pretending to be of lower status to gain sympathy? Or perhaps the shoes are stolen?"

"Both are good guesses, but I'd gamble neither is correct." I looked back at the woman's lopsided pregnant stomach. "She's not actually pregnant. You can tell by how quickly she moves for someone that far along and how her belly is shifted too far up. She's likely faking to be offered a better seat on a ferry tomorrow. You can also tell because no pregnant woman would bother tying up so many laces with a belly that big, not unless they had a servant to do it for them and she appears to be traveling alone."

Shep looked at me in astonishment, his eyes wide and cloudy at the same time, like he could see me but couldn't process everything that was happening.

"Incredible..." he breathed. "I see what you mean by noticing the parts that don't add up, but still, that's an impressive skill."

I smiled, and for once, didn't curse the butterflies that took over my stomach. Shep wasn't playing a part right now, so it was okay if I allowed myself to feel special around him... right?

"Now it's your turn." I hastily changed the subject, grabbing him by the arm and pulling him into the center of the room where we had more space. "Teach me something! I want to know how to fight more offensively, rather than just using defensive maneuvers."

Shep laughed, the sound sweet and warm in the cozy suite. "Alright, but just a quick one for now. You need to get cleaned up before our crooks get into town." He swiped a comb from the nightstand, holding it up like a fake dagger as he took a step back. "Here's what we'll do. I'll show you how to disarm an attacker and use their weapon against them."

Excitement rose inside me like floating soap bubbles, flooding me with energy as I trained my eyes on the dastardly comb. "Yes! What should I do!?"

Shep bit back another laugh, making slow movements forward to demonstrate the incoming attack. "It's simple, but you need to move quickly. Watch the direction the blade is coming from, then move your body in the opposite direction and throw your back against your opponent. From there, you can latch onto the hand with the weapon, twist the blade free from their wrist, and thrust the knife into your attacker."

He acted out the entire movement, playing both the part of the attacker and the victim as best he could, but it was difficult to follow.

"Here, why don't you give it a try, and I'll help you with your form." Shep waved at me to come after the comb, and I followed his instructions in slow motion. "First, determine the direction of the blade. Good. Now press your back into your opponent and seize their wrist with both hands."

I spun around, forcing my weight against Shep as I took his wrist into my hands. His familiar warmth enveloped me, reminding me of our time together on the horse and clouding my thoughts with the uproar of my finicky heart.

"And then twist the blade out of my hand before I—"

I wasn't paying attention, my thoughts once again distracted by Shep as I startled back into the moment. I tried to twist his wrist like he instructed, but I was moving too frantically. He fought against me like a real opponent would, and when I tried to get the upper hand by blocking him with my foot, he pressed forward and knocked my leg out from under me entirely. I pulled my hands to my chest as I braced myself for impact with the floor, cursing myself for not taking the training more seriously.

But I never hit the floor... only an equally hard, equally sturdy pair of arms that I always seemed to find myself winding up in. I opened my eyes, feeling my breath hitch as I caught

Shep staring straight at me the same way he had all day—the way he looked at Lyla Herder. He was looking at me like I was someone he cared for again. It was that unmistakable doughy-eyed look that always felt too real when he used it. Why is he suddenly looking at me like this now?

What's happening? Did someone see us in the window or something? Is he trying to slip back into character?

"Are you alright, Evie?" His use of my real name squashed any chances of this being another act, which only assured me that the look he was giving me now was real. Maybe even *more* real than the looks he'd given me before.

"Y-yes," I stuttered, unable to move even though I was safe from falling.

Shep made no motion to release me, his grip on me just as stiff and unmoving as my entire body, as if we were both locked in a scenario we hadn't ever expected to unfold. I suddenly became acutely aware of all my senses. The carpet felt too soft, the room was too hot, and every place Shep gripped me felt like it was on fire. The crisp scent of the inn's soap and his fresh sunshine-bathed clothes almost left me dizzy, but it was the kind of dizzy you wanted to soak in before coming back to your senses.

"Good," he said softly, finally aiding me to my feet one graceful inch at a time. "Would you like to try again?"

Would I?

It was more than clear to me now that I couldn't keep my heart in check. So did I dare let myself grow closer to this man... this *spy?* Shep wasn't some suitor I could tote back home with me and keep around whenever I pleased. He was a valuable asset to our kingdom and likely had far bigger goals in life than spending time with a girl who had a knack for finding lost things.

I should stop this now before I get any more entangled than I already am.

"I'd love too." My lips betrayed my better judgment as I pulled away from Shep, fully expecting to end up in his arms once again.

Goodness Evie, since when did the girl who was good at finding things ever get so lost?

chapter seventeen

"Wow, black suits you," Shep said as I stepped out of the washroom.

The dye felt sticky on my scalp, and the earthy scent was so overpowering, it made my eyes water. I looked down at my freshly trimmed locks, trying to see if I'd missed any lopsided ends when I cleaned up my chop-job. My hair wasn't too much shorter, maybe just a touch above my shoulders now, but it felt completely foreign. My new dress was similar to my old one—a soft, light blue cotton dress with wood buttons down the front. I wondered if choosing blue was a mistake now that I had the dark hair, but I suppose it wasn't an awful combination.

"At least I won't be quite as recognizable." I flicked my new dark curls, inspecting the tips for any patches of blonde I may have missed. "I know how hard it was for bystanders to ignore my adorableness."

Shep rolled his eyes, but I could see the hint of a smile tugging at his lips. "Well, *your adorableness*, you may want to get some sleep while we have a little spare time. You haven't fully rested since we first set off on this trip, and I'm doubtful you slept much at those inns."

He pointed toward the unoccupied bed, and suddenly, every lesson in propriety, modesty, and general ladylike behavior came crashing down on me like an armload of books. My mother would certainly disown me if she ever found out Shep and I had traveled alone, and she would probably kill me if she ever heard that we slept in the same room. Every fiber of my manicured noblewoman alter ego resisted the urge to acknowledge the sleepy droop of my eyes and the exhausted ache of my bones.

Nope, no way. Not letting Shep have a chance to see me drool!

"How about I take first watch while you rest?" I offered with a cool tone. "It'll be easier for me to pick out the robbers if they're in disguise, and you need to be well-rested in case we have to go up against Wolfe again."

Shep folded his arms, and a slight gleam of irritation burned in his retinas like a growing spark. "Evie, you need to sleep." He sounded sterner than I'd expected him to be, and maybe even annoyed.

Clearly, I'm not the only one who's tired.

"You need to sleep, too," I said with an equally stern frown. "I'm sure you're worn out after teaching me all those techniques."

"So are you." Shep stood from his chair, that intense frustration returning in his tone. "I could tell how quickly you lost your breath during all that practice. You need to sleep, and I need to stay right here."

The snap in his tone actually startled me, and his eyes darkened like there was more than just sleep clouding his emotions. Why was he acting so harsh? Was he really just tired?

"Shep..." I said softly, reaching out to gently touch his arm. "Please, I'm not sure I could even sleep..."

His entire demeanor changed from the simple touch. He blinked rapidly for a moment, and the hazel tone of his eyes brightened briefly, as if they had just looked past a fog. He rubbed his temples with a sigh.

"I'm sorry, Evie. You're right. I need to rest, too." He stepped away from the window, letting my hand fall from his arm like he was simply brushing by a tree branch. "Just promise you'll wake me up the moment you notice something, alright?"

"Of course," I said in a quiet voice, my eyes following him as he tucked himself into the bed without any further hesitation.

It took me a moment to return my focus to the window with how wildly my thoughts were racing. I'd never seen Shep so tense before... He'd been shocked when we first came across Wolfe, but other than that, he was usually so collected. I wonder what could be bothering him.

Was it my hair? Oh no, did it really look that bad...?

I fiddled with the ends of my darkened curls as I studied the crowd out the window, watching as the soft snores of Shep slowly filled the room. I should have felt awkward knowing that a man was sleeping right behind me, but to my surprise, it didn't feel nearly as taboo as Mother had always made it out to be. I suppose we weren't both sleeping, or sharing a bed, and it was also still broad daylight out, but above it all... it was only Shep.

He may have been suave, and a far too skillful flirt, but even when he was mildly grouchy and sleep-deprived, I felt safe having him around. Perhaps I should have taken him up on his offer of letting me sleep after all...

Hearing Shep's gentle breathing and sitting in the warm sunshine made it torturous to keep my eyes open. Shep was right about me barely resting at the inns. I kept the candle burning all night—busy studying maps, twirling my dagger, and trying to think of ways to prove I was superior. I'd slept some those nights...

Hopefully, the bandits will take their time...

then maybe I'll get a turn to sleep after She—

My wish was crumpled up and tossed into the waste bin as my focus latched onto a group of three men pushing through the crowd. They had changed their clothes, and one of them had even shaved his beard, but there was no mistaking the towering build of the half-blind man I'd encountered in the sheep pasture. At a second glance, I noticed a group of the other four men who were sticking closer to the alleys, led by the dark-haired man I'd only seen once before from behind.

Wolfe...

"Shep!" I raced over to the bed to wake him, but his eyes were already wide open when I got there, as if some vivid nightmare of his father had alerted him of his presence.

Dang, he's such a good spy, he even has super-human senses! I need to learn that trick, too...

He sat up without missing a beat, his eyes glassed over and focused like he was still partially asleep, but also fully ready to face any foe. "They're here, aren't they?"

I nodded. "Yes, there's a group of three heading for the docks, and a group of four who seem to be investigating the town. I bet they're hunting for the other cloaks."

"Which group is my father with?" Shep asked coldly as he tossed the covers aside and grabbed his boots.

"The larger group. I can't see the cloak anywhere, so they might have stashed it," I explained as I ran back to peek through the window. The group of four was starting to explore the market now, and the group of three was nearly out of my view.

"You take the smaller group, and I'll follow daddy-dearest," Shep said as he knotted his last boot. "If they're hoping to board a ferry, they'll have to go back for the cloak at some point."

Something writhed in my stomach as I digested Shep's plan. I wasn't entirely fond of the idea of splitting up, nor was I eager to go up against Wolfe's goons again, especially after the weird way they abandoned me last time...

But Shep knows what he's doing. I need to trust him as my partner instead of arguing against his ideas. There's no time to waste.

"Got it," I said as I ensured my dagger was safely tucked inside my boot. "We can meet back up at the docks before the first ferry leaves if we don't find each other sooner. That way, we can cut off the robbers if they try to sneak aboard with the cloak."

My head throbbed at the idea of missing another night of sleep, but I would just have to deal with the discomfort like any good spy would. It was just another hazard of the job.

"Sounds like a plan." Shep reached for the door, pausing before opening it to look back at me. His expression was shockingly tender, like he had forced his adrenaline to pause just for this one moment. "Be *careful*, Evie."

My heart jolted, and that familiar fluttering sensation returned to my stomach. Something about the way he spoke was different than his usual words of warning. He had always been so good at conveying what he needed to say through his tone, but this felt different... He spun back around without so much as another blink and briskly walked through the halls, but I lingered in the doorway as I chewed on his words like a bitter taffy.

That voice... what made it so different? And why did it unsettle me so much?

I shoved the thoughts aside and followed Shep's trail out the door, keeping a few steps behind him since I no longer looked like the sunny-haired wife he had stepped inside with. I snuck past the lady at the front desk and hurried out into the humid market, scanning the crowd for the group I'd seen earlier. Shep was already slipping into the crowd, and a moment later, he was out of my sight, hot on the tail of the more dangerous half of the group. It didn't take long to spot Wolfe's goons at the far end of the market. The three men blended in fairly well, but the beastly man with the one white eye made them a shining beacon.

Don't get too close... I don't want to start another fight; just find the last cloak.

They made their way to the docks, and spoke to the same friendly boatman who had informed Shep and me about the ferry schedule. The man we'd seen as the nightguard last night scowled, then followed minion number one—the one with the funny eye—back into the crowd.

I tried to get a closer look at their attires as I trailed them. They each had a small bag, but none of them looked full enough to be hiding a scrunched-up cloak. Now that I thought about it, it was more likely that Wolfe would keep the last cloak close to himself.

I hope Shep feels more prepared to handle his father this time.

My chest wound tight as a top as I slunk through the crowd. I pretended to browse a jewelry stand while keeping an eye on the men who were enjoying the same chicken skewers I'd eaten earlier. They seemed so normal out in the open, nothing like the numb soldiers who had turned away from an easy hunt and marched back to their master.

Even if they don't have the cloak, maybe I can catch them acting strangely again.

I thought back to how Lex had described the other men's emotionless behavior. They didn't seem emotionless at all now that they were happily indulging in an early lunch. It felt like I was missing something in this puzzle... like I had all the pieces, but the angle was all wrong.

What is Wolfe really up to...?

I stepped away from the spice table I was browsing, feeling slightly refreshed after inhaling a strong waft of peppermint. I glanced back at minion number one, and suddenly I didn't need the peppermint to feel alert.

The men had all frozen as stiff as carved marble, bites of chicken still pressed behind their lips as they slowly set their skewers down in unison. My heart rate spiked as I watched their pupils dilate like a spreading drop of ink. It was like someone had flipped a switch and they had shut off their entire brains—just like I'd seen in the forest.

They swallowed their mouthfuls and stepped back into the street, walking in a single file line with the stiffness of tin soldiers. I followed behind them a good ten paces, though I wasn't even sure if they would see me if I stepped in front of them. Their expressions were completely vacant as they moved wordlessly through the crowded streets.

Where are you going now?

I stuck close to their trail, following them around the streets, through the village, back through the streets, past the docks, and even through the back alleys. My body screamed at me for staying on my feet for so long, warning me I was far more tired than I allowed myself to believe. Their mindless stroll continued for hours, never pausing for more than a few minutes before choosing a new destination and wandering aimlessly like a pack of lost puppies. I couldn't make sense of it. It was as if their minds had been swapped out with that of a directionally challenged blood hound who was blindly following any scent he caught wind of.

The day dragged on, and the chase continued. It was starting to occur to me that they may have been suspicious that I was following them, and their odd movements were a test to see if I remained close by, but it was hard to believe that was their intention when they never even glanced back. My head throbbed, growing dizzy from chasing the bandits in circles while already feeling depleted.

It's official... I'm a fool. I should have taken that nap when I had the chance.

The sun began to set over the river's horizon, marking another full day I'd gone without sleep. I was debating going back to the inn and just cutting them off at the docks in the morning when, all of a sudden, they decided on a new direction. Minion one led the group just outside the town, arriving at the edge of the forest before disappearing into the trees. The new location piqued my interest, and I followed behind them at a safe distance.

The sky began to darken, and I was grateful that my dark hair didn't stand out so much under the fading glow of dusk. They continued into the forest for a long time, straying off the path and weaving through the trees so intricately, I was surprised they weren't following a map.

Is this some sort of meeting spot? Or maybe even where they stashed the cloak?

"Okay, men, this should be far enough." Minion one stopped abruptly, his voice dull and echoey but still sounding somewhat like his grouchy self. "Let's get this over with."

I crouched in the bushes, peering through a sparse collection of leaves as my heart raced a mile a minute. Minion one started glancing around the forest, looking for something, or someone, until he finally gave up and called again, "Jonty, you got her?"

Her? Wait a moment...

My blood turned to ice, and every sleepy cloud sprang from my mind when I heard a rustle behind me. I jumped to my feet, my heart hammering and lungs clamped shut as I stood face to face with a jagged silver blade.

"Oh yeah, Brone." Jonty, the crook I'd last seen

in the group Shep followed, grinned at me with a crooked smile. "I got her."

chapter eighteen

Jonty forced me into the clearing under the threat of his crooked blade. I staggered back, finding myself standing between the four men who all shared the same bloodthirsty look. My throat went dry and my veins heated like they were being stewed in my flaming panic.

They shouldn't have noticed me... I was never in their line of sight, and I was confident I didn't draw any attention to myself. But even so, this wasn't just me getting caught; this was a trap. Was I really that bad of a spy that I didn't even recognize how long I'd been compromised?

"What's the matter, little lady?" Brone asked, narrowing his unsettling eyes on me. "You're not looking as tough as you did last night."

I clenched my jaw, trying to stiffen any part of me I could to keep myself from quaking. This was bad. Somehow, these crooks had stayed a step ahead of me, and now it was four against one, with no one within earshot to even hear me scream.

"Is this the brat who escaped you by

chopping her hair?" Jonty laughed, flicking the ends of my hair with the tip of his blade. "She's certainly got spunk. Must be working for someone pretty important to have that much backbone."

Brone shoved Jonty aside, whipping out the same dagger I'd had the pleasure of meeting last night when he used it to embrace my throat. "Let's make this easy, shall we? Why don't you tell us who you are and who you're working for, and then maybe we'll let you keep your pretty face."

He traced the blade up the side of my cheek, but I didn't even flinch. My adrenaline numbed me to the pain as a warm rush of blood dripped down my face. Brone wasn't nearly as graceful with a blade as Shep had been, and he didn't seem to be as merciful, either.

"My name is Lyla," I said coldly. "And I don't work for anyone."

Something is off here. Why are they asking about me instead of the other cloaks?

"That's a cute alias," Brone growled, "but the boss already knows you have deeper connections than that. If you didn't, then you wouldn't be partnered up with that prodigal son."

I lifted my chin, fire burning behind my eyes as I discreetly studied each man's position. From what I could see, only two were armed, but that didn't mean the others weren't concealing weapons. I still had the dagger in my boot, but they'd notice if I tried to reach for it.

"If you know so much about my partner already, then why bother asking me?" I asked while I mentally mapped the distance between Jonty and the goons behind him. "I presume if you cornered me, then you already cornered him as well."

I bit the inside of my cheek, hoping that wasn't the case at all, and Shep was already hiding out in the inn with the last cloak in hand.

"Don't worry, dear. We've already taken care of pretty boy." Brone chuckled, causing my stomach to drop faster than a falling anvil. "The boss said he had something special in store for him."

I felt sick, my knees wavering more than wheat in a windstorm. Shep couldn't have fallen into a trap. He just couldn't have... He was the strongest one between us, so he definitely would have fought his way out, right?

My mind flashed back to the last moment I'd seen Shep, and his voice rang through my mind like the lingering echo of a graveyard's bell.

"Be careful, Evie."

Why did he sound like he was already defeated when he said that?

"What did you do to him?" My voice was

filled with venom, lashing like a flaring cobra as I stared straight into the point of Brone's blade.

"Shouldn't you be worried about yourself, dear?" Brone murmured darkly, his voice accompanied by the cracking of knuckles behind him. "The boss told us we don't *have* to get you to talk, but we do have to keep you silent."

A brisk shiver rolled down my spine. "What about the other cloaks? How do you plan to find them if I never tell you?"

The men shared a pleased look, one that made the shiver I'd felt earlier feel like a warm breeze compared to the deathly cold that chilled me now.

"Why do you think we kept you company all day?" Jonty grinned. "It wasn't to take you sight-seeing if that's what you were wondering."

My breath caught in the back of my lungs, and I fought to keep my eyes from widening.

All this time, they were just trying to distract me? But how!? How did they know I was following them?

They couldn't have gotten to the cloaks already, could they? The bank was sealed, and the code was something only Shep and I knew. *Shep!* They hadn't forced the code out of him somehow, right? He was far too tough to give up that easily. Maybe they were still planning to break into the vault some way... but that still didn't explain how they found out where the cloaks were hidden.

My mind spun and my breaths came out short and ragged as I tried to push my thoughts aside. I needed to get out of these woods, find Shep, and find the cloaks as soon as possible, and there were four minions standing in my way.

"Geoff, throw a gag on her so she doesn't scream." Brone jabbed a finger at the shorter of the other two men. "Let's make this quick. I just hate dealing with whiney little girls."

Excuse me?

I pressed my weight against my back foot, gathering every remaining scrap of energy I had. I may have been whiney at times, little, and even a girl, but I was downright insulted that this man thought that my screaming would be the most annoying thing about me. Unfortunately for him, my skills at irritating others were far more refined.

"I agree. Let's get this over with," I said as I noticed Geoff move behind me. I kept repeating Shep's lessons in my mind, mixing them with the sleepy remnants of my problem-solving skills. "I have a partner to find."

"Sweetheart, the next time you see your partner, it will be from beyond the gra—" I kicked the air out of Brone's lungs with a heel to the gut. Before he could catch his breath, I slammed my back into him and elbowed him in the tender place I'd just kicked as I twisted his blade free.

Shep, you better not be dead, because I need to brag about how awesome I just was.

With Brone's weapon now mine, I turned my focus toward Jonty, who was the only other man with a visible weapon. He slashed toward my torso, but there was no real force behind his swing and his aim was terrible. If I didn't know any better, I would have guessed this was the first time he had ever wielded a weapon.

Our blades clashed, and I was only a second away from shifting to elbow him in the throat when something caught around my neck and pulled me back. The air was crushed out of my windpipe as Geoff slid the gag over my throat instead of my mouth and started choking the life out of me. I coughed and sputtered, clawing at the fraying scrap of fabric while trying not to lose focus on Jonty's dagger. Brone was now standing upright after recovering from my blows. The fourth man, who's name I hadn't learned yet, lingered in the back, ready to jump in at any moment, but fortunately he was still not armed.

"Slippery little brat." Brone coughed. "I'll show you not to mess with me!"

He swiped the dagger from Jonty, and right as he swung for my gagged throat, I threw all my weight to the side. I latched my free hand around Geoff's leg, pulling him off balance and dragging him with me as we both fell to the ground. The fabric dug into my skin, definitely leaving a nasty bruise. Blood oozed beneath where the gag cut into me, but knocking Geoff down with me was enough to make him loosen his grip.

I ripped the gag from his hand, freeing my throat with a massive gasp as I rolled away from the incoming stomp of Brone's boot.

"Alric, grab her!" Brone called to the man who I had nearly rolled into.

The fourth man, Alric, reached down to grab my hair, but I wasn't about to go through the hassle of another haircut. I sprang to my feet, knocking my head straight into Alric's chin— another trick from Shep. He yowled in pain, and Jonty raced up to try grabbing me by the arm, but I was too fast.

I pushed past Alric and dashed into the woods, my heart racing and neck bleeding as I pumped my legs with an inhuman amount of energy. I could hear the men scrambling behind me, but there was no chance I was going to let them catch me, not when I needed to find Shep. My small frame had the upper hand when it came to maneuvering through different terrain. I used my internal compass to recall the twisted path I'd been led down, grabbing onto my tender throat to try to block the cool air from rushing against it. My vision went blurry as my adrenaline began to fade, growing hazy from exhaustion and the shock of being nearly choked to death.

Even with my scrambled mind, mapping the forest came easy, allowing me to cut through the extra twists Brone had added during our journey and run straight back to the edge of town. It was past dark by the time I made it out of the woods, and my entire body felt like it was on the verge of crumbling to pieces.

Shep… I need to find Shep.

I stumbled into town, constantly glancing over my shoulder. I pulled up the hood of my cloak, attempting to hide both my face and the patches of blood on my cheek and throat. Everything felt blurry, like I was wading through a dark ocean where all sounds were muffled and a shark could snag me in its jaws at any moment.

Shep and I were supposed to meet at the docks in the morning… but it's too early for that. Where else would he go?

The streets were nearly empty under the moon's glow, with only a few rosy-cheeked men waltzing out of the taverns and a scattered few who were enjoying the evening air. I thought back to what the men had said about the cloaks, and how they already knew where to find them. Maybe they were planning to force Shep to open the locker? Or perhaps they already had?

I started for the bank, my neck still stinging in the cool wind and my throat burning like I'd inhaled gulps of smoke. The bank appeared to be closed, but I wasn't about to let a locked door stand in my way. What if Shep was inside?

I was just about to start looking for something to pick the lock with when a familiar voice cracked through my last wall of strength.

"Evie!"

I spun around, nearly tripping on my feet as I blinked up at Shep. Tears blurred the last of my vision, tightening my sore throat even further as I took in a sobbing gasp. He ran toward me, not even bothering to use my false name as he pulled me into his arms.

He's alright.

"Thank the kingdoms you're alive!" He pulled me close, gifting me the strength I no longer possessed, as I melted into his embrace. I rested my uninjured cheek against his chest, trying to control my breathing so I didn't start fully sobbing in my partner's arms. His finger brushed the edge of the cut, careful not to touch it as he inspected the injury. "You're hurt."

Shep took in a sharp breath as he traced the injury until his eyes landed on my swollen neck. He stopped breathing entirely, his eyes glassed over like they were fighting between pulling me back into his arms and hunting down the men who did this. After a moment, he gently pulled me back so he could inspect the purple bruises that were likely forming, tenderly lifting my chin as he bit his lip.

"I'm going to kill him..." he growled, his voice so sharp it could have easily run through any man.

While he was looking over my neck, I took a second to inspect him for any similar injuries. I clenched my teeth as I prepared to see a bloom of crimson spread across his abdomen or a gash along his leg, but no matter how closely I looked, I couldn't find a single injury. I should have expected as much as from someone as perfect as him. Thank the kingdoms he was unharmed...

"I'm just glad we both got away," I said in a raspy voice, my throat still raw from having the air choked out of me. "It was all a trap, Shep... Somehow they knew we were following them, and they even said they knew where to find the cloaks."

A tear streaked down my face, breaking past my defenses and mixing with the blood on my cheek. I'd never felt like so much of a failure until now... I should have been smarter or better than I was. What kind of spy let herself waltz into a trap?

"I know," he shushed me, gently pulling me

back against his chest as he stroked my hair. The soothing motion only increased my desperate urge for sleep as his heart beat lulled me, despite its growing speed. "It's going to be alright."

I should have felt embarrassed in how I allowed Shep to hold me up, or at the very least, frustrated that I'd let myself get so weak, but I was too tired, too sore, and Shep's embrace was a remedy I couldn't replicate. He took my weight effortlessly. We had taken on the same villain, fell into the same trap, and only one of us was still standing straight... I really was a pitiful excuse for a spy.

"They may have outsmarted us this time, but we'll get the cloaks back, I'm sure of it," Shep soothed, still combing his fingers through my hair.

Get them back?

I looked up at him, my eyes too glassy to truly see him. "They took them, didn't they?"

My lip quivered, making my ragged voice almost impossible to keep clear, but the broken look in Shep's eyes was enough for me to know that he'd heard me loud and clear. He glanced toward the locked bank doors, a grim look staining his features as he tightened his hold on me.

"They did..." he said dryly. "I don't know how, but they had all eight when they cornered me in the woods. After getting away, I tried to look for you, but wasn't having any luck. I decided to come back to the bank to figure out how they got the cloaks out, but thankfully, I ran into you on the way. I was so worried."

They got all of them...?

I bit my lip to keep from crying, and instead burrowed my face into Shep's chest, where he held me without complaint. I'd failed... All I had to do was keep track of what I'd already found and gather one more, but not even the walls of a bank could keep them safe. How was I supposed to compete with a villain like that? The answer was simple... I couldn't. I, the great Genevieve Rayelle Palleep, was a failure of a spy. This was Shep's chance to prove he was more than a traitor's son, and my chance to prove I was more than just a clever, pretty face. We'd nearly had it, too.

I'd lost the wools... and for once, I didn't know where to find them.

chapter nineteen

I don't remember when I fell asleep. I don't even think I made it out of Shep's arms before my body collapsed against his. All I remember was feeling him cradle me, pressing me close against him as my throbbing skull slowly calmed itself. My throat burned, making each breath feel like it was rubbing against an internal lesion. At some point during my sleep, I felt something cool and damp brush across my neck. At first, it stung enough that I nearly jarred from my sleep, but after a moment, the cold liquid began to soothe the pain and my breathing became smoother.

With the pain eased, I couldn't help but fall back into a deeper sleep. This time, I couldn't sense any movement at all. When my senses finally returned to me, the crisp scent of moving water and a chilling breeze coaxed me to flutter my eyes open.

The first thing I noticed was the sky, and how the clouds were moving far too quickly for me to be stationary. The sun's rays blanketed me in a luxurious warmth, and the soft chatter of people acted as white noise that threatened to pull me back into sleep. I had nearly given into the temptation when I finally noticed what else I was looking up at.

The sunlight silhouetted most of his features, but there was no mistaking Shep's glittering hazel eyes. They burned into me, gripping me like they were terrified to let go. I blinked again, clearing the sun from my eyes as I tried to figure out why he was leaning so far over me. It was then that I finally noticed the comfortable pillow I was resting my head on... but it wasn't a pillow at all.

I'm sleeping on Shep's lap.

I jerked awake and tried to sit up, but Shep held me down by the shoulders. "Evie, calm down. You're safe." He tried to keep me from rising too quickly, forcing my head back down in his lap as a rush of red flushed through my cheeks. "Don't get up until you're ready. It's okay to rest. There's no rush."

There was no time to be calm! I was lying on Shep's lap... There was no such thing as resting now. How long had I been here? Why wasn't he rushing to track down the rest of the cloaks, and what happened since I blacked out?

My head began to spin, and I realized Shep was probably right to keep me down for another moment. "W-where are we?"

The sun seemed brighter now that the haze had cleared from my vision, and I could see the shadows of people walking by. The fresh air spurred me even more awake. The curiosity of our location, and the desperation to get out of Shep's lap had me itching to sit up.

How is he so calm about this!? What kind of man is so chill while being used as a pillow? Oh, no... I didn't drool, did I? Oh, kingdoms, I might faint again...

Shep brushed a strand of hair from my eyes, the touch surprisingly sweet. "We're on the ferry. We should arrive in Sarnold in a few hours."

The ferry? No wonder the clouds are moving too fast.

It was then I noticed the wood planks under my back, the sound of rushing water, and the iron railing only five feet away that was crowded with passengers looking out at the river. Shep was resting against a smokestack, where, upon closer inspection, I could see the plumes of orange smoke float out the top.

"Wait a moment. The bandits were planning to get on the ferry. Are they on the boat too!?" I started to rise, feeling my adrenaline kick back in as the images of Brone and the others flared in my mind like a fever dream.

"No." Shep sighed, bracing my back as he aided me into a sitting position. "They likely took the first ferry out. I was only able to get us on the second one. The market stands didn't open until sunrise, so I had to wait to buy some medicine and bandages."

My hand flew to my throat as I recalled the cool sensations I'd felt in my sleep. In place of the swollen cut on my throat, there was a delicate satin ribbon tied around my neck in a dainty bow. I slipped my finger beneath the ribbon, finding a soft cotton bandage laced around my tender throat.

"I hope you like blue..." Shep ran a hand through his hair. "I figured it would be a good idea to get something to cover the bandage with, so I picked out a ribbon that I thought suited you."

My heart fluttered as I toyed with the smooth ends of the ribbon. *Oh, Shep...* He had really delayed the mission just to take care of my injury? I looked down at my hands, still noticing a few flecks of blood under my nails from when I'd touched my neck. It was the last remnants of a nightmare that was now tied up with a perfectly neat bow.

"I'm sorry, Shep..." I closed my hands, bunching them into fists as I pressed them against my knees. "It's my fault we missed the ferry. I shouldn't have been so careless about not getting rest, and I shouldn't have been so foolish not to notice the robbers' trap."

I crinkled up my skirt, squeezing the fabric as I funneled all my frustration into my pitiful grasp. I wasn't strong, wasn't intimidating, and I wasn't even smart enough to avoid an obvious trap. After losing the wools, I couldn't even claim I was skilled at hunting things down, especially if I couldn't even bring them back. In an effort to prove I was a worthy spy, I only proved how much of a failure I was.

"Perhaps I'm fooling myself," I said hoarsely. "Genevieve Palleep was never born to do anything more than marry a wealthy lord and carry on the family name. Maybe that's what I should stick to. At least then, I won't be endangering anyone else."

Trying to think I was anything more was a mistake. I may have loved being a spy, but was it really something I was meant to do? Perhaps I should stop kidding myself.

"Evie." Shep took my hand, holding it as tenderly as if it were a wounded dove. "Don't talk like that. One failed mission doesn't define how incredible your talents truly are."

My hand tingled in his touch, sending sparks through my blood as I felt a sudden urge to squeeze his hand back. "What about you? You've never failed... Even last night, you escaped unharmed while I was too hurt to even make it to the first ferry on time."

Shep opened his mouth to respond, but strangely enough, he didn't say anything. Instead, it looked like he choked on his own breath for a moment. It was like he was going to reply, but decided against it a moment before it passed his lips. He furrowed his brow, clacking his teeth together with a pained look in his eyes that felt directed toward me... as if the thing he wanted to say was still needing to be conveyed.

"I shouldn't have escaped as unscathed as I did," he finally said. "My father is a wicked man, and unfortunately, I think very similarly to him. I escaped because I was able to read his mind in a sense, and the only reason I could do that was because we think in the same horrific ways."

He took in a ragged breath, like saying that much was almost too painful to admit. It looked like he was fighting with his words, fighting with the truth of what he was afraid to admit. At that moment, he reminded me a lot of my old handmaiden, Lacey, who struggled with speaking her truth a lot, too.

"You may think the same, but you're nothing like him," I said softly. I squeezed his hand, unable to hold back the urge when it felt so needed. "Just because you think similarly doesn't mean you share a mind."

A cloud passed overhead, shadowing Shep's eyes and washing the deck floor in the orange hue of the magic stone fumes.

"But it feels like we do," he said with a monotone drop of his voice, his eyes growing shadowed and dull. "I can still hear his voice in my head. It's hard not to follow his commands, even now."

My heart cracked as I watched the strength he used to mask his pain crumble into dust. Kingdoms, his eyes... They hadn't truly been the same since we first came across Wolfe in the pasture, but was that something that had changed within Shep, or something that had simply resurfaced?

As different as our upbringings were, I could still understand how he felt. Shep was groomed to become a heartless spy, and I was bred to be a perfect lady. We'd both found ourselves in a job that allowed us to become anyone we chose, but that didn't mean that our pasts didn't still overshadow our futures.

We're both more than what we were made to be.

"Then let's discover more of *you*." I met his eyes, staring past the broken shards of his father's influence in search of the suave partner I'd grown to rely on. "You've already started learning how to think around situations instead of approaching them with intimidation and force. That's not something your father cared to teach you, so that's a part of you he hasn't touched. Maybe if I teach you more of my tricks, you can combine them with the skills you know and become more like... more like Shep."

He looked at me for a moment, his grip on my hand growing more natural by the second, until I'd nearly forgotten we were touching. He studied me in the same way I would look at a new map—uncertain of what he was looking for exactly, but still intrigued by all the different elements he actually found.

"Has anyone ever told you how incredible you are...?" He brushed his thumb against my hand. "And not some snotty suitor, or brass-buttoned noble who was only looking at your frills; I mean, someone who truly knew *you.* The stubbornly amazing spy and woman who never fails to make me look like a rookie. *That* person deserves far more praise in her life, and I sincerely hope I'm not the first to give it."

My breath hitched, completely stolen by Shep's perfect, and I mean *perfect,* voice. It was smoother than the one he used with my parents, stronger than the tone he took against Lex, and more adoring than any of the ones he used on Genevieve or Lyla.

I don't think I will ever get tired of that voice...

"I'm not much," I said shyly. I hoped he couldn't hear my heart over the sound of the lapping water. "Just a girl who can't keep track of a couple of wools."

"But you have kept track of them," Shep

countered. "And this time, we're going to find them all. They may have escaped us once, but we'll drag those wools back home, one shred at a time if we must."

I smiled, my heart uplifted as his encouragement refilled my emptied cup. He may not have thought he was perfect, but I couldn't think of anyone else who ever made me feel this way.

Does he feel the same? Oh goodness, this is bad... When we met, I never thought I would tolerate him, let alone...

"Let's do it, then." Shep stood to his feet, pulling me with him slowly enough that I could steady my sea legs. "We have a few hours until we disembark, so why don't we continue those lessons we were giving each other at the inn?"

"L-lessons?" My cheeks burned as I recalled how many ways I had stumbled into Shep's arms in the room.

"Well, maybe only verbal lessons." He winked. "We don't want to frighten any of the other passengers. Maybe you can talk me through your next prediction on where the wools are going? Unfortunately, we weren't able to prevent them from making it into Sarnold, but maybe there's another way we can—"

His voice choked off, his pupils dilating as he suddenly looked like he was struggling for air. He looked like he'd been struck with a rush of intense pain. My heart skipped a beat as his face suddenly paled the exact moment a woman brushed up behind him.

"Oh, pardon me, sir," the woman apologized as she continued past us without a second thought.

"Shep?" I took his hand, jolting as I realized he felt ice cold.

What happened? Did that woman do something to him? Why wasn't he speaking!?

The color started to return to his face, but he still wasn't breathing, his eyes glued to the woman who had barely brushed his shoulder.

"Shep!" I grabbed him by the shoulders, giving him a light shake as he took in a solid breath. He began to cough, and I felt like I could scream with relief. A second later, his hand warmed, and the paleness that made him look like a blink from death had vanished as quickly as it came.

"S-sorry," he sputtered, clearing his throat as if he had merely had a coughing fit and nothing more. "I think that woman's perfume aggravated my senses. I've admittedly felt a little off since we boarded the ship and started inhaling the fire stone fumes."

The fumes?

"Shep, that looked like more than an irritant.

You couldn't breathe!" I pressed a hand to his cheek, checking for fever and satiating my need to feel that he was alright.

"It's nothing, Evie; I promise." He pulled my hand from his cheek, giving me an easy smile as if it truly were just a bad inhale of fumes.

But that couldn't have been it. I'd seen that type of reaction before…

"So, what were your thoughts on the wools' next location?" He carried on like nothing had happened, and I gave him some vague answer, but was hardly paying attention as my mind clicked together everything I had just seen.

It can't be…

I glanced over at the woman who had brushed past Shep, analyzing the side of her body that would have made contact. I hadn't noticed any perfume on the woman when she walked by, and even the magic stone vapors were nearly scentless when used correctly. But what I did notice was the woman's bracelet on the arm that would have touched Shep…

It was a fairly simple ornament, with a braided silver chain and a basic clasp, but that wasn't what drew me in. At the center of the chain was a bright emerald-green stone— a balance stone, often used for preventing sea sickness. My stomach plummeted as I looked back at Shep's smiling face, recalling the brief moments he had gone deathly quiet. I'd only seen one other person react that way around a magic stone... But I'd seen Shep around magic before, hadn't I? The cloaks were magic.

But Shep wanted me to carry them... he didn't want to touch them.

Shep said something else about the dock port, and I forced a smile as my heart surged with the ferocity of a lunging snake.

The only people who can't come into contact with magic stones are the ones who already contain a hazardous fragment of their power.

I thought back to my handmaiden Lacey, and how weak she became after coming in contact with magic stones. Her body couldn't handle being near refined magic, because she carried unrefined magic in her body from a curse.

I looked back at Shep, noticing the hidden look behind his eyes. The cry for help that had always been there, but I had never truly seen. It was the same look I'd seen in Lacey's eyes when I discovered she was cursed to only speak in lies. Shep was capable of speaking the truth, but I couldn't deny how his body reacted around the stone. There was unrefined magic trapped inside his body, which could only mean...

Shep is cursed.

chapter twenty

It made perfect sense, yet at the same time, it made none at all. I knew that curses came from unrefined magic stones, and that after an individual was cursed, their body would rebel against sources of refined magic. Lacey was cursed by a truth stone, which turned all her speech into lies. Was Shep cursed with something that affected his speech, too?

No, that wouldn't make any sense. He was far too skillful with words to have his tongue magically tied. There had to be something else that his curse was affecting, but what? And why did he never tell me about it?

We funneled off the ferry and were instantly greeted with another port market that was even larger than Willen's. The crowds were thicker, and the Sarnold locals were far pushier when selling their wares than the folks in Reclusia had been. A kaleidoscope of colors filled the market, with brightly-dyed fabrics on one end, a rainbow of fruit stands on the other, and hundreds of people all rushing around in a blur. Voices called from every stand, luring shoppers into their stalls in any way possible with samples, displays, or simply physically dragging them by the arm.

"Fresh dates! Nuts and seeds on sale, two pouches for one coin!"

"Hand-dyed silks! Perfect for that special someone!"

"Magic-stone necklaces! Verified by Sarnold's top miners!"

My head whipped toward the jewelry stall, my attention fully stolen by the glitzy necklaces. Shep heard the vendor too, but he kept his eyes trained on the street without even glancing toward the refined jewels.

"We should probably go somewhere a little less crowded to make a plan," Shep said as he guided us to the opposite side of the market, far from the magic stones. He snuck a quick peek back at the table, and I could see the slight tense in his shoulders.

So, it's true... He really is cursed with something. He can't go near the stones.

Despite ensuring we were away from the jewelry vendor, I noticed Shep still didn't seem relaxed. His eyes flicked around the market like a paranoid pickpocket, and his breathing seemed far too heavy for just a brisk walk. I followed his gaze, noticing that he was eyeing all the flashy jewelry glittering off the locals.

There are magic stones everywhere.

It wasn't surprising. Sarnold was the number one producer of magic stones with the largest mine in all the kingdoms, so stones were more affordable and worn even by the common folk. Many used energy stones to work more efficiently or magic stones that were rumored to bring luck to the wearer. The stones worn by the commoners were still fairly small and weak compared to the gaudy gems reserved for nobility and royals, but there were still enough that the entire crowd was peppered with the radiance of magic.

"Shep, are you alright?" I couldn't help but reach for his hand, and nearly jumped when I realized how clammy it was. *How many magic stones had he brushed up against already?*

"Me? Oh, I'm fine." Shep gave me a reassuring smile, but the beads of sweat on his brow exposed what was stirring inside him. "I suppose it is a little warm with all these people around."

I gave his frosty hand another squeeze and pulled him through the crowd with a little more haste. He definitely wasn't wanting to admit what I'd discovered, but that didn't mean I couldn't still help him get to safety.

"Come on, I see a clearing this way." I dragged him by the hand, feeling his skin flash between hot and cold as we brushed by any number of people who could have been decorated with magic.

Shep didn't argue and allowed me to guide him without a word as he discreetly wiped the sweat from his brow. It pained me to see him try to hide his distress from me. Had he been cursed ever since we'd first met? Did it happen during a training incident as a child? Other than the cloaks, I had never seen him interact around magic before now, so there was no telling how long he'd been hiding this secret from me.

Although he did pull the cloaks off the sleeping men in the sheep pasture... And he interacted with Lex's cloak, too.

I suppose it was possible that someone cursed with unrefined magic could interact with other sources of unrefined magic fairly easily, but if I was to guess, even that had limits. Otherwise, he wouldn't have been so insistent on me carrying the rest of the cloaks. Did he have a certain threshold he could meet before unrefined magic began to harm him? Is that the real reason why he failed to collect the last cloak from his father in the pasture?

My mind flashed to the guilt Shep had displayed when he let Wolfe escape with the last wool. Something had seemed off about him then. Was it because he felt guilty that his curse got in the way?

Oh, Shep... Why didn't you tell me?

We finally came to a stop in the back alley of what appeared to be a furnishing shop. I finally let go of Shep's hand, and he instantly used it to brace himself against the dirty clay wall. Shep's face was completely flushed and his lungs heaved with long, slow breaths. He cleared his throat, attempting to distract from his sickly appearance, but there was no way I could pretend not to notice.

"Shep, is there something you haven't told me?" I asked. My stomach twisted, knowing perfectly well that he would have told me about his curse if he wanted to. I shouldn't be prying, but this wasn't just some stranger I was looking at too closely. This was my partner, this was Shep. This was the man I felt safe around, and I wanted to make him feel safe, too.

Shep's breath hitched, and something about his expression turned to iron, as if I had knocked on a steel door he hadn't expected to be found. His skin returned to its natural color and with another long breath, he looked just as healthy as he did when we stepped off the boat.

"What do you mean?" His tone was distant and cold, but at the same time, it didn't seem like he was trying to avoid the question. His eyes were deep and complex, like a mass of wool twisted on a loom that was tangled beyond repair.

He's never talked about this before, has he?

"Something is off with you," I said gently, my heart pounding wildly as his pupils shrunk to the size of pin pricks. I didn't want to be the one to say it first; he needed to admit it when he was ready, but I couldn't hide the fact that I already knew. "Your reaction around the market just now, and the woman on the boat... Shep, you know that you can tell me anything right? It won't change how I see you."

Talk to me, Shep...

The air went dead around us, freezing us in time as I locked eyes with the man I desperately wished would confide in me. It wasn't that I needed him to admit his flaws, but more that I wanted him to trust me enough to know I'd support him despite the curse he carried. I wasn't sure why it tugged my heart so much, but I couldn't fight the pull to be there for Shep, to help fight against his curse and prove to him that I still cared for him, even if it was a burden he carried.

I care for him... Is that why I'm so bothered that I never knew?

"You're right." Shep's voice cracked, his gaze so intense that I couldn't even blink away. "Something has been off about me, and I've been too afraid to tell you."

He sounded so jumbled, like he was fighting

between the urge to admit his secrets and keep them bottled inside. Was it some sort of reaction caused by his curse? I wish I knew what type of stone he had been infected with...

"You don't have to be afraid, Shep." I took a step forward, shrinking the distance between us to prove I wasn't going anywhere. "We're partners, lovers, rivals, and even husband and wife. There's nothing you can tell me that's going to make me see you as any less."

He looked at me with so much severity, his jaw clenched shut and his eyes gripped me like they were trying to give me one last warning before I prodded any further.

How bad can his curse really be?

"Evie," he said my name so purposefully, his voice stronger than I'd ever heard it before. He took my hand into his. At first, I felt a rush of elation pulse through me at the touch, but when I noticed his fingers were quaking, my heart froze. "Something is very wrong."

His tone left me unsettled, causing me to squeeze his hand back as I knit my brows. "What's wrong, Shep?" I whispered. "What can I do to help?"

He squeezed my hand so hard, I feared he might bruise it, but I wasn't going to pull away. He needed someone right now, though I still didn't fully know why.

"Do you trust me?" His voice cracked again, his eyes desperate and pleading like there was a specific answer he needed to hear.

"Of course," I said assuredly. I placed my second hand on top of his, trying to steal some of whatever had him so frantic. "I trust you with all my heart, Shep."

His hand twitched in sync with my frantic pulse, and I wondered if my face looked as red as it felt. It had been too easy to say I trusted him —the words had just flown off my lips before I could even filter them—but I didn't regret it. I wanted him to know that I, Genevieve Rayelle Palleep, hater of all men, trusted my partner with every piece of my stone heart.

I would say "curse you, Shep." But little did I know, someone had already beat me to it. Looks like I was doomed from the start.

"Then I need to show you something." Shep gripped my hand, his eyes still flooding me with too many signals to read. I just hoped one of them wasn't disgust after my corny confession...

"Alright." I nodded, barely even getting the word out before he started dragging me with him. He led us out of the alley with a brisk, almost mechanical stride, his grip on me both firm and shaken at the same time. "Where are we going?"

He didn't say anything, didn't even look back

as he guided me out of the buzz of the market and onto the main roads. He kept his grip on my hand, still squeezing me like I was a life source he couldn't release. We were starting to move away from the town, off the road and along the edge of the river, where only a few fishing shacks dotted the banks. I started to worry that taking this much of a side trip would impact our mission, but I meant what I said about trusting Shep. If he needed to show me something this badly, then I was going to see it.

He finally stopped just in front of another fishing shack, this one made of scrap metal with blue paint chipping overtop chunks of rust. The smell of fish still lingered around the building, and twisted nets and shards of hooks were scattered around the ground. It was completely quiet this far out from town. There was no more shouting, no more vendors, and only the peaceful sound of the river rushing in the distance. If Shep needed peace and quiet for whatever he wanted to show me, then he certainly had found it. I just wish it wasn't so fishy...

"We're here," Shep said ominously as he finally released my hand. "I'll need you to step inside."

He turned to face me, and my heart stopped when I noticed the bloodshot color of his eyes. He looked terrified in a way I never thought was possible for him. My stomach churned as I glanced at the mysterious shack, wondering how it could possibly tie into Shep's curse.

"Okay, I can go in." I swallowed, putting on my bravest face as I lifted my hand to the door.

Before I could even touch the door, he grabbed my shoulder, and I whipped my head around to see Shep gripping me. His nails dug into me, burrowing into my skin with a silent desperation that seared into my core.

"I-I'm sorry, Evie." His voice was choked, almost as if he was fighting off the effects of another magic stone.

"Why? What's the matter?" My throat was dry and the stench of fish burned my eyes.

He cleared his throat, then shut his eyes and opened them once again with a far calmer demeanor as he let his hand fall from my shoulder. "Just go inside," he said. "Then you'll understand."

I bit my lip, feeling anxious to turn my back on Shep while he was acting so shattered.

I'm ready for you to show me, Shep. We'll get through this together...

With a fortifying breath, I pushed the door open, washing my senses in the old smell of rust and fish. The shed was dark, with no windows letting light into the metal walls, but just enough cracks in the ceiling to let me make out the silhouette of a figure... and then another, and another...

The shack wasn't empty. This wasn't just a space for Shep to show me something... It was a hiding place for someone to lie in wait.

No...

I staggered back a step, but Shep was already at my back, standing in the doorway with his stiff frame blocking my escape. His warm aura suddenly felt as cold as the metal walls. Standing in the cramped shack, were seven men... And all but one were wearing glittering gray cloaks.

"Well done, son." Wolfe stepped into the light, his hazel eyes a terrifying replica of Shep's. "I knew I could count on you."

chapter twenty-one

Ryder Wolfe, the most dangerous spy to ever double-cross Reclusia, looked so much like his son. They had the same dark hair, rich hazel eyes, and chiseled jawline, though Wolfe's was framed with trimmed sideburns. He shared the same devilish smile I'd seen Shep wear, and his voice was a sharpened tool that could carve straight down into your soul.

He wore pressed slacks and a tight-fitted linen shirt that hugged a set of muscles that were even more impressive than Shep's. He looked approachable enough that you'd be willing to trade your soul for the right bargain, but also viperous enough to stab you in the back after he collected his payment. Just looking at him made me uneasy, and not just because he had Shep's eyes, but because they seemed to know so much more than I could have ever guessed. All those times I had felt inadequate, or like I was always just a step behind, these were the eyes that were seeing ahead.

His, and his son's...

Standing behind him were all six of his lackeys, each sporting one of the magic-infused cloaks with glassy stares. They were lined up like soldiers, each standing at perfect attention and barely even blinking. It was beyond unsettling the way their eyes felt completely unseeing, even as they stared straight at you. The other two cloaks were poking out of the saddlebag hanging on Wolfe's shoulder, the exact same bag I had sealed tight in a vault.

A vault Shep had known the combination to.

I couldn't move, couldn't even breathe. I could still feel Shep behind me, his stone-cold presence acting as a dark shadow that was looming over my shrunken form. This couldn't be happening... it had to be some sort of misunderstanding or accident.

But it wasn't.

Shep had led me here, and now he was standing between me and the door. My stomach seized, and the stench of the air mixed with the raw betrayal in my gut nearly made me hurl. The man I had trusted, taught my tricks, and even feared for his safety was working hand in hand with the man we were meant to be fighting together. Like a perfect fool, I followed him. A sheep to my own slaughter.

"W-what is this?" I don't know why I even asked, but the silence was too heavy on my crumbling heart and the eyes of the enemy were far too piercing. "S-Shep?"

I could hear him intake a sharp breath when I spoke his name, but I couldn't bear to turn around to face him. The sting of his betrayal burned beneath my skin; I couldn't handle letting him see how much it affected me. But then I heard him close the door...

I jumped around, facing his dead stare as he scraped the metal door closed against the wall and latched it shut. My adrenaline spiked as the room darkened, locking me inside with the row of mute tin soldiers and the beady-eyed Wolfe. Shep didn't look at me, but I could still see the shake in his hands—the small sign that part of him didn't like what he was doing. Yet he still did it...

"You... You were working with your father all this time?" I asked, my voice barely a squeak. "How could you...? After all that you said about wanting to prove yourself trustworthy?"

And after how much of my trust I'd given you...

It all made sense now. Why he'd acted so strange whenever his father came up. How he walked away from an ambush unharmed. How the cloaks were magically removed from the vault... Shep was behind it all. All this time, he'd been just like his father—playing the other side and making a complete fool out of me. He told me he wanted guidance, but in reality, he wanted me to be oblivious. I was the foolish sheep led astray this time.

"You betrayed me... Why?" I asked as my heart crumbled into dust at my feet.

Shep's eyes went glossy, but he still didn't say a word. It was like he hated every minute of what was happening, but even so, he was too stubborn to stop.

"Why, Shep!?" I shouted.

"Don't blame the boy, Miss Palleep," Wolfe interrupted, his voice low with a slight rasp that differed from Shep's. The blood drained from my face at the mention of my real name, like hearing the grim reaper rattle your name off his collections list. "He's only being obedient. Isn't that right, Shepherd?"

Shep barely met my eyes. His expression was completely emotionless, but his gaze looked agonized, like every glance at me ignited him from the inside out.

"I-I'm so sorry." Shep's voice quivered, but his tone was stark. It barely even sounded like him at all.

What happened to my partner?

"Oh, don't apologize, Shepherd; that's a nasty habit," Wolfe said as reached into his pocket. I glanced back at his sickening grin as he held up something round and vibrant in his palm. "I command you to stop apologizing."

My breath choked in the back of my throat as I watched Wolfe speak into his palm. Tucked between his fingers was a massive yellow-gold stone, glittering and sparking with magic so chaotic, there was no way it could be refined.

"Yes, Father," Shep said blankly, his muted tone a shadow of his former self.

"That's a good boy." Wolfe smiled as he tossed the stone into the air, catching its wild sparking in the small fragments of sunlight. "I bet you're well-educated on magic stones, are you not, Miss Palleep? From what I recall, you were rather close with a young woman who bore the curse of a truth stone."

A lump formed in my throat, too dense to swallow back as I forced all my confidence into my glare. *A magic stone... Could that be the one that cursed Shep?* I already felt nauseous just looking at it. Wolfe's smile twitched, clearly enjoying watching his prey squirm now that she was trapped in a cage of monsters.

"Well, allow me to introduce you to one of the rarer stones found within Ebonair's soil." He held out the stone for me to view, but I didn't dare approach it. It was the size of an apple, with a golden hue that sparked, but dim enough to show that some of its magic had been drained... drained into Shep. "This, my dear, is an obedience stone."

Obedience?

I'd only read about obedience stones, but had never seen one. Refined versions were used for self-discipline and helped wearers stay on task and keep their minds clear. An unrefined version would have to be far more powerful, and more dangerous...

"You cursed Shep, and now he has to obey you?" I asked.

"Ah, so you are clever. Shep was right about you." Wolfe chuckled with a low rasp. The idea of Shep telling this man anything at all about me made me want to squirm. *How long has this been going on? Was he cursed from the day we met?* "To put it simply, yes, though that wasn't the initial plan."

He tugged the corner of a cloak out of the bag, comparing the shine to the fading glitter of the obedience stone. My heart skipped a beat as I recognized the sparkle. The cloaks were a bit brighter when held up to the light because the magic wasn't drained, but they still possessed the same golden shade.

"The cloaks are infused with the same magic," Wolfe said proudly as he glanced back at his silent army. "Anyone who wears them takes on the temporary effects of a curse, but it fades within a few days if they take the cloaks off.

Fortunately, I was able to get my property back before any of my men gained too much of their autonomy."

He patted Brone's shoulder, and for the first time I actually felt a wave of pity crash into me as I looked into his good eye. These men hadn't been attacking me under their own free will?

"You forced them to join you?" I asked numbly.

"They certainly *joined* me willingly," Wolfe said as he brushed a piece of lint off Jonty's shoulder. "The payment I offered was too tempting for most of them to refuse, so they helped me retrieve the cloaks of their own volition, though I can't say much about their thoughts after I encouraged them to try on our new wares... The cloaks were all made with remnants of this stone, which was a lot bigger before it was shaved into magic dust and twisted into the wool. Because the magic in the stones and cloaks are connected, whoever wields the stone controls those who are in contact with the rest of the particles. Not a bad way to amass an army, if I do say so."

They're all his puppets...

I looked up at the statuesque men standing beside their boss, and suddenly everything came crashing through my mind all at once. The way Lex had described the other robbers... How the men had been normal one moment, then lost their humanity the next. How the men had walked away when they were mere moments away from knocking me loose from the tree.

Wait a moment, that was around the same time Shep first started acting strange. Right after we ran into Wolfe for the first time...

My racing heart came to a screeching halt as I recalled the blast of white and gold light that had blinded Shep in the pasture. The gold color was the exact same as the stone in Wolfe's hand and the shimmering color of the cloaks.

"You cursed Shep in the forest," I said, my voice tight and dry. "When we tried to steal the cloaks back from you... You panicked and cursed him with your stone to make him obey you."

I turned back to look at Shep, my heart practically bleeding out of me as I finally understood the chaos I could see behind his eyes. All those times he was telling me to be careful, and acting distant when I claimed I trusted him... It was because he *didn't* want me to trust him, not while he was a *Wolfe* in sheep's clothing. Ever since that night, I felt like there was something off about him, but I just assumed it had to do with seeing his father again for the first time in years.

"I can still hear his voice in my head. It's hard not to follow his commands, even now."

He'd been trying to tell me all along... And just like Lacey, I couldn't tell until it was too late.

It hurt. It burned me alive. The guilt gobbled me up and spat me back out in a useless lump as I stared into the trapped soul behind my partner's eyes. I was meant to be observant; I was meant to be the one who noticed things that had changed.

But I was lost when it came to Shep, and now I'd lost so much of him, I wasn't sure how to find what was left.

chapter twenty-two

Ryder Wolfe had cursed his own son, and now we were all trapped in a smelly fishing hut with the world's most awful family reunion. I hated how pleased Wolfe looked when he gazed at his brainwashed son. The worst part of it all was that the real Shep was still inside... still fighting to break free and forced to feel the pain and guilt of his actions.

There's a special place in the afterlife for people like you, Wolfe.

"I had preferred to use a cloak on him," Wolfe continued, not even phased by the lifeless marionette his only son had become. "Curses are finicky and cause people to stick out in the crowd. I had hoped to use his position in the crown's agency to get me closer to the more off-limits black-market goods, but what use is a black-market spy when he can't even go near the gems? Sure, he can approach the unrefined ones without too many consequences, but even those might cause him to combust after too long. So I had hoped to catch his loyalty with one of the cloaks. But I trained him too well, and when he snuck up on me in the night, my instincts took over. He's still useful, I suppose, just not in the way I had originally intended."

I wanted to *no peep* him so hard, he wouldn't wake up for weeks, but Shep never taught me that move... And I doubted it would work on the man who likely invented it. The great Ryder Wolfe, whom I had even admired as a young spy, was now nothing but a scumbag crook who couldn't even see his own son as more than just a tool.

"You were planning to brainwash Shep all along, then?" I asked through gritted teeth. "Is that why you trained him to be like you? So one day you could overtake him and order him around like your slave!?" My veins burned, steaming from the inside out.

"I can't say I had envisioned it would work out as smoothly as it did." Wolfe shrugged as he stuffed the stone back into his pocket. "But the black market makes the best toys, so I was hoping something offering mind-control would pop up some day. It would seem fate was in my favor. I will admit it was rather satisfying to have Shepherd not only follow me, but hand deliver the stolen cloaks to us, and even instruct us on how to lure you into an ambush not once, but twice. I wanted to have you killed the first time, but I was impressed that you managed to escape with your life, so here we are now."

What is he going to do with me, then?

I could sense Shep take a sharp breath behind me as if his father's upcoming thoughts had already passed through his mind, but his lips were pressed tight. Wolfe eyed me like fresh meat, determining if I had a use or if it was best to devour me.

"Are you planning to kill me?" I asked boldly, praising myself for hiding the shake in my voice.

"A clever girl like you?" Wolfe tilted his head at me with a sideways smile. "Of course not. Not when you'd look so ravishing in a fresh new cloak..."

Oh no.

He motioned toward the cloaks stuffed in his bag, and I felt my entire body turn to lead. I should have taken Lex's advice and burned those cloaks the moment I had them in my hands... If he put one of those on me, I wouldn't be Evie, Genevieve, or even Lyla anymore. I would be a traitor's puppet.

"Is this your way of recruiting me?" I scoffed. "Because I hate to break it to you, but even if you control my mind, I don't think my stubbornness will ever actually fade."

Shep could fight the magic, I'd seen him do it with his veiled warnings, though I hadn't been clever enough to figure them out until it was too late... Even if Wolfe stole my mind, he wouldn't steal it all. If Shep could continue fighting, then so would I. Even if it meant walking myself and the cloak into a fire that would destroy us both.

"Don't worry, my dear. I can be rather persuasive when I want to be. Magic or no magic," Wolfe said slyly, reminding me of the moment I had seen Shep interrogate Lex with the delicate use of his blade. I didn't want to find out the type of interrogation tactics Wolfe used. "But there's no need to fret so soon. I still have a buyer to flaunt my finds to. Once I show off the cloaks and collect the buyer's payment, I'll stage a little accident for him and come back to crown you in your new finery. You'll make such a wonderful little addition to the team." He stepped forward and his grimy hand reached for my chin, lifting my face until I was looking into his murky eyes. "There's always good uses for a pretty face in our line of work, wouldn't you agree, Shep?"

Shep didn't say anything, but I could feel the heat radiate off him from behind me. Wolfe laughed and dropped my chin with a jerk before he turned to pat his son on the shoulder.

"Don't look so cross, my boy. I promise to take care of your darling partner." Wolfe chuckled. "Actually, why don't *you* take care of her? We'll need someone to safeguard our newest recruit while the rest of us take the cloaks. Since your obedience has a more flexible leash, you can stay here and keep watch. I know how much you were worried about her when I sent my men to attack her when she was alone. So, this time, I'll let you be part of the action."

He pulled Shep's blade from his belt and placed it in his hand, his eyes as cold as the steel that reflected in the metal. Then he pulled the obedience stone back out of his pocket with a wicked smile.

"Both of you will stay here until we return," Wolfe commanded. "If she makes even the smallest attempt to escape... kill her."

My blood snapped colder than the bottom of the river. Wolfe snapped his fingers, stirring up the six lackeys who had been patiently waiting for their next command. Brone and Jonty approached me, and I tried to back away, but Shep stopped me by gripping my shoulders from behind.

My skin rippled under his touch while simultaneously shivering at the thought of his actions not being his own. Despite it not being his will, his touch was still the same. He held my shoulders firmly as the other men took my wrists and bound them with scraps of an old fishing net, but even so, his touch was as gentle as the compulsion of the curse could allow. He was still in there, trapped, but fighting to rebel at every chance he got.

Shep...

Shep pulled me against the wall, and Jonty moved my bound wrists above my head. He snagged the make-shift rope on an old hook nailed into the metal that was likely used for hanging fresh catches on, effectively pinning my wrists above me.

"You two play nice now," Wolfe said as he summoned his minions out the door. "This will be your first test of obedience, Miss Palleep. If you sit still and be polite, you'll get to live to join my forces. If you decide to be a bit rebellious... well, I'm sure Shepherd would be disappointed if he had to murder you. So, let's try to put him first, okay, dear?"

"How noble of you," I spat. "Looking out for your son..."

Wolfe flashed me a wicked smile, his low laugh ragged enough to peel paint. "How could I not look after him when he's such a perfect child? Obedience is such a rare trait nowadays, don't you think?"

chapter twenty-three

My arms went numb from being pinned above my head, so I had to keep twitching my fingers in order to keep the blood flowing. Shep stood at the far end of the room, arms folded and head down as he dug his nails into his arms so deep, I wondered if he was going to make himself bleed.

"Are you allowed to talk to me?" I asked, my voice echoing against the metal walls now that we were alone. "Or were you commanded not to speak to me, too?"

Shep glanced up from the floor, his expression tense, like he was fighting through an intense pain. "I am instructed to keep you here at any costs," he said in a stoic voice. "I am not permitted to share any more information than what the boss has already told you."

His eyes shook as he tried to meet my gaze. It was like I could actually see the mental tug-of-war between what he truly wanted to say and what he was permitted to speak. It was just like Lacey... Only he had even less control over himself than she did.

I guess I'll just have to navigate conversations with Shep the same way I did with Lacey.

"He commanded that *you* can't share information, but he didn't say you couldn't confirm or deny information that *I* spoke, correct?" I nodded my head slowly with each word, watching his pupils widen behind his statuesque expression.

"That's correct," he said with the slightest lift in his tone.

Relief flowed through me like a breath of fresh air each time I caught a piece of the real Shep hiding behind his cursed mask. Every curse had loopholes somewhere, and Shep's was no different.

"Did you know you were cursed?" I asked with a tug in my chest. "When it first happened, I mean."

"Yes," he said, his eyes glassed over. "I could see the stone the moment he woke up. I didn't know what kind it was, or what it would do, but immediately after it happened, I was unable to say anything about it."

He can explain his experiences as long as they don't expose any more of Wolfe's plans. Good, that means I'm not limited to only yes or no answers.

"How much of your actions after that were Wolfe's?" A lump formed in my throat, thinking back to the tender moments we'd shared at the bank vault and even in the inn. Was that all an act put on by his father?

I shivered at the thought. I didn't want the trust I'd built with Shep to be fake...

"It was still me, Evie," Shep said breathlessly, his chest heaving as he forced the words out like they were choking him alive. "I was instructed to act normal so you wouldn't expect anything amiss."

He started coughing, and I instinctually lurched forward to help him, nearly forgetting I was pinned to the wall. When I jerked forward, the tiny sound of a string snapping alerted my ears. While Shep was recovering from his coughing fit, I glanced up at the hook my bindings were hanging on and noticed that it wasn't just any hook... it was a fishing hook with a sharpened tip.

"I did his bidding." Shep cleared his throat, still sounding hoarse as he managed to straighten. "And I couldn't tell you what was going on, but I promise... It was still me."

Warmth flooded through me as I met the desperate look in his eyes. He knew what I was fearing and was fighting with everything he had to tell me the truth. He may have had his father's voice in his head, but his heart still belonged to him.

Thank the kingdoms...

"So all our conversations, all the time we spent together..."

"Real," he said assuredly, his eyes glistening like a dying star he needed me to see before it burned out. "I wanted so badly to protect you from myself, but I couldn't warn you. His control was too strong."

I bit my lip to keep it from wobbling, trying to draw Shep's eyes to my emotion as I silently sawed away at my restraints.

"Can your father hear us somehow? Does he have access to your thoughts or what you say?" I asked with an anxious dart of my eyes.

"No," Shep replied. "Though he can make me tell him whatever he likes."

Like the bank locker passcode...

"In that case, can you tell me what you'll do if I try to escape?" I continued sawing at the knotted fishnets binding my wrists, hearing another few cords snap.

Shep's eyes darkened, his entire demeanor stiffening like clay left out in the sun. "Evie... He'll make me kill you."

"Yes, I'm well aware of that," I said dryly as I forced myself to swallow. "But can you tell me *how* you'll try to kill me? That way I can know what to expect."

His entire body jolted for a moment, as if the Shep trapped inside had tried to kick his way out for a moment. "I can't say," he said in his dull tone. "I'm simply instructed to kill you by whatever means necessary."

Another cord snapped. I watched as the sweat beaded across Shep's forehead, and his fists shook like he was on the edge of a seizure. I may have been the one bound, but he was the true prisoner.

"Do you truly think you'd do it?" I asked softly, my voice more haggard than I'd expected. "Could you really kill me?"

He took a slow step forward, closing the distance between us with a towering glare that would have been intimidating if I was actually afraid of him. His intimidation had startled me in the past, but even with the curse flowing through his veins, I couldn't find myself afraid of the man who had cracked through my prideful heart.

"I fear so," Shep said in a daunting voice that was laced with a low tremor. "I am *terrified* of what will happen if you try to leave."

He raised his hand to my chin, his touch gentle and strong as he adjusted my head to meet his imprisoned gaze. When he looked at me, I had expected him to glower with the intensity of a proper guard, but even though he was scowling, his eyes were so different... The way he looked at me was similar to the way he'd captivated my heart while we were crafting our fake relationships, but at the same time it was unique. He didn't look at me like he was a lover, or a husband, or even a partner. He looked at me like a spy would... A spy whose mission was right in front of him, yet still out of his reach. Like he would take on any persona, or fight through any enemy it took to achieve his objective.

"Don't you dare run," he breathed, running his hand up the side of my face and cupping my cheek. "Because even though I know you're capable of escaping, I can't promise I'm not capable of catching you."

My skin tingled beneath his touch and my heart hammered relentlessly. I wanted these touches to be more than a warning; I wanted this moment to be more than just a threat. Because it didn't feel like a moment I should be afraid of. It was a moment I wanted *more* of.

"Have you ever resisted the stone's pull before?" I asked, my voice barely a whisper as I carefully cut free another section of the binding.

"Once..." His gaze lowered to my neck where the bandages and satin bow were still tied. "I was commanded to stay with Wolfe until we heard if you'd been killed, but I couldn't bear it. My emotions went wild, and for the briefest moment, I couldn't hear his voice, and I ran."

So the magic can be resisted? With a strong rush of emotion?

"That was when I realized just how afraid I was of my father," Shep continued solemnly. "And just how afraid I was of what he could make me do... Even with the brief flicker of freedom, he still clawed me back into his command a moment after. It was only because he assumed you were already dead that he let me leave. Not long after I'd bandaged you he commanded me to get on the ferry and bring you to him. I suppose I was able to fight him a bit when I brought you here. I was afraid then, too."

"Were you really that worried about me?" I glanced up at him through my lashes. "I never imagined you'd care so much about such a sloppy partner."

Shep brushed one of my darkened locks from my eyes, the color already half-faded from the boat's water spray. "Evie... I don't think I could convey how much I care, even if my words weren't being tampered with."

My breath hooked, and everything inside me went quiet as I watched the honesty pour out through his gaze. A rush of butterflies filled my stomach, and for a moment, the dingy fishing shed felt as regal as a Reclusian ball, and the cursed guard brushing my skin looked like a dark prince. Any methods I used to restrain my heart before were officially useless as it threatened to pound out of my chest.

Shep cared about me... and for kingdom's sake, I cared about him too, and I wasn't going to keep pretending I didn't. I may be the infamous Lady Genevieve who couldn't keep a man around for longer than twenty minutes, but this time I was willing to do anything to make him stay by my side...

But first, I need to leave.

"I care about you too, Shep," I said as I cut free all but one thin string of my bonds. "Which is why I'm going to get back those cloaks, and that stone."

Shep's hand went cold just before he dropped it from my cheek. "Evie, if you try to escape then I'll be forced to—"

"Underestimating me again, are we?" I gave him a teasing smile, my hands twitching as I tried to build up the courage for my grand escape.

If I can cause his emotions to flare for even a second, then maybe that will be enough to delay his attack.

"Evie, please." He took a half step back and he tightened his grip on his dagger with a quivering hand. "I'm not sure you can handle me."

His words circulated through my mind, teasing a smile on my face as a memory brushed my lips like sweet honey.

"You said that once before," I said slyly, pressing my heel against the wall as I prepared my next move. "Right before you kissed me in the rain. You told me I couldn't handle you then, either. I've been waiting to prove you wrong ever since..."

I snapped the remains of the net free, and pressed off the wall with all my strength. Shep's shock lasted only a second, and he quickly reacted by whipping out his blade. I grabbed for his wrist, forcing the direction of the blade away from my chest and held it out to the side as I slammed against Shep's chest. With one hand holding his blade away from my throat, and the other gripping him by the back of his hair, I pressed up on my toes and met his lips with a curse-shattering kiss.

chapter twenty-four

Even cursed Shep had perfect kisses...

As a spy who couldn't help but notice everything, this was a rare moment where the world truly faded around me. My hand burrowed into Shep's thick dark locks, while the hand holding back his wrist floated to my side with his weapon. I had intended for the kiss to merely be a distraction, but it was so much more than a brush against a cursed puppet's lips. Shep was right... I wouldn't have been able to handle this when we first met.

The blissful moment almost made me forget the risk I was taking, so much so that I let it go on for just a second longer, and then a second more. He seemed just as oblivious to the world as I was. He stopped fighting me, and his entire body melted against me like we were puzzle pieces meant to fit together all along. When I finally noticed his hand start to twitch around the dagger, I knew I needed to make my escape, but I still counted one final slow second before pulling away.

His gaze was mystified, like he was somewhere between cursed and enchanted as his muscles started to regain control of his blade. I let my hand slide from the back of his hair, brushing my thumb against his jaw for one final second before curling my hand into a fist.

"I'm sorry about this." With all the force I could muster, I punched Shep directly in the jaw I had just embraced. He reeled back from the shock, and I took the opportunity to swipe the dagger from his hand and dash for the door.

"Evie, run!" Shep growled, his steps only a few feet behind me.

I pushed the metal door open and kicked it closed behind me as fast as I could. Shep rammed into it on the other side, smacking the door into my back and causing my entire spine to rattle from the impact.

"Block the door!" Shep shouted just before ramming the door once more.

It took all my strength to keep him from bursting through. I dug my heels into the sandy ground as I searched for something to bar the door with. A long strip of metal roofing caught my eye, and I grabbed it just before Shep pounded the door with another relentless attack. Another wail of pain shot up my spine, but I didn't wait around to feel the bruise form. With the metal scrap in hand, I whirled around and wedged it between the door slats, effectively barring him inside. Shep rammed the door again, and the metal vibrated from the force, but it didn't budge.

"I'll come back for you, I promise!" I said through panting gasps as I rubbed my freshly bruised back.

"Don't worry about me!" Shep huffed as he continued kicking the door. "I don't think I'll be in here long. Go, Evie! You can do this."

I bit my lip, still feeling the heat of his kiss as I fought my heart's urge to stay by his side. He hit the door again, and this time, the metal bent under the force. He was right, it wouldn't keep him in for long.

"Do what you do best," Shep said with a heavy breath, his voice throaty and deep. *"Find them."*

Oh, I will.

My feet flew across the sandy path as I clutched Shep's dagger to my chest. I sprinted as fast as I could, barely managing to follow the footprints left behind as my head swirled like a flower in a windstorm.

I had kissed Shep, really kissed him. Why had I waited so long to do it!?

I smacked my blushing cheeks to try to rattle some sense back into my mind. Shep may have been the most perfect kisser known in all the kingdoms, but he was still under the control of a dangerous traitor, and he was currently trying to kill me...

Not exactly how I imagined my first kiss to go, but... you know what, never mind. This is exactly how I expected my wreck of a love life to end up.

Shep was the type of man I never truly thought existed. Someone who could hold his own against my family, and more importantly, hold his own against *me*. It wasn't until now that I realized how deeply I enjoyed the moments he had to pretend he cared for me, because in reality, it gave me glimpses into how I had always dreamed a man would show his affection. Not just the sappy words or the sweet touches, either... Shep challenged me. He wasn't someone I felt I could pick apart in an afternoon tea session, but someone I could spend a lifetime learning more about.

And what a lifetime that would be.

But right now, his life was tied to a big dumb rock. It's a good thing I'd always had a knack for drawing out stupidity around me—the men Mother sent to court me being a prime example, of course.

The footprints led back to a main road before blending in entirely with all the other footprints, carriage tracks, and hoof prints. I paused to take a breath, clearing my mind as I tried to formulate a mental image of Sarnold's maps. I hadn't studied Sarnold nearly as much as Reclusia, mostly because I'd been brash enough to assume our crooks wouldn't even make it this far, but it would seem my wishful thinking hadn't calculated for a traitorous, yet charming, partner. I knit my brows together as I formed the map in my mind, using the river as a starting point and retracing my steps from the fishing shed to where I was now.

There should be a stable about a half mile down this road... Even if Wolfe didn't decide to go on horseback, acquiring a mount will help me catch up to him.

With my mind made up, I continued running, only slowing when the stitch in my side burned too much to keep pushing. A small lake caught my attention on the side of the road, and the glittering water drew me in. I paused to take a long drink and splash my face with its icy water. A dribble of black dye ran down into my hands, reminding me of my dark locks. I took an extra moment to dunk my whole head into the frigid water and hastily scrubbed at my hair. It felt amazing to wash out the itchy dye and all the other flecks of dirt that came from running around through the forest.

When I came back up, an inky plume of black clouded the water. When the dye finally dissipated and my reflection came back into view, I could finally see my familiar blonde curls again. I wrung out my hair and stood to return to my chase, but paused when I noticed something catch off the sunlight.

Sitting in the dirt along the bank was a tiny fleck of gold dust... Nearly undetectable unless you had spent days obsessing over the glittering fabric it was usually attached to.

They were here.

I wandered around the perimeter of the lake, searching for any other clues, flecks of dust, or even a footprint. It only took a minute before I spotted a discreet trail tucked between two crooked hickory trees. A smile spread across my face as I located fresh footprints dotting the path, along with another loose fleck of gold dust...

Found you.

Down the trail I went, forgetting to look for a mount entirely as I decided to try to catch up on foot. As I walked, I tried to remember where this specific trail would have been located on my maps. This wasn't a path I had ever seen marked before, but based on the location of the lake, it should have connected to the town of Cracin.

Most of the more affluent cities were close to the kingdom's capital, but Cracin was one of the few more rural ones. The town bordered the river, so it was a hot spot for trade and mercenaries, just like the port towns were, but Cracin had a few noble estates that made its location stick out more on most maps.

It wouldn't surprise me if Wolfe's buyer was a noble. Those with money often looked for new exotic ways to spend it, even to go as far as experimenting with black market sales. I couldn't help but wonder if the buyer even knew what the wools were capable of, or if they were just trusting Wolfe to put something flashy in their greedy palms.

Either way, it wasn't good. Wolfe made it very clear he had no intention of actually giving up the wools, which meant this was a rescue mission as well as a fetch mission.

I followed the path for hours, stopping once more to collect a few nuts to gnaw on in hopes of silencing my growling stomach. Shep and I had eaten the last of the fruit we purchased on the ferry, and it was already quickly approaching suppertime. When the path finally opened up, I found myself stepping into a vast garden full of orchids, climbing roses, and a dozen other flowers I didn't know how to name. A tall iron gate blocked me from exploring any farther, so I skirted around the edge until I found the front of the property. A very *decorative* property.

Oh no... Anything but this.

An expansive manor, probably larger than

my own, stood proudly in midst of the trees like a rose in a weed garden. Some sort of party must have been ongoing, because there were dozens of people flooding the doors, all dressed from head to toe in the finest gowns, suits, and glamor only a proper noble could afford. The entire sight was like a flashback to my childhood nightmares of being dragged by the wrist into similar parties so I could be guilted into dancing with boys who had sweaty palms and bad breath.

Music poured out through the doors, and haughty laughter rang through my ears like an out of tune harp. I had officially stepped into another universe... and I was already starting to miss the smelly fishing shed.

Noblemen threw parties all the time as a way to amuse themselves, flaunt their wealth, and allow the other affluent families to showcase their unmarried daughters. But another, lesser known, use for parties, was to provide a flashy distraction for the less flauntable parts of a nobleman's life—like purchasing an illegal black-market item, for example.

I needed to find out whether the buyer was the host of the party or a guest taking advantage of the chaos. Though it would be rather difficult to walk in unaccompanied while looking like I came fresh off a boat, complete with the lingering smell of old fish.

In the midst of the lineup of people, a group

of three men caught my eye, urging me to step back into the bushes. Wolfe was at the head of the group, but he looked different than when I'd last seen him. His hair was combed back, and his ruggish attire had been swapped for a silk suit and top hat. Jonty and Brone followed behind him, both still sporting their flashy cloaks that blended in exceptionally well at a party like this.

Well, at least I know for certain I'm in the right place, but did Wolfe have to pick a place so fancy? Why couldn't he have made the trade in a sketchy back alley, or on top of a half-rotted roof?

I cursed under my breath as I slipped back into the trees and stared down at the simple dress I had bought at the Willen marketplace. It was still in fairly good shape, but the stench of fish and river water wouldn't go unnoticed by the footmen at the door. That, and Sarnoldian nobles were far glitzier than Reclusian's, which meant that even my finest gown at home may not measure up to the dress code.

Looks like I'm going to need to find some ruffles.

I growled under my breath, kicking up a few fallen twigs as I hurried around the back side of the manor to look for a second way in. Maybe I could *borrow* a gown from one of the residents? The idea of wearing something so fluffy and frilly made me groan. All this time, I had been so thrilled to finally rely on the skills I had learned as a spy and adventure out into a world where I could be whoever I wanted to become. But, when it came down to the final match... I still needed the skills of Lady Genevieve.

At least all those etiquette lessons weren't for nothing... Looks like the wools have brought me back home. *Time to dust off your manners, Genevieve.*

chapter twenty-five

Warm nights were always the best time for a break-in. The cooing birds covered up any unusual sounds, the soft breeze kept your senses active... and the nice weather meant that everyone left their windows open!

I crept into a first-story window with so much ease I almost considered climbing to the second floor for a bit more of a challenge. The room I'd entered was some sort of study, with a sturdy oak desk, rows of crisp books, and a rather perky desk plant. The room smelled of dried ink and expensive hand creams, with the thick fragrance of an old cigar burning the inside of my nose. I took a moment to browse the scattered papers on the desk and found multiple signatures with the name *Edward Dranger.*

Dranger? Wasn't he a member of the Sarnoldian king's court of advisors?

I wasn't particularly up to date on all the politics outside of Reclusia, but it was hard not to overhear the mounds of gossip surrounding Sarnold and its infamous *blood princess*. Princess

Amirah was the only surviving member of a brutal attack against their monarchy. She was found nearly unharmed amongst the carnage, so there were multiple rumors that she wasn't quite as innocent as one would believe. Her uncle had taken over the throne until the princess came of age, so he utilized a collection of advisors to help keep the kingdom stable.

This must be Dranger's party, then. I suppose it's not uncommon for court advisors to flaunt their wealth.

I slipped out of the study and snuck through the halls with the same light movements I had been trying to copy from Shep. The brief thought of him made my lips burn and sent a *thud* so hard against my chest, it nearly knocked me off balance. The incoming chatter of servants pricked my ears, silencing my heart altogether as I ducked into a random room.

I pressed the door shut, peering through the crack as I watched the two maids calmly pass through the hallway. The room I'd selected appeared to be a bed chamber, filled with ornate furnishings, and almost as much frill as my room back home. This meant it was likely a woman's room...

A wardrobe sat in the far corner of the room, elegantly lit in the dwindling evening rays like a golden chest on a sandy shore. I raced over to the wardrobe and threw the doors open, unveiling a dozen gowns with so much glitz, it looked like the stars had thrown up all over them. I flipped through the dresses, trying to find one that wouldn't stand out *too* much while simultaneously trying to avoid ruffles at all costs. My favorite color caught my eye, and I pulled out a baby-blue satin gown with sparkly lace stitched across the top and not a single ruffle in sight.

Jackpot.

I changed into the gown and left my old dress behind in the packed wardrobe. The gown was a bit too large on me, and the skirt dragged on the floor, but it was still better than what I came in with. I snagged a brush off the vanity and ran it through my hair a few times to try to appear a little less homeless, then hurried back out to find the party.

The manor was big, but it had a similar layout to most of the others I'd been in. Using my natural sense of direction and the growing sound of music, I found myself wandering into a grand foyer flooded to the brim with ballgowns, top hats, and half-hearted laughter.

Rich marble floors made everything echo in the cramped space, but the tall diamond-paned windows helped keep it from feeling too claustrophobic. The foyer was sweltering compared to the rest of the house, likely from the mass of bodies, who all kept clustered together like they needed to socialize in order to survive. I tried to look out for the glittery cloaks, but the blinding shimmer of gowns, jewels, and magic-stone accessories made it nearly impossible to find anything.

I crept farther into the room, intentionally avoiding eye contact while keeping my head tall as a proper lady would. A table full of refreshments caught my attention, flooding my senses with the mouth-watering aroma of beef wellington, roasted nuts, and something covered in gravy. My stomach growled, gravitating me toward the table. I swallowed back a glob of drool as the rich Sarnoldian spices saturated the air around me. I plucked a bite-sized meatball of some sort off a platter and popped it into my mouth. Flavor burst across my tongue like an array of fireworks, offering me a brief reminder of why the noble life wasn't *quite* so bad.

"Excuse me, miss?"

A young man jolted me out of my bliss. I choked down the last swallow of the meatball and whirled around to find a finely dressed man with tanned skin, dark eyes, and two glasses of bubbling drinks in his hand.

Two drinks? Oh no...

"I noticed you from across the room and wondered if you might be in need of a drink," he said in a thick Sarnoldian accent. "I don't believe we've had the pleasure of being properly introduced."

I hadn't thought of it until now, but blonde hair and blue eyes weren't a particularly common trait in Sarnold... Perhaps I shouldn't have washed out the hair dye quite so early.

I took the drink from him with a gentle smile, mostly because I was actually pretty thirsty after gulping down that meatball. "Lyla Herder, pleasure to meet you, Mister...?"

"Xavier Dranger," he said with a proper dip of his head. *Dranger? He must be Edward Dranger's son. Oh drat.* "Where is your family from Miss Lyla? I don't believe I'm familiar with the Herder family?"

He swirled the drink in his hand, his eyes raking over me with a mixture of suspicion and intrigue.

Goodness, I despise noblemen... Always thinking they have the higher ground.

I took a slow sip of my drink, keeping eye contact with the young Dranger as the bubbles sparked against my tongue. If he didn't recognize my name, then that meant there was a guest list I wasn't on—a guest list that Wolfe *was* on.

So, Edward Dranger invited him here... Looks like I found my buyer.

I needed to find the host, but first, I had to shake off his snoopy son. It had been a while since I'd had some proper fun with a stuffy noble.

"I beg your pardon?" I snapped through a tense smile. "Did you just imply that you haven't heard of *my* family?" I fluttered my lashes with a steel lock in my jaw, challenging the man to repeat what he said.

He did an impressive job of keeping his smile fixed in place, but the slight knit in his brows betrayed his confusion. "Forgive me, I mean no offense. It's only that—"

"That Xavier Dranger, *son* of this evening's host, doesn't even know who's on the guest list?" I scoffed, looking him up and down with the well-practiced 'noble glare' all ladies had to master at some point if they wanted to convey their distaste without saying it. "My word... When my father hears about this, I'm certain he'll—"

"Please, Miss Lyla," he cut me off, and I made certain to give him a pointed glare for silencing me. "It was my mistake. I apologize for not recognizing your esteemed family's name. Might I inquire where the rest of your family is so I might have the ability to introduce myself?"

Drat. Who here can I pawn him off on?

I glanced around the room, acting as if I was looking for a specific man, and not wildly searching for someone he hopefully didn't already know. I did not have time to get thrown out of a party...

"Well, you see my father is—"

"Xavier, are you done pestering this young woman, or shall I inform your mother that you're being rude to your guests?" Out of nowhere, a young woman stepped up from behind me. Her tone was soft and airy, but there was a bite in her voice that couldn't be ignored. "Not every woman wants a man to meet her family right away. You shouldn't be so presumptuous."

I had no idea who this woman was, but in that moment, she was my new best friend— though I'd never tell Lacey. I turned around to look at my rescuer and nearly gasped when I saw her stunning appearance.

She had red eyes... not dark brown or even violet, but red. Her skin was paler than milk, and just as flawless, and her hair was a bright white that couldn't possibly have been faked. It was as if her body lacked all pigmentation but in a beautiful way, as if crafted by a master painter with her features as the canvas.

"Ah, Lady Brietta. so lovely you were able to make it this evening. I do hope your health has improved." Xavier bowed, though he still kept a wary eye on me. "Miss Lyla and I were merely chatting. I wasn't trying to make her uncomfortable."

"No man ever *tries* to make a woman uncomfortable," Lady Brietta said with a dainty fold of her arms. "Now, if you'll excuse us, I've been trying to find Lady Lyla all evening and don't wish to have you hanging over our shoulder as we speak."

She what?

Xavier looked between us, his suspicion on me settling the more Lady Brietta claimed to know me. "Of course." He gave a slight bow, eyeing me one more time before finally turning to leave. "I hope you ladies enjoy your evening."

He slipped back into the crowd, and I waited for him to vanish before turning back to face my mysterious rescuer. The second he left, she dropped the prim lift of her chin and rolled her eyes in a rather vulgar manner for any young lady.

Oh, I like her.

"Sorry about that," Brietta said. "You looked like you were in need of a rescue. I'm guessing you came here alone?" She glanced down at my unfitted dress, and I bit the inside of my cheek as I looked around to see if I'd caught anyone else's eyes. "Oh, don't worry, I'm not a tattle-tale or anything. We've all got our secrets, you know?" She winked at me, her blonde lashes almost as white as her snowy hair.

"That I do." I laughed wryly, feeling slightly

more at ease with how calm she was about a stranger wandering around at an exclusive party. "Thank you for your help... Lady Brietta, was it?"

"Just Brietta is fine." She smiled back at me. "I'm not much of a dancer, so I'll be hanging around the edges of the room if you need another save. Oh! And if you're trying to steer clear of the hosts, Lord Dranger is in the far corner by the servant halls."

My head pricked up at the mention of the lord, and I eagerly scanned the crowd for him.

"Or... if you *are* looking for him," Brietta said with a knowing lilt in her voice, catching onto my search.

"Like you said," I shrugged as I hoisted up the front of my extra-long skirt, "we all have our secrets."

"That we do," she said quietly, waving me off as I disappeared into the crowd. "Good luck."

What an interesting woman.

It would have been nice to actually chat with her for a bit—she seemed different than most noble girls I'd ever met, especially considering her appearance. Her accent was a bit too mild to be a true Sarnoldian, so I wondered if she was visiting from another kingdom, like Ebonair or Bellatring? Either way, I hoped I would get another chance to thank her for her help at some point.

Now to find those cloaks.

I combed through the crowd, dodging eye contact with anyone who looked at me as I made my way to where Brietta had pointed. When I finally found Lord Dranger, he was moving toward the back of the room, cutting off a few conversations while setting his drink on a passing serving tray.

"Ha ha, yes, of course! We'll have to chat about it more once I return to the festivities." He pressed a thumb to his temple, scrunching his brows with a pained look as he made another move toward the door. "I'm afraid I've come down with a headache. Please excuse me for a few moments while I get some fresh air."

He waved to his guests and slipped out into the hall while nursing his head with a twinkle in his eye that was more eager than pained. I followed him, keeping a safe distance back. Once away from the crowd, he stopped nursing his head entirely, and his posture straightened. He snaked through the halls, dodging servants and glancing behind him just as I darted behind a corner. Finally, he burst out of a servants' exit, stepping straight outside. The fresh night air blasted down the hall, and I pressed myself behind another wall to ensure he didn't notice me when looking back. My adrenaline kicked up as I waited for the door to shut. It reminded me of when I was waiting in the bushes outside of

Willen's perimeter, spying on a conversation I had believed I was invisible to, but in truth, was waltzing straight into a trap.

Is this something I can really handle on my own? Finding Wolfe and the cloaks is one thing, but stealing them away from a vicious traitor...?

I crept up to the door, my heart pounding and muscles tightening as I glanced outside to see the unmistakable smirk of Shep's kingdom-forsaken father. He held his hat under his arm, revealing his slicked-back hair, while his two lackeys stood proudly behind him. Each man wore a cloak, and held a folded one in their arms, displaying their wares like proper salesmen.

I found them, now it's time to bring them home. For Reclusia, and more importantly, for Shep.

"You're looking well, Dranger." Wolfe grinned as the man stepped out into the polished garden. "Let's do some business."

chapter twenty-six

"You sure kept me waiting long enough," Dranger huffed, his eyes drawn to the cloaks like a raven to sparkle. "Is this really them?"

Wolfe snapped his fingers and Brone approached Dranger with the folded cloak stretched across his arms like he was selling a fine silk. Dranger eyed Brone's glassy expression with a fascinated tilt of his chin, then turned his attention to the cloak.

"Exactly as promised," Wolfe said with a sly smile. "Magic capable of controlling even the most stubborn of minds. Fresh from the black market."

Dranger brushed his finger over the cloak, inspecting the tiny specks of ground magic stones infused into the wool. "Impressive." He waved a hand in front of Brone's eyes, smirking when the man didn't even blink. "And you got all of them, correct? I don't want this product to be in anyone else's hands but mine."

"Of course." Wolfe placed a hand over his heart with a gentle bow. "I wouldn't dream of leaving behind any loose ends. What you see now is only half of the cloaks. The other four are with the rest of my men. I'll command them to join us once we receive the full payment."

A pit lodged into my stomach as I watched Dranger smile without an ounce of worry. Those men weren't waiting around to offer up their cloaks... they were waiting to come deal with Dranger.

"And how do you control the wearers?" Dranger tapped his chin.

"With this." Wolfe pulled the obedience stone out of his pocket, and my entire body felt like it had plunged into an icy river. It was like Wolfe was holding his son's heart in the palm of his hand, carved straight from his chest and flaunted in front of a buyer without a second thought. "The cloaks were created from fragments of this stone, so all their magic is connected."

Dranger approached the stone, his eyes reflecting the chaotic spark of light simmering beneath the stone's surface. "Remarkable." He reached out to touch the stone, but Wolfe pulled it out of his reach before he could even brush a finger against it.

"I'd be happy to let you see it and the other half of the cloaks *after* I've received the promised payment," Wolfe said with a dark shift in his tone.

Dranger scowled at him, but ultimately backed away from the stone. "Yes, yes, you'll get your money. The agreed upon price was two million gold, correct?"

Two million!? Where did a court advisor get that much spare coin?

"Two million, plus a few hundred thousand extra for all the trouble." Wolfe gave a sleazy grin. "The job was a bit more finicky than I had anticipated."

"Oh, come now, that wasn't in the bargain." Dranger tapped his polished shoe, his voice stern and callous from a lifetime of getting what he demanded.

"I like to think bargains are more... *guidelines.*" Wolfe raised the stone to his lips with an eerie shadow in his eyes, then whispered into the stone. Brone and Jonty stepped up on either side of Dranger, towering over the man with a silent threat. "Besides, you and I both know you didn't get that money on your own... Since someone with a far larger pocketbook wants the cloaks, I think it's only fair that they pay the extra fee to keep me from nosing around to find out who *actually* wants the power to control men like mindless sheep."

Someone else's money?

Dranger paled and his shoulders tensed

stiffer than a stone wall. "I'll be back shortly with your coin," he hissed. "But know this, Wolfe... the money you're swindling comes from someone who isn't to be trifled with."

The hair on my neck stood on end as Dranger's warning turned stale in the quiet air. It was hard to imagine who would be more powerful than one of the king's closest officials... unless it was the king himself.

"Trifling with dangerous people is what I do best," Wolfe said proudly.

Dranger passed him another grimace, then moved back toward the door I was peering through to retrieve the coin. I slid behind the door, pressing my back against the wall as he swung it open, hiding me behind the door entirely. He briskly moved down the hall, muttering to himself about how he hated working with uncultured vermin.

Now's my chance.

Ducking down so the garden's foliage would hide me, I slipped out the door before it swung shut and crept behind a thick juniper bush. Wolfe toyed with the gem in his hand as he patiently awaited his paycheck, tossing it around like a meager hacky-sack.

I need to get that gem.

From how Wolfe explained it, whoever controlled the obedience stone, controlled everyone in the cloaks—even Shep. That single rock's magic had been carved up and spread between multiple different points of control... so if I had the gem, I could turn Wolfe's men against him.

But how do I get it from him?

I crept around the edge of the garden, moving as quickly as I dared. My heart buzzed like a raging bee, and my body felt light and airy with all the newfound energy inflating me. My dress, however, was putting a serious damper on my elegance, ironically enough. The extra-long skirt kept snagging on rose thorns and bush branches, and the glittery bodice forced me to stay low to the ground so I wouldn't get caught sparkling.

I hunted for my boots under the voluminous skirt until I found the familiar hold of my dagger grace my palm. The blade had always had a bit of weight to it, but it felt particularly heavy tonight as I envisioned running it into Wolfe's back...

You can do this, Evie... One strike from behind, and then take the stone. Then Shep will be safe.

"Once he shows us the money..." Wolfe whispered into the stone. "Kill him. His death will be a message to the *real* buyer that I don't work with middle-men."

My lungs clamped shut as I crept behind where Wolfe was standing. The lightness I'd felt earlier completely left me. The blade felt too heavy, my skirt too big, and even the air I breathed threatened to choke me like it was laced with smoke. I'd never killed anyone before... never even truly harmed anyone outside of a black eye or broken nose.

But this was my job.

When I agreed to become a spy, it wasn't to just become mysterious, or cool—though admittedly, that was part of it... It was to protect my kingdom and the people within it. I may not be in my kingdom right now, and the nobleman about to walk into his death wasn't one of my citizens, but this was still my mission... No, it was *our* mission. Shep and I were going to finish this job together, even if it meant I had to kill his father to free his mind.

I stepped out of the shadows, my blade glinting in the moonlight and reflecting the determined look in my eyes. One step at a time, I moved closer to Wolfe. My brain went wild trying to navigate another option, another direction, or a different path I could take that didn't involve driving my dagger into this man's empty heart. But there was no more searching left to do... I had found what I was looking for, and this time, it wasn't getting away.

This is for Shep.

Every nerve in my body went numb as I

raised the blade in the air, but I never plunged it.

I don't remember screaming, but my voice still reached my ears even through all the ringing. Warmth rushed down my wrist as the blade clattered from my hand and the crimson wound spread across my palm. Everything went blurry, but I could still see Wolfe's sickly smile as he turned to face me with that horrid stone held directly in front of the heart I'd hoped to pierce.

The blade that had sliced my palm raised to my chest, pausing inches above my heart as the wielder's other hand grabbed me by the shoulder. It was impossible not to recognize the touch of the man a fraction away from running me through. It was the same man who had already stolen that same heart...

"Evie..." Shep's voice shook as much as his hand did, vibrating faster than a spooked hummingbird's wings. "I-I can't stop."

chapter twenty-seven

"Shep..." My eyes watered as I stared down at his clenched hand, fighting with all his strength to stop it from plunging into my heart. "You can fight it, Shep. You're stronger than he is."

My palm felt like it was on fire, but the cut didn't feel as deep as I first thought it had been. I looked down at my crimson fingers and the smears of blood I'd already stained the satin gown with. The cut in the center of my palm was extremely precise. Shep had somehow managed to slide his dagger underneath where I was holding my own and cut me just enough that the shock forced me to drop the blade.

I thought back to how gently he had threatened Lex with a blade, never once letting the weapon out of his control.

Shep is in control... Only a little, but enough where he didn't take my whole hand off.

His free hand squeezed my shoulder, using me as a brace as he fought the will of the dagger pointed at my chest. "I-I—"

"Kill her, Shepherd," Wolfe commanded into the stone, his eyes practically glittering with bloodthirst. "Be a good boy, just like you always were, and obey your father."

Shep flinched as the stone flickered, and the dagger jerked, the tip barely brushing the edge of my satin neckline. I grabbed his wrists, trying to help him pull the blade away the best I could. My hand screamed in pain as I rubbed the fresh wound raw. The blade moved back another few inches, and I took the opportunity to duck and slip out of Shep's hold.

Shep let out a massive, strained gasp, but it only lasted a moment before his eyes went black and he raced back toward me. I dodged the first swing of his blade by ducking, then swept my legs underneath his to send him tumbling over me.

"Thanks for teaching me that one," I huffed as I scrambled to my feet.

"Shepherd, grab her," Wolfe commanded, his voice far more tense as he gave the stone a rough shake. "Obey me, Shepherd, and grab the girl."

Shep's arm reached out and grabbed me by the skirt, jerking me back to the ground faster than gravity could ever pull. I tried to push away from him, but he was too strong. He grabbed my arm and yanked me to my feet, catching my other wrist on the way up and pinning them both behind my back.

I didn't understand… One second, Shep was able to fight off the stone's commands and the next, he was following through with each one with the force of a soldier.

"Forgive me, Evie," Shep croaked behind me, his hands cold and stiff like he was nothing more than a hollow shell.

"Ah, what did I say about apologizing," Wolfe scolded. He turned the stone over in his hands, inspecting the pulsing magic within with a furrowed brow. "Something isn't right here… You shouldn't be able to fight against my commands this much."

I watched the stone flicker like a fading candle. Its magic had been spread rather thin…

"Brone, Jonty, and the others are doing just fine, so why is it that *you*, my boy, are being such a troublemaker?" Wolfe scratched his finger across the stone with a shrill screech. "I thought I raised you not to be so weak."

My skin flared as the blood rushed to the tip of my ears. "Shep is not weak!" I thrashed against my partner's hold, and as if to prove my point, he tightened his grip on me. "The only weak person here is the one whose hiding behind the power of stupid rock."

"Dear girl, power is always behind whoever has the biggest stone." Wolfe laughed. "Do you think our kings can fight for themselves? Or do they hide behind stone walls and send out magically-equipped soldiers to fight their battles?"

"I didn't think you liked kings," Shep seethed behind me, his voice hot and bitter in my ear. "After all, you did betray one."

Wolfe narrowed his eyes on his son. "That's because I spent my entire life helping pass power onto our king, and never once was I allowed to keep any as my own." He glanced back at the cloaks draped over his mindless minions, basking in their glory like they were trophies on display. "I decided I wanted to live a life where the jewels I collected could remain my own... So, I started training up the one fragment of power I knew the king could never truly keep from me."

He gave Shep a wicked smile, and I could practically feel his skin crawl where he gripped my wrists.

"I always planned to get you back, Shepherd," Wolfe continued. "It just took a little time to find the proper methods."

"You *cursed* him," I spat.

"I didn't want to." Wolfe glared at me. "Shepherd was always such an obedient child... Never complaining when our training sessions lasted until morning, never refusing my instructions, and always surpassing my expectations. I had hoped his loyalty would last, but unfortunately, he made the choice to go against me."

"Because *you* made the choice to go against our kingdom," Shep said with fire in every breath, his grip on me loosening just a touch as his emotions went back to clouding his father's control.

"There you go again, being difficult." Wolfe flicked at the stone and sparks shot off around his finger. "For some reason, your curse reacts differently than the cloaks." Wolfe glanced up at me, his eyes raking over me like I was a red stain on a white suit. "Is your little friend being too much of a distraction for you to listen, Shep?"

"Don't you dare touch her!" Shep growled, his hands vibrating.

"Oh, *I* won't touch her..." Wolfe said with a devilish laugh as he raised the stone to his lips. "But you, Shepherd, you're going to slice her throat."

"No!" Shep's dagger crept to my throat in stiff, jagged movements while his other hand remained latched around my wrists. His entire body tensed like he was fighting off a beast with his bare hands, but instead of a beast, it was his own mind. "I-I won't do it!"

My breaths came fast and heavy as I tried to yank my wrists free from Shep's hold. All his resistance was going into stopping the blade, so his grip on me was fiercer than a pair of iron shackles.

"Yes, you will..." Wolfe said coldly, his eyes reflecting the point of Shep's blade. "Show me the obedient son I raised; the one who always wanted to be just like me."

The blade inched closer, and Shep's strength wavered with each taunt his father threw. "I will *never* be like you."

"You already are." Wolfe laughed. "The only thing left is to make you my perfect follower."

"Don't listen to him, Shep!" I gave my wrist a yank so hard, I nearly dislocated my shoulder, but the force managed to free all but three of my fingers. "Fight him! The curse isn't as strong as you think. Just look at the stone."

I could see Shep's reflection in the approaching knife, his eyes going wide as he noticed the dimming flicker of the stone. It hadn't occurred to me until now, but Shep's curse wasn't made up of the obedience stone's full power. A large portion of the magic was dispersed amongst the cloaks, and another part still resided in the stone itself. That was why he was capable of fighting it.

"Well, aren't you the observant one? I suppose he is a little low on magic," Wolfe said in a grim voice as he studied the stone's weakened glow. "It's no wonder he's been acting up so much. No worries, my boy. I know just how to fix you up!"

Shep's shaking stopped as we both stood locked in fear. Everything felt too quiet as Wolfe raised the stone to Shep's head, summoning the same brilliant glow I had seen when we first encountered him in the pasture.

He's going to curse him again... Can he even do that?

I didn't wait to find out the answer. My body moved on its own, pulling the rest of my fingers free from Shep's grip and then elbowing him in the ribs so hard, he doubled over. The light grew brighter, and the shine of gold flared in my eyes like a second sun. I didn't have to think, didn't have to plan, or even look for any other details. I jumped in front of the incoming stone, shielding Shep as the white-hot fire poured straight into me.

chapter twenty-eight

My eyes were wide open, but I was completely blind. White light burned my retinas, but I couldn't force my eyes closed. It was like someone had shot lightning through me and the energy was convulsing my every muscle while simultaneously paralyzing me. The heat shot from the forefront of my head, all the way down to my toes. There was some pain, but most of it just felt like I was being destroyed... like the magic was dissolving everything inside me and building it back according to its new schematics.

When the light faded from my eyes, the burning ceased and a stone-cold rush left me numb as I finally managed my first blink. Wolfe's fist was clenched around the stone. He looked only an inch away from cracking it with his bare hands, steam practically rolling off his skin in the humid air.

"You foolish girl!" Wolfe pushed me back with a harsh blow to the shoulder. I crumpled to the ground, too unstable to fight after having the magic fuse with my soul. "Look what you've gone and done!"

He shook the stone in front of my face, but it took me a few blinks to stop seeing three of them. The golden glow had faded to a measly spark in the center of the stone. The once vibrant rock was now cloudy and resembled a dull chunk of citrine, aside from the fuzzy light in the middle. It was actually kind of beautiful, like a soft burning star in the center of a dim sky. It was nice seeing something so tame when there was so much chaos flickering in my chest.

Is this what it felt like to be cursed?

I pressed a hand to my buzzing chest, wondering if it felt as warm on the outside as it did within. The magic may not have been tangible, but it truly felt like there was a rock burrowed beneath my skin that glowed far brighter than the one in Wolfe's palm.

"Instead of having one flawless follower, I now have two half-witted dogs." Wolfe kicked up a spray of dirt to shower over me. "Stand up, girl."

His command rang through my ears so loud I was shocked he wasn't standing over my shoulder. The last thing my body wanted to do was stand—my legs ached, my skin still felt numb, and I definitely didn't want to do anything Wolfe asked of me. But it didn't matter what I wanted... or even what I felt capable of doing.

The strange warmth in my chest flared, compelling my body to pull itself from the dirt. My legs wobbled and my head throbbed as I stood up far too quickly for someone who was still seeing double. I wavered for a moment, and the curse responded with a sharp pain in my heart, jolting me straight and forcing me upward one inch at a time.

It was horrible. It looked so mindless when I watched Shep obey commands, but in truth, it was full of quick flashes of pain and heat. It was like being directed on puppet strings made of razor wire, and if you dared go against the pull, you would instantly pay the price.

"Evie... what have you done?" Shep's voice rattled me, cracking my heart and piecing it back together in a single beat. I knew what I did was reckless, but hearing the humanity in his tone made it easy not to regret.

"I couldn't let him overtake you." My lips tingled with each word as if my very breath was laced with the sparking magic. "You're my partner, Shep. We look after each other, no matter the cost."

I won't let your father ever hurt you again, even if it means taking on a lifelong curse.

"But you're more than just a partner!" Shep took a few steps toward me, but a cruel glare from Wolfe caused his legs to stiffen before he could reach me. "Y-you're Evie. You can't be replaced like some random partner can. I can't lose you to him; he doesn't deserve to control your mind."

"He doesn't deserve you, either," I said through a cracked voice. "I can't lose any more of you than I already have, so stop pretending I'm more important because we all know I'm a massive pain!"

"Now there's something we can agree on." Wolfe rolled his eyes, faking a gag as he spectated. "Brone, go check on our buyer and keep him inside for a few minutes longer. These two need to be sorted out, and I can't promise it will be a clean affair. Everyone else come lend me a hand."

Wolfe's bloodthirst trickled in through the stone, filling my head with sparks of awaiting requests that flooded me with nausea. I felt like half of my mind was consistently being invaded, and every time I tried to refocus my thoughts, a shepherd's crook smacked me back in the direction it wanted me to go. The stone didn't just affect your actions, it affected your head, too... I could only imagine how much it would have taken over had Shep received the full force of the stone.

Brone wandered back inside the house, and the other four cloaked men stepped out from the shadows and joined their boss. They all shared the same dead expression, and for the first time, I wondered if any of them were truly crooks at all. Sure, they had agreed to do a sleazy job for some extra cash, but had any of them wanted to leave when they realized what they were taking? How long had they been blindly following their leader without even the comfort of their own minds?

"I don't need two cursed imbeciles in my arsenal, so why don't we have a little challenge to see which of you is more useful to me?" Wolfe tapped his fingers against the stone, and the simple action *thudded* in my head like a hammer. "While I know you're talented, Shep, you seem to have gotten rather soft in my absence. Miss Evie isn't quite cutthroat either, but her intelligence may prove useful... Let's settle it like this."

He raised the stone, holding it out like a statue displaying a forbidden jewel, as a crooked smile darkened his features. I risked a glance at Shep, his skin paling as he met my eyes with a desperate look that shared the same fearful command I was already hearing.

"I command both of you to fight to the death," Wolfe said. "Clearly, your half-dosed curses give you some resistance to my more *intense* commands, so we'll just have to see who's saturated with enough magic to actually follow through with the request. The loser can rot here and serve as a reminder to everyone of what happens when you disobey."

Fight Shep?

The heat in my chest surged, and my legs felt like they were being dragged toward Shep by hot iron chains. Shep and I locked eyes, the fear of our shared compulsion feeding into each other like a silent request for forgiveness.

Kill Shep.

The command repeated in my head, urging me to reach for my dagger that had fallen in the grass earlier. I fought against the pull, my arm burning like it was holding my entire weight off the edge of a cliff. I tried to fight the pain, to pull away from the awaiting blade, but the curse was too strong, and the dagger slid into my injured palm.

Kill Shep.

I bit my tongue, trying to ignore the compulsion. My blade was a magnet to Shep's heart that I could barely keep away.

"I-I can't hold back for long," Shep stuttered, his teeth gritting as he endured the same internal battle that was tearing me to shreds. "Listen to me, Evie. I want you to kill me."

"What!?"

Kill Sh—

The command was smothered under the flare of my heart, flooding my thoughts with a brief rush of clarity. My body stiffened, and the urge to pierce Shep's heart was eclipsed by the overwhelming desire to see him live. I needed him to live. He still had to prove himself to the kingdom. There were still so many things he needed to teach me...

"I can't kill you!" I argued. The burn in my chest started to return, stinging my heels the longer I stood in place.

"You have to!" Shep clawed at his chest, his perfect face contorted. "He trained me to be a killer, Evie. If you don't kill me first, then I'll—" He swallowed hard, biting off his words with a seething breath. "Don't make me do that, Evie... I can't bear to hurt you any more than I already have. Not when I... I—"

His cheeks burned a fiery shade of red, and I wondered if it was an effect of the curse.

"Kill me, Evie. Please."

Kill Shep.

"I won't!" I stamped my foot, sending a jolt of energy up my leg that caused me to stumble closer, my blade raised high.

"Oh, for kingdom's sake, will you two love birds hurry this up?" Wolfe huffed, tapping the stone and sending another rattle through my brain. "Hurry up and attack each other!"

The pull in my chest grew stronger, almost unbearable, as I dug my heels into the dirt to keep from pressing forward. Shep was clutching himself so tightly, he was basically making his own straight jacket, fighting against the stone with every ounce of his will.

Think, Evie, think! This can't end like this. I can't kill Shep! There must be a way to work around this curse. Another loophole, a different path... something!

Kill Shep.

I won't! Whatever it takes, I will fight for mine and Shep's life—

That's it.

"Make it stop!" I whined, faking a few tears that admittedly may have been a *little* real, but the drama was added. "There's too many voices in my head!"

"Then get on with your task and stop complaining," Wolfe growled. "It can't be hard to follow a simple command."

"It's not simple, you moron!" I snapped. "You told us to *fight* each other to the death, then *attack* each other. The curse doesn't know which way you want us to proceed!"

Despite the contortion in Shep's face, I could still see the subtle twist in his brow. He knew as well as I did that the command was perfectly clear, but that was the problem. The command was *too* direct, and I needed it loosened.

"Just tell us to stop holding back or

something!" I begged, shedding a few extra tears for good measure. "To fight for our lives!"

I stumbled forward another step, with Shep only a mere foot in front of me and in full reach of my blade. Another tear streamed down my cheek, but this one was hot and fueled with the rage I was itching to redirect.

Come on, Wolfe...

"Fine! I command you to fight for your blasted lives, then! Just get this over with so I can get back to my business," Wolfe shouted into the stone, and everything in my mind switched.

Shep's eyes widened with mine as our brains rewired to the new command one fiber at a time. The ache in my chest was still there, and the urge to attack hadn't faded, but my target had officially changed.

"You heard him, Shep," I said softly, my eyes turning to Wolfe with a fire so intense, I could have scorched him where he stood. "Let's fight for our lives."

"With pleasure." *That* was Shep's voice, the voice that wasn't choked out by anyone else's desires but his own. The desire to fight for his life and the man holding it in his palm.

Wolfe's distracted fury faded faster than Shep's mercy, his eyes snapping wide open as we sprinted toward him and the stone. "Hold on, that's not what I—"

Shep clapped a hand over his mouth so hard, he nearly knocked him to the ground. Wolfe tried to twist Shep's wrist off his face, but Shep was too strong—he was fighting for his life after all. Even so, Wolfe was strong. With only one hand, Wolfe had nearly freed his mouth. Shep's muscles strained from the force of keeping his father silent, but we only needed a second more.

"Evie!" Shep darted his eyes between me and the stone clutched in Wolfe's hand, but I was already a step ahead of him.

"I got it!" I clawed the stone out of Wolfe's grip, my entire body pulsing as the stone made contact with my skin just as Wolfe pried Shep's hand free.

"No!" Wolfe lunged to grab the stone, but he was no match for the one and only Lady Genevieve Rayelle Palleep, who was blazing madder than an irritated ram.

I raised the stone in the air, and with the strength of its magic, I commanded myself, "Stop this."

And then, I smashed it to pieces.

chapter twenty-nine

"What have you done!?" Wolfe dashed to the ground, picking up the shattered remnants of the stone, only for them to fall through his fingers like gravel. Despite the stone being broken, I could still feel the pull in my chest as he touched them, but like the stone itself, it was a mere fragment of what it was before. "Do you have any idea how rare that—"

His shouts were cut quiet as a pair of strong hands yanked him to his feet. The five mindless spectators who had been standing loyally by his side only a moment ago had now surrounded him with glares cold enough to freeze even the brightest flame. They circled him like ravenous sharks, each one only one prod away from sinking his teeth into their former boss.

"I think the real question..." Jonty stepped on the scattered remnants of the stone with a satisfying *crunch*, "is what have *you* done? And what should we do with you now?"

The men closed in on him, two of the more burly ones latching onto Wolfe's arms as they pinned them behind his back. "Hey! Watch who you're dealing with! You all agreed to work with me, meaning I am still your boss!"

"You're only our boss if you pay us." Brone's familiar voice entered the fray as he popped out of the door with a very ashen Lord Dranger standing behind him. "And this scrawny man won't be buying anything you're selling, isn't that right?" Brone smacked the lord on the shoulder, causing him to jolt so violently he nearly fell to the ground.

"Y-yes," Dranger stuttered. "I don't know what is going on out here, but it is beyond clear to me that whatever control you had over these... men has long since vanished." He glanced over at me and Shep, and his skin turned visibly green when he saw my blood-stained hand. "I want you all off my property immediately. No deal is worth this much mess; surely even royalty can understand that..."

Royalty?

He barely mentioned the word under his breath, but it still pulled my attention stronger than the curse's will. Did that mean that the real buyer of the cloaks was one of the royals after all? The king? Or maybe even the blood princess?

Before I could shake down the weasel for more answers, Brone stopped in front of me, his towering figure and ferocious glare sending off all the warning signals in my brain. "You, blondie." He pointed at the shattered remnants of the stone. "Was this your doing?"

My spine stiffened, unsure if there was a *correct* answer in this situation. "Uh..."

"It was her, Brone," Jonty called over while gagging Wolfe with one of the men's yellowed socks. "She and the kid broke the stone."

Brone turned his eyes back on me and Shep, and within a blink of his blind eye, I could sense Shep sweep up behind me in a defensive position. Oddly enough, Brone didn't look like he wanted to smash my skull to match the stone; instead, his eyes almost looked... misty?

"Thank you," Brone sniffled, and in a sweep of his massive arms, pulled us both into a suffocating embrace. "I haven't seen my daughters in weeks, and I was starting to think I'd never get to again." The monstrous man who had plagued my nightmares and nearly murdered me twice was now bawling on my shoulder like an overgrown infant. "Lyla, or was it Evie? Sorry, my head was pretty cloudy up until now. How about I just call you blondie? I'm so sorry for everything we did to you, blondie. Even without the cloaks on, the power still lingered enough that the boss was able to use us to get them back. Our minds were basically just an extension of his. Every thought, desire, and action was one we couldn't control. I think

I speak for all of us when I say we never wanted anyone to get hurt, only to earn a few shady dollars."

So, they really were trapped...

My mind raced back to the moments in the forest when some of the men had been sloppy with their attacks. They were never trained to fight, nor did they have any true motivation to do so. It was all fueled by Wolfe.

"I'm just glad everyone is okay." I smiled shyly, then curled my fingers around my bleeding palm. "Well, mostly okay."

He released us from the embrace, but Shep didn't pull away from me, keeping close to my side like the curse was somehow still drawing him near me. Brone joined the other men who were busy tying up Wolfe with whatever they could find, leaving Shep and me with our first moment to breathe since we arrived in Sarnold.

He turned to face me, his skin beaded in sweat, and his eyes shadowed and exhausted from fighting off the command of the curse, but he never looked so alive. He reached out for my injured hand, gently coddling it as he raised it with my palm face up.

"I'm so sorry, Evie." He winced as he inspected the wound, and I could see the pain he felt from hurting me was far worse than anything he had actually inflicted. "I fought it as hard as I could, but in the end, I still couldn't stop myself from doing as I was told."

"It's not your fault, Shep," I said. "That stone was no joke; I can still feel it buzzing inside me even now."

Shep gazed into my eyes, his look deep and searching as if he were looking for the curse that was now buried inside me—a curse we now shared. He reached his hand up to the side of my face, brushing a stray lock of hair from my cheek and tucking it neatly behind my ear.

"I still can't believe what you did," he said in a low voice, his hand lingering on my cheek as he gazed into my cursed soul. "You know what comes with a curse... After seeing both your friend endure one and then me, I can't understand why you would willingly place yourself in front of one."

Oh, come now, Shep... I know I'm the smart one, but still.

I leaned my cheek against his hand, his touch warm and soft and finally free of the cold chill of his father's grasp. "Isn't it obvious?" I smiled up at him through my lashes. "I needed you to stay you. If Wolfe had hit you with the rest of the curse, there's no telling how much of your mind would be left. I couldn't lose you, Shep... So, I decided I'd rather follow you."

"Follow me?" He let out a soft laugh, a

real one that wasn't shrouded by any weird controlling forces I couldn't pinpoint. "Well, that certainly sounds like a foolish decision for someone who's usually so smart. But then again, I'm not much better. I stopped thinking wisely the moment I believed I could play the part of a lover without getting attached."

Attached?

He brushed his thumb across my cheek, the simple touch radiating through my skin like a slow-moving firework that crackled with warmth. I wanted to stay under his gaze forever, or at least until the exhaustion finally hit me and I crumpled back into his arms like I'd done before. We had done it; we'd found the cloaks, found each other, and now we just had to bring them home.

"Shep, what should we do about the stone?" I turned toward the shattered pieces of glittering rock. "It may be broken, but I don't think it's completely useless."

"I feel what you mean." Shep raised a hand to his chest and clutched his shirt. "I'm guessing the wools were tied to the stone's power as a whole, hence why the wearers could all be controlled in unison. Breaking the stone severed the connection to the cloaks and weakened its hold on us, but that doesn't mean the magic is necessarily gone."

Shep approached the scattered shards, each gem sparkling like a fallen star as he sifted through the pieces to find a chunk about the size of a pea. "May I?" he asked me.

"Okay, but don't ask for anything ridiculous," I warned.

Shep gave me a mischievous grin that made me already doubt my agreement. "Evie, come here." Shep spoke softly into the stone, and the soft buzz of magic spurred to life in my chest.

It was calmer than it had been before, like a gentle nudging instead of an aggressive pull, but nonetheless, it wasn't something I could refuse. I didn't bother resisting since my energy was already too depleted, and I calmly approached Shep until I was directly in front of him.

"Well, that answers that." Shep sighed as he began to scoop up the remaining shards. "The wools may be useless, but we aren't. We'll need to keep these close in case anyone ever gets any funny ideas."

"Oh, like you?" I bent down and started scooping up the pieces with him, not leaving a single shard behind. "Don't think I'm just going to let you walk away with those pieces now that you know they can control me."

"Why? Is there something you don't want me to make you do?" He raised a brow, but for some silly reason, my gaze landed on his lips.

Evie! So, help me, girl, we are going to have a serious self-talk about this later.

My cheeks blushed, and I could hear a stifled giggle come from Shep as he stood with the last of the stone pieces in his pocket. Thankfully, Jonty stepped over before Shep could attempt any further teases with a tall stack of cloaks in his arms.

"Here." Jonty offered the cloaks to me, placing them directly in my arms. "I don't know who you work for, but seeing you break that stone tells us that these are going to someone who doesn't want them used."

I looked past the stack of cloaks to the other men, who nodded in agreement. Wolfe was slung over Brone's shoulder, thrashing and flailing, but ultimately failing to even wiggle his bonds loose. I must admit, it was a satisfying sight, though I kind of wished I could have given him just a *little* black eye.

"We'll be taking him, if you don't mind." Brone shifted Wolfe on his shoulder, causing the man to mumble against his gag. "We'll hand him over to the guard, but first, he's going to explain to our families and villages where we've been all this time."

I shared a quick look with Shep, wondering if he had any more detailed plans for his father other than passing him off, but Shep gave them a stiff nod of approval.

"Our mission was only to collect the cloaks, nothing more," he said plainly. "Do whatever you want with him. He's no threat to me anymore."

My heart soared as I watched the confidence pierce through Shep's eyes. Shaking free from his father's shackles was more than just being freed from his curse, it was also Shep's decision to release the non-magical control he put over his life. Shep could finally be his own person now, free from his father's past and his cursed future... well, mostly free. There was still some curse left to deal with.

I set the glittering cloaks down, but on second glance, realized their sparkle had faded a large amount, and the natural warmth they'd radiated before had faded. I looked down at the stone shards in my good palm, wondering how many of them still had the strength to control me if I ever lost even one.

"We should get these back to the agency; they'll know what to do with them," Shep said softly.

"And what about us? Will they know what to do with two cursed spies?" I asked, curling my fingers around the crumbs of magic. "The effects of the curse are manageable as long as we have these stones, but what about the parts the stone didn't control? We can't risk going around refined magic anymore; the confliction between the magic we carry and the stones could kill us."

Would I still be able to act as a spy like this? So much of my job is tracking down magic stones. What would happen now that I can't go near them?

"They'll have something for us," Shep reassured me as he pressed his hand over my closed palm. "They'd never let go of you over something as silly as a curse, especially when they hear about how skilled you are at working around them. I must say, you really left my head spinning with that distraction of yours back in the fishing shed."

The distraction...? Oh, that *distraction.*

"R-right... W-well I had to be certain it uh, it would work..." I babbled as my cheeks grew hot enough to fry an egg. *Kingdoms, Evie! Speak! Make words!* "Sorry if it was a bit much, I was only trying to—"

"To best me?" Shep guessed, his head tilting with the cocky lean of his smile. "Because if that's how you best your rivals, I'd be happy to lose to you anytime."

Really? Oh man, play it cool... play it cool!

"Oh, so are you finally admitting defeat to me?" I asked with a slow cadence, despite the fact that my heart was raging behind each breath. "Not going to be a sore loser, are we?"

Shep inched closer, the growing smile on his

face making me wonder if he could see how much I was screaming behind my calm. "Not when I'm winning so much more."

"So, you think you can handle it after all?" I breathed, his face only inches from mine now as my heart pounded without restraint. "Falling victim to the great Evie Palleep?"

"Only if you promise not to punch me this time." He laughed, the smile still staining his lips as he drew his face closer to mine.

He cupped my cheek, drawing me into a kiss so blissful, not even magic could command it to be better.

chapter thirty

"We've gone through your report, Evie, and before we send you home, there's just a few things we need to go over." Jillian Croon, owner of the Little Bows shop and agency handler for two dozen of the kingdom's finest agents, said as she straightened the papers on her desk. "Let's start with your partner, Shepherd."

I leaned back into the leather armchair, trying to keep my silk skirts from squeaking against the seat while I shifted. Shep and I had already given our full report together when we had handed over the cloaks and stone remnants. Now all that was left was the individual questioning and details on when we'd be getting our next assignment.

If I'd be getting a next assignment.

My chest buzzed as I looked over at the glass bowl of obedience stone shards that sat on Jillian's desk. They looked so harmless in the delicate bowl, like glass beads ready to be strung on an anklet, or even little candies that no child should ever actually eat.

"In your report with Shepherd, you claimed that, despite working alongside his father Ryder Wolfe, you never believed he had any true loyalty to him." Jillian dotted a quill and the fresh scent of ink brought me back to our time in the bank when I had unknowingly shared the lock combination with Shep's traitorous mind. "Now that you two are separated, you can answer more honestly. Do you still feel the same? As you know Shepherd has been kept under close eye ever since Wolfe's betrayal, so it's imperative for us to know if there's any chance that he remains loyal to his father."

Jillian scribbled something on the parchment, the soft flutter of the quill wafting the scent of drying ink into the air. I had expected this sort of questioning at some point. After all, it was rather suspicious that Shep was cursed to do exactly what his father said, and his partner somehow returned under the exact same curse of obedience, agreeing with everything.

Their suspicion will just make proving Shep's innocence even sweeter.

"I stand behind everything I said alongside Shep," I said. "While it's true he did betray the mission on multiple occasions, his betrayal was never truly his own. Up until Shep's encounter with the stone, he had been nothing but reliable and was even spiteful toward his father. When he finally unveiled his betrayal, it was clear that he was fighting the curse's pull with everything he had. Those are not the actions of a traitor, madame."

Jillian scratched out another note with her quill, then tucked it back into the brass inkwell. "And what about *your* curse, Miss Palleep? Is it true that you placed yourself in front of Wolfe's attack? Or is there any chance your partner used you as a shield to protect himself."

I bit the inside of my cheek, itching to jump up and defend Shep, but knowing perfectly well that was not the best response. The agency was always particular—they had to be—because if they weren't then more people like Wolfe would exist.

At least this is one in particular I can stop them from questioning.

"Why don't you confirm my story for yourself, Madame Croon." I motioned for the bowl of stone shards with a polite smile. "You've already heard the details of my curse and how the remaining gem pieces affect me and my partner. Why not use them to confirm my story?"

Jillian eyed the stones, her brow arching as if she was inspecting them for some sort of trick. "Would it be of any offense to you if I ran a few test commands to ensure their legitimacy first?"

"None at all. Please, help yourself." I nodded

toward the bowl, suddenly wishing there actually was candy hidden with them.

Jillian reached into the bowl and selected a small shard the size of maybe a pebble. I could feel my blood warm the moment she touched it and the familiar tug in my chest ready to do whatever she commanded.

"Genevieve Palleep," she spoke into the stone, her dark eyes glancing up at me as I anxiously waited for her instructions. "I command you to kill your partner Shepherd Ryde for treason against the Kingdom of Reclusia."

I choked on a breath as the curse stirred to life inside my muscles, already coaxing me into moving from my chair. "What!? Madame Croon, please reconsider. H-hold on—"

My legs pushed me out of my seat, but I still dug my fingers into the leather to try to hold myself back. The pull wasn't nearly as intense as it had been while the stone was fully formed, but it was still difficult to fight.

"Shep is innocent!" I argued, my blood blazing as Jillian only watched me with wide eyes. "I won't kill him. I-I won't!"

I lost my grip on the chair, and my body practically flung itself toward the door. I locked my knees in place, forcing my legs to remain stiff, hoping I could tense them enough to maybe even pass out. My foot shifted forward another inch, and my hand stretched out toward the door where Shep was patiently waiting on the other side.

"No!"

"That's enough, Evie. You can stop." Jillian spoke into the stone, and my entire body relaxed as I took in a massive gasp. It took all my effort not to crumble to the floor, but I managed to brace myself on the back of the leather chair as I tried to catch my breath. "I'm sorry for the distress, Miss Palleep, but I think I've seen all I need to."

Wait, what?

"Are you saying *that* was the test?" I asked with another short breath.

"Yes, of course. You gave me your permission, did you not?" Jillian said innocently, earning a sharp glare from me. "Forgive me for selecting such an intense test, but asking you to rub your stomach and pat your head at the same time wouldn't have proven that the stone can force you to do anything. I needed to command you to do something that you clearly wouldn't want to do. Your resistance to kill your partner also proved that you truly believe he is innocent, it wasn't something he commanded you to believe."

Drat. That was a good test; why didn't I figure it out sooner? I could have worked up some tears or something to really sell it.

"Glad it was helpful?" I said half-heartedly as I sank back into my seat.

"It was. As a matter of fact, all of what you have accomplished is," Jillian said. "Miss Palleep, your service to our kingdom has been invaluable, which is what brings me to our next topic of discussion... your curse."

A lump formed in my throat, and I tried to swallow it back behind my pinned smile. Even though Jillian had put the stone shard down, I could still feel the heat flaring in my chest, like the curse was trying to remind me that I was still a victim to its control.

Will it be enough to stop me from working?

"To put it blatantly, we don't want to lose you, Evie." Jillian steepled her fingers. "After what we learned about Shep, we don't want to lose him, either. You two have performed better than we expected, under far more intense circumstances than we anticipated, and those are the exact types of agents we want protecting our kingdom. The only issue is that your curses prevent you from being around magic stones, which make up a large portion of our missions. We do have occasional non-magic-oriented mission that we can devote a single agent to, but not enough that we could devote two agents."

My lungs clamped shut, robbing me of my

breath as I pieced together what she was trying to explain. "So, what you're saying... Is you could still utilize either me *or* Shep, but not both of us."

Jillian gave me a sympathetic look, her shoulders shrinking with a long sigh. "I'm sorry, Evie. Unfortunately, your cover story with Shepherd as lovers won't work long-term with your family since courtships often lead to marriage and meeting another's family. Partnering you two together won't be an option after today."

She was right. Shep couldn't keep sweeping me away from my family unless he intended to actually marry me and throw a fake family together. If the job was only open for one of us, then the answer was clear.

"Let Shep stay with the agency," I said firmly, clutching my skirts as I fought my heart from crumbling.

Jillian raised a brow. "Is that what you want?"

I want Shep to be happy. That's more important than me.

"I'm fortunate enough to have a life outside of the one I've built in the shadows," I explained. "Shep doesn't have anything else. His entire life was formed around being an agent, and now that his father is officially gone, he can become the spy that *he* wants to be. Besides, he's always been better than me, anyway." I smiled down at the floor, remembering how desperately I wanted the opposite to be true when we first met. "I can go back to being Genevieve Rayelle Palleep, so please, let Shep continue to be himself."

Jillian shifted her papers together, rising from her seat with an understanding nod. "Very well then, Miss Palleep. If that is what you wish, then it has been an honor having you in our service." She dipped her head to me, and I took the moment to blink back the tears while she couldn't see. "I'll inform Shepherd of your decision after his final briefing, and as for the remainder of the obedience stone, I can assure you we will have the pieces destroyed by the kingdom's finest jewelers."

"Thank you, Madam Croon." I curtsied to her, blinking slower to keep my eyes from misting. "It has been an honor working for Little Bows."

I turned to step out the door, pausing to gather myself before facing Shep one last time. Once I walk outside this office, I won't be a spy anymore. I would only be proper lady with a piece of her heart always trapped with the man who shared her curse.

I hope you save the world time and time again, Shep.

I stepped into the hall, the air feeling staler somehow than it did in the office. Shep was seated in a hardbacked chair, his eyes lighting up like polished tourmaline when he saw me step outside.

"How did it go?" Shep jumped out of his chair, his eyes lingering on mine for a moment as he, no doubt, noticed their red rims. "Is everything okay?"

"Yes, everything is just as it should be." I smiled. It was a real smile, yet the tears in my eyes were real, too. It was strange, feeling so happy for someone's accomplishments while also so broken knowing I couldn't witness any more of them. *Is this what love is like? Kingdoms, it hurts...* I pressed my hand up to his cheek, letting the feeling of his warmth map its way into my skin so I could always have it for reference on the days I was lost. "You're going to do amazing things, Shep. Thank you for letting me be a part of a small piece of it."

Shep opened his mouth to respond but couldn't get a word out before Jillian stepped back into the hall. "Shepherd? I'm ready for you now."

Goodbye, Shepherd. Thanks for the adventure.

"Good luck." I leaned forward and kissed him on the cheek, wishing I could linger there for a thousand minutes more. But our time was up, and all the lost things had finally been returned home, so I pulled back and disappeared into the only life I had left.

chapter thirty-one

"Evie, darling? Are you sure there was nothing else you wanted to share with us about your trip?" Mother asked as she joined me on the couch. Her tone was light and tender, not prodding like she had first been when I arrived home. "I know you said that things didn't really work out with Shepherd's family, and you were alright with that, but... Well, you don't really seem alright."

I put down the book I was reading. Now that I didn't need to keep my mind as fresh, I'd starting actually *reading* the romance novels that Mother always bought me but never believed I would open. I'd always thought they were so sappy before, but now I just thought they were ridiculous. No blissful romance truly had a happily ever after.

"I'm sorry, Mother." I forced a smile, going so far as to crinkle my eyes in the hopes it looked more sincere than it felt. "I suppose I've just been tired since getting home. It's only been a week since I returned, after all."

A week since everything... Since being cursed, losing my job, and leaving Shep. I suppose I shouldn't be shocked that Mother can recognize my aching heart.

"Yes, darling," Mother said gingerly, moving closer to me. She placed a gentle hand upon mine. "But are you sure it's only that? I tried to speak to Elaine, but she didn't seem to know much about the details of what happened. I don't mean to pry, sweetheart, but ever since you ended things with Shepherd, you really haven't been yourself."

My smile twitched, and I could already feel the gloss of tears wetting my eyes. It had only been a week since I'd stopped being a spy, and I was already losing my touch. I used to be able to fake a smile better than this, When did it get so hard?

"Oh, Evie." Mother wrapped me into her arms, and with that motherly magic all mothers somehow possess, she drew the tears right out of me. I sniffled and swallowed to try to keep them back, but just like a curse, there was no fighting mom magic. "Darling, it's alright to feel heartbroken. Shepherd was a wonderful man, and I'm so sorry his family made things difficult for your courtship."

"You have no idea, Mother." I sniffed, burrowing my face in her shoulder as I let the hurt I'd kept buried finally burst free. "You should have seen how controlling his father was. Shep didn't deserve that."

Mother stroked my hair, holding me tight as my cries started to settle. "That's terrible. I can only imagine how hard it was to watch him go through that," Mother cooed. "Is that why you broke it off? Because you didn't want to marry into a family like that?"

I shook my head, pulling back to face her with my bleary eyes. "No, not exactly," I said with a ragged breath. "Shep actually had to leave his family behind in order to become his own person. He's starting fresh, and I'm really happy for him... but it's not a life I can be a part of."

I cleared my lungs with a long sigh, gathering myself and dabbing my eyes with a lacy handkerchief. Crying wasn't befitting of a lady, and since I wasn't a spy anymore, I needed to ensure I fit the part of my permanent role in life. I suppose being a lady wasn't all too different from being a spy—both involved a lot of faking.

"I'm not quite sure I understand." Mother furrowed her brows. "Did Shepherd not want you to be a part of this new life?"

I opened my mouth to reply, but found my words catching in my throat. *Would he have wanted me to remain his partner? Or even remain a part of his life at all?*

"I don't know," I answered honestly. "I didn't

ask."

Mother gave me a gentle smile, reaching out to brush a damp curl from my eyes. "Well, maybe he does. He sought you out once, didn't he? Who's to say he won't do it again?"

If only he could…

I managed a weak smile, allowing myself to cling to Mother's hopes for just a moment. "I suppose only time will tell. But in the meantime, may I request no more suitor visits? At least for a little while until I've had some time to clear my head."

"Of course, darling," Mother said, giving my hand one last squeeze before standing back up. "I'll inform Dedra that—"

"Lady Genevieve!" Dedra practically burst through the door. "You have a visitor, and it's—"

"Hold on a moment, Dedra." Mother held up a hand to quiet the housekeeper. "Evie is not quite ready to see more suitors at the moment, so please, kindly tell the gentleman that now is not a good time."

I smiled, my shoulders relaxing as I watched Mother defend my wishes. The last thing I wanted to do was entertain some snobby noble brat.

"But, my lady, it's not just any suitor." Dedra glanced at me, her eyes enormous with some sort of bizarre excitement. "It's Sir Shepherd!"

"What!?" Mother and I gasped in unison, though hers was more swoony and mine was far more shocked.

"Shep is here?" My jaw dropped so wide, I was shocked I didn't feel it hit the floor.

What is he thinking!? We aren't supposed to cross paths now that I'm no longer an agent.

"Oh, I just knew he loved you too much to leave, Evie dear! Dedra, bring him in at once!" Mother fluttered after her toward the door.

"What!? Hold on a moment, Mother. I'm not —" She vanished out the door before I could finish.

Shep is here... Shep is here!?

I rushed over to the nearest mirror, taking a moment to make sure my eyes weren't too puffy and my curls weren't too wild. My heart throbbed violently in my chest, and my stomach churned like someone had filled it with gravel. I gulped down a large drink of my herbal tea to calm my nerves, then waited the most agonizing minute of my life as I tried to piece together all the reasons he would have come.

Is he in trouble? Did something happen with his father? I know he was delivered to the Reclusian guard a few days ago...

My eye caught the cover of the romance novel I was reading, and a soft flutter whirled in my chest before I could silence it. Mother's whimsical thoughts were starting to wear off on me, and I needed to keep my head together.

"She's right in here." Mother's voice filtered through the doorway, and every thought I had vanished as my head went blank. "I'll just give you two a few minutes to speak."

Shep walked into the room and all the pain I'd just let loose around Mother melted into a puddle at my feet when I met his deep hazel eyes. He always looked good, but seeing him cleaned up without scratches on his cheek or leaves in his hair made him look just like the prince on the cover of my book. I hated my heart for betraying me so quickly, but I couldn't deny how much I'd been longing to see him ever since we split off.

But now it's going to hurt all over again when he leaves.

"Hello, Miss Palleep." Shep's voice... Oh, Shep's voice. How I'd missed how smoothly he could fill a room with the silky touch of his words. He waited for Mother and Dedra to clear the room, but his eyes didn't leave me for even a second as he stepped in. It was like he had been commanded to find me, and the curse refused to let him look anywhere else.

"Hello, Sir Stocklan." I dipped my head, glancing up through my lashes as I watched his lips twitch at the familiar code name. Stocklan suited him better than Ryde after all, plus it wasn't tied to his horrid father. "To what do I owe the pleasure of this visit?"

Shep stepped forward, the hungry look in his eyes consuming every inch of me like he'd been starved for a week. "Am I not allowed to come visit my partner?"

"You would be, *if* we were still partners," I said. "What are you doing here, Shep? Didn't the handler tell you about the new arrangement?"

Shep stuck his hand in his pocket, fiddling around until he pulled out a note. "They did, which is why I asked them to consider a new proposal." He handed me the letter, and my eyes furrowed on the familiar seal.

The Little Bows Shop.

"Evie, I don't want to keep being a spy if it means I can't be with you," he said wistfully, jerking my eyes up from the note as he crept forward another inch. "And that's exactly what I told the handler."

My breath caught. "You what!?" I hissed. "Shep, did you give up your job!? You couldn't have."

I tore the letter open, my heart pounding wildly as I scanned the contents. It only took me a second to read through the letter, but the more I read, the more puzzled I grew.

"I didn't quit." Shep chuckled softly. "I knew you'd never let me, so I found a way for us to keep working together."

I felt light-headed, the air far too thin as I reread the letter.

To Our Loyal Customer,

> *We apologize for the confusion on our newest business policy, but our new supplier has presented us with an alternate business plan we believe will work in everyone's favor. With the blessing of our loyal customers, we are hoping to propose a working union with our supplier, so we may continue to work alongside them as a paired unit.*

New arrivals will be coming in soon! So stay tuned for more fabulous stock.

Sincerely,

Little Bows

I tried to make sense of the note, but the codewords weren't ones I was familiar with. *Union?* What could that possibly mean?

"I don't understand... Have they decided there's enough work for me to come back on?"

"Not exactly," Shep said as he reached back into his pocket, this time pulling out a tiny wood box. "The reason we couldn't work the available jobs together was because our cover story had already run its course and we couldn't keep up the charade with your parents. But that didn't seem like a good enough reason for me to never see you again."

He opened the box, and my eyes widened when I saw the beautiful golden ring sitting inside. The braided band was adorned with a soft glowing stone the size of a pea, one that looked very familiar...

"Is that...?" I pressed a hand to my lips.

"One of the two remaining shards of the obedience stone." Shep held up his hand, revealing an identical stone mounted onto a gold ring on his own finger. "The rest were destroyed, but I asked if I could keep two. As I'm sure you remember, aside from giving commands, they also allow the person wearing it to connect to the mind of anyone cursed with its magic. When I explained this fact to the handler, they agreed it would be an excellent tool for two cursed agents to utilize. It's not often you can know exactly what your partner is thinking, or what they need you to do."

I looked over at the ring on Shep's finger, realizing that, despite the fact that he'd been wearing it, I'd never once felt a command. "So, you're saying you want a partner you can better control?" I asked with a quirked brow.

"If I did, I wouldn't be offering you the other ring." He smirked. "If we both hold a stone, we can sense the other's commands, but we can also command ourselves to disregard them. It's a perfect balance."

I looked at the beautiful ring, my chest already burning with the desire to wear it and feel the connection to Shep and his thoughts.

"Does this mean I get to keep working?" I asked hopefully.

"Yes... but there is one more stipulation." He pulled the ring out of the box, taking my hand in his as he met my eyes with a gaze that made me feel like the most valued magic in the kingdom. "In order to continue working together, we need to make our cover story last longer than a seasonal fling. A *union,* if you will."

There's that word again. Does he really mean...?

"Genevieve Rayelle Palleep, I love you more than any stone could ever command me to say, and I want to spend the rest of my life saving the world with you," Shep breathed. "Will you be my partner in more ways than one and marry me?

Bliss poured through me, causing my fingers to shake and my breathing to stop entirely as I nodded mutely with a growing smile.

"Y-yes." I flung my arms over his shoulders, nearly exploding from the inside out as he encompassed me in his arms. "I love you too, Shep."

He ran his fingers through my hair, pulling

me so close I couldn't even breathe, but I didn't care. Shep was mine forever, and I got to spend the rest of my days bickering about who was the better spy.

"Now we just need to fabricate a story for your parents." Shep laughed as we pulled apart just enough that our noses brushed. "I was thinking that my family moved overseas and decided to remain there, what do you think?"

"Oh, that won't do." I giggled. "I already told Mother that you split off from your family, so we'll have to build off that. Maybe say you got a new job at the local dress shop in town?"

"I heard Little Bows has some excellent employees." Shep brushed his hand along my cheek, and I leaned into his touch. "Although, I also heard some of them are cursed..."

"You don't say?" I gasped. "Those poor souls... they must be absolutely *miserable*."

Shep smiled, his eyes twinkling as he reached for my hand and slid the delicate golden ring on my finger. Warmth filled me as I felt Shep's curse meld with mine, our hearts both yearning to follow the other's as loyally as faithful sheep.

"Tragically so." He smiled, pulling me closer until our lips were only a touch away. "Could you imagine what it would be like if someone said, *I command you to kiss me*?"

My chest warmed at the veiled command,

urging me to follow through, but at the same time, I could sense the ring's strength, allowing me to override the command if I so chose. But I didn't stop it, I didn't pull away. Why would I, when my greatest desire was pulling me closer with a magical tug.

"I imagine it would be like this," I whispered.

And then, we shared our first, truly magical kiss.

epilogue

Kingdom of Sarnold, The Royal Palace

The Blood Princess, Amirah

"I'm sorry, princess, but the deal fell through. I was unable to acquire the magic you requested." Dranger bowed, his pathetic pleas causing the magic in my necklace to buzz in discontent.

"The task should have been simple," I said bluntly. "I still fail to understand how you managed to not only lose the products I requested, but also the full sum of money I gave you to purchase it."

I tapped my rings on the edge of my seat, the clattering echo of metal on wood filling the empty study like the grim ticking of a clock. Dranger pressed his lips together. Sweat beaded down his brow and his eyes darted around fearfully, like a mouse who knew he'd been cornered.

"I-I don't know what happened to the money, Your Highness. Honest," Dranger pleaded.

My earring warmed with magic, sparking my

sympathy as I looked into his wide eyes. He didn't appear to be lying, which simply meant he was a fool.

"It must have been stolen," Dranger continued. "I know it's hard to believe, but I can't figure out where else it would have gone. One of the party guests must have noticed me carrying around the money and followed me to its safe."

"A party guest? You mean, one of the rich nobles who already lives advantageously?" I narrowed my eyes. "That seems unlikely."

Of course, it was stolen.

I should have expected as much. The heads of the black market were experts at sniffing out major trades. They probably had someone waiting to take advantage of the deal as soon as they heard the cloaks were in motion. There must have been a black-nosed mole in the party...

Dranger dabbed at his brow with a handkerchief, his breathing growing short. "I don't know, Your Majesty. The men I was intended to deal with didn't leave with the money, so it had to be someone else... maybe a servant or a thief who broke in! Please, allow me the time to find the culprit or even gather back the funds that were stolen. If I need too, I can sell my estate and cash in my investments, but I'm sure I—"

"It's not the money that I want," I said coldly.

"I wanted the obedience stone..."

Dranger bit his tongue, nodding silently as a darkness sank over his eyes. "To... to control your uncle? Because if that's the case, I can always offer you my loyalty within his court. Whatever you wish, princess, just say the word. I will do whatever it takes to persuade him."

This is useless.

I stood from my seat, my heavy skirt swishing across the ground as I started for the door. "I didn't need the stone to control my uncle," I said under my breath. A headache breached my skull, telling me I had already had enough disappointment for one day.

They are all the same... Always assuming they know what I want.

"I don't understand," Dranger said, his voice echoing behind me as I left, and the guards swept up to his sides. "If you're not hoping to control your uncle, then what use do you have for the obedience stone? Who are you hoping to control?"

I stopped in the doorway, my skin bristling as my bracelet flared against my wrist.

They'll never understand.

"Myself."

Thanks For Reading

Ready for more Once Upon A Rhyme? Keep reading for a sneak peek of book three.

Hush A Bye Lady

Hush A Bye Lady

Prologue

What have I done...? What will happen to me now?

I started to wake up, but I was too afraid to open my eyes. I didn't want any of it to be true... The first thing I noticed was that I was being cradled, but the arms wrapped around me were anything but comforting. The cold, boney limbs clutched me in stiff manner, like chains shackling me in place. They must have expected me to want to run away after what had happened. But even if I did, where would I go?

My lashes fluttered open, slow and sticky from the dried tears clustered around the edges. It was my mother who was holding me, but her arms felt nothing like the embrace of anyone maternal. I wanted to squirm free or even be thrown to the floor. It didn't take more than a glance at her viperous glare to know I wouldn't make it far before being snatched back into her claws.

"She's awake, finally." Mother tightened her grip on me, digging her nails into my frail arm. "Can you stand, Sasha?"

I bristled at the way she said my name. Her tongue flicked like a barbed whip, and I felt the full force of the sting. I didn't respond, my body still shaking as the memories of last night made me revisit the shock.

"Speak, girl." Father's voice echoed from the edge of the bedroom, and I jumped when I realized he was here too. "After all the trouble you've caused, the least you can do is answer a simple question."

I scrambled to my feet, tripping over the frills of a nightgown I didn't recognize. It was a little big on me, but I was small for my age. Once I was free from Mother's arms, I straightened as stiff as a board in hopes of stopping my quaking.

"He told you to speak, Sasha," Mother hissed. "And don't stand so straight. You look like a tin man."

"I-I'm sorry," I said in a small voice.

"No mumbling, either." She snapped her finger an inch from my eyes, startling more tears from me. "If you can't speak clearly, then it's best not to speak at all."

"Give her a few hours to adjust, Yolanda,"

Father said in a cooler tone, though his eyes were still burning at me. "She's only five, and this is all so sudden—"

"We don't have time for her to adjust." Mother's voice was so close to screaming, yet she managed to keep it within her control. It terrified me how easily she could command a room without intentionally striking fear. "Last night's events must never be heard or spoken of, and in order to accomplish that, Sasha must never raise questions. She must be flawless. Anything less means we're ruined, and she's worthless."

Flawless... Worthless...

Those were such big words for my tired mind. Could I really cover up what I did? And was I even capable of doing it? Why did everything have to go so wrong? I just wanted to play in the treehouse...

My lip wobbled as the memories resurfaced, streaming thick tears down my dirty cheeks.

"You're right." Father sighed. "This doesn't work unless—Sasha. Sasha! Stop that crying at once!" He stormed beside me, snatching my hands and squeezing them until I swallowed back my tears with a gasp.

"Oh, for kingdom's sake." Mother rolled her eyes. "She's hopeless!"

Hopeless? No, I can't fail already… If I fail, then…

"We should just get rid of her and count our losses." Hearing Mother say that so easily nearly made me sick. I felt like I might faint, or at the very least, cry again, but that wasn't an option. I had to be perfect. I had to prove I could keep everything a secret.

I didn't cry, I didn't speak, and I didn't waver.

"We don't have to decide that now, dear. Let's give it some time." Father dropped my hands, looking a touch impressed that I had stopped crying on command. He got on eye level with me, his yellowish-amber eyes reminding me of a crocodile. "Listen closely, Sasha. What happened last night has to stay a secret. Not a single person can ever find out what you did."

I swallowed and nodded to show my understanding. I didn't trust my voice not to crack or mumble.

"You know what will happen if anyone finds out, don't you?" Father's eyes narrowed, and a grim shiver tickled through my ribs.

I nodded again.

"Good." He rose to his feet, casting his long shadow over me like a dark cage trapping me within. "If you can stay silent, and obey, then your mother and I are willing to give you a second chance."

Be silent and obey...

"This is your last and only chance, Sasha," Mother said in a frigid tone. "If your little secret ever gets out..."

"It won't," I squeaked, surprised I even had a voice inside me.

Mother tilted her chin, nails tapping on her crossed arms. She studied me for a moment, as if deciphering if a five-year-old little girl was capable of keeping such a horrid secret to herself. I pressed my lips tight, stuffing the terrible memories down my throat so they could never cross my tongue.

"Good," she finally said. "For the family's sake, I hope you mean it."

Follow me

For more updates on Once Upon A Rhyme

 Abigail Manning, Author

 Abby Manning Author

Abigailmanningauthor.com

Special thanks to my little brother, Isaac.
He doesn't read my books, but he'll be
annoyed if I never thank him. I suppose he
did get me a birthday present once...

Made in the USA
Middletown, DE
11 July 2023

34856283R00201